"NO PROVISION CAN SAFEGUARD
THIS STRANGE MARRIAGE."

Grace Morrisson's softly spoken words puzzled Sir James Troyes. In spite of them, she had accepted his proposal and indeed seemed surprisingly determined to marry quickly. Though there was not the slightest hint of love or affection between them, he had his reasons for desiring the marriage and for enduring Grace. For so vast a fortune as Grace Morrisson ruled, a man could overlook the flaws in any woman's personality...

He would marry her and abide with it all for his beloved home, Lyndley Waters. Lyndley Waters deserved the best of everything—the finest of architects, painters, gardeners, decorators. With Grace Morrisson's fortune, he would make Lyndley Waters outshine any house its size in the British Isles.

Yes, he knew why he so desperately wanted this loveless marriage, but why did Grace...?

House of Sorrows

Marjorie Bowen

ZEBRA BOOKS

KENSINGTON PUBLISHING CORP.

ZEBRA BOOKS

are published by

KENSINGTON PUBLISHING CORP.

521 Fifth Avenue

New York, N.Y. 10017

First Printing: March, 1976
Second Printing: June, 1977

I
THEME

JAMES TROYES smelt mischief in it from the first, but it amused him, and he was in the mood for an adventure. The countryside was not at all to his taste, nor was the castle as he supposed it must be called, and there was something of southern contempt for the crude north in his reflection of a very majestic aspect. But many circumstances, some fine as cobwebs, combined to halt Sir James Troyes and his servant before this grey residence and ask of the porter if he might have a night's hospitality. This was easily accorded by the servant, whose accent was so harsh as to be hardly comprehensible to the English gentleman. The interior of the building was as rude as the exterior, but to a man harassed, anxious and exasperated, had a certain severe dignity that was soothing.

The master or laird, Robert Morrisson, appeared at once and gave appropriate welcome. There was nothing in his appearance (as Sir James afterwards with bitter rancour recalled) to suggest evil; he was an ordinary better-class Scot, as the rude castle was an ordinary better-class Scots residence; but Sir James continued to sense, though he was not a man who was easily disturbed, that there was (the only way he could express it to himself) mischief about the old place, and this feeling was strong even when the supper had been eaten, the drink handed round, the harper and the piper brought in to offer entertainment.

The traveller did not intend to stay more than one night in this Moffatt glen. He was on his way to

Edinburgh, were he hoped, and a vain hope he feared it was, to do something to patch up his tattered fortunes, he said as much, staring into his horn tankard.

Robert Morrisson looked wistful at the traveller's mention of the capital.

"It is a long while," said he, "since I have left my own land, Drumquassel here, but I have a lady daughter who is being educated in Edinburgh, and if you had the leisure you might pay your respects to her and her guardians."

It seemed to Sir James a curious thing, even though he was not very interested in any circumstance save those directly bearing on his own affairs, that this man should live alone in a well-appointed if antique house—for there was no sign of wife or housekeeper—and have a daughter educating in Edinburgh, and he remarked as much in a drowsy manner, watching the blue rings from his clay pipe ascending into the darkness of the ceiling. There was no light save what came from the faggots on the cavernous hearth, and his host, the other side of the rough table, had sunk back into his chair with arms, in some moody meditation.

"Grace," he said. "Grace Morrisson, that is my daughter; she is being trained like a gentlewoman at a grand house in Edinburgh."

"I suppose she is a very young girl, sir, or else you would have her here to play mistress for you?"

"She is near her twenty-first birthday, but I keep her apart—my wife was a Spaniard and the girl is like her mother. I suppose that seems an odd sort of story to you, but you see there is a large—a very large fortune attached to Grace, and she is only partly in my bestowing. She has her foreign guardians." He leant forward from the darkness of his chair into the circle of firelight. "These Spaniards have to be consulted about everything, and when they were asked if she should come to live with me, with such rude companions as I might obtain for her ... well, they disagreed ... it was the Edinburgh mansion for them. She is a rare heiress for some man's solace," he added flatly. "And the gentlefolk who care for her keep her free from the wordly taint."

Sir James Troyes felt he was being crudely jested with, for he had himself for some while been in search of an heiress. It was not easy, even for a man with a baronetcy, a respectable estate and a comely person to find a woman of tolerable appearance who was also very wealthy, willing to accept a man whose fortunes were in the state that his were.

He continued to regard the smoke rings, and Mr. Morrisson, as if amusing a large and invisible audience, murmured on about his courtship and marriage of the Spanish lady. To his solitary listener, absorbed in his own affairs, his own speculations that became, with his increasing drowsiness, more and more vague, this tale had the likeness of a ballad that he surely had heard sung or recited some time in the past—a Spanish lady and the Scot who went seafaring and landed at a Spanish port ... and behind a grille of twisted iron saw a fair face looking down. ... Well, that would be the beginning of it and what would be the next step? ... He would contrive to be entertained by her father, and she, closely guarded by *duenna* and music masters, would nevertheless be permitted to receive him, and he would lose his heart to her uncommon good looks as she stood before him

7

in her gown of silver with rows upon rows of narrow gold braid round the wide skirt.

Sir James Troyes sat up with a jerk. He had been falling asleep and dreaming. What did this stranger or his daughter or his tale matter to him, who had such considerable burdens on his mind; but he said as a matter of courtesy, as he rose, his host also at once getting to his feet:

"Sir, of course I shall be pleased to wait upon your daughter, although I do not know whether the mansion where she is being educated is willing to receive strangers like myself. Mistress Graçe Morrisson, I can remember . . ."

The other added the name of the street . . . near Holyrood . . . a decent house of a flat, grey stone with a garden behind that was famous for pear trees. "They'll be coming to their best just now—ask her to give you a sample of the pears."

* * * *

Sir James found his chamber too primitive for his liking. It was ill heated, too, and he slept badly. When he woke in the morning he rose with a sense of curiosity that was not altogether pleasant. In his snatches of slumber he had had incoherent dreams, and the room, though large and stately, had an air of unreality. The curtains at the tester hung slack and thin . . . a poor place Castle Drumquassel seemed by daylight. His own appointments, though by no means fine by southern standards, appeared too handsome for these surroundings. He glanced at them where they had been placed on the wooden settle by the window, and then rose and dressed himself with some eagerness, too keen to be gone to wait for Thomas Pratt, his body-servant.

From the window, that was uncurtained and unshuttered, for the chamber was high, he looked over a country where changing mists seemed to shift even the contours of the landscape so that nothing was abiding . . . the hills and valleys seemed to interchange with pastures scanty and mean, and long vistas that appeared to stretch into an unfathomable distance.

* * * *

Mr. Morrisson was cheerful at the breakfast he shared with his guest. He now added some details to what he had related the night before of the history of his daughter. At least his guest supposed that they were added details. For himself he could not have been sure what had been told him as they had sat together alone in this same room, which had then been so full of shadows, with merely the glow from the logs on the wide charcoal hearth to light them.

Mr. Morrisson now emphasised, with a good deal of jovial dryness, that his daughter's fortune was entirely from her mother's house and that a distant relative would inherit Drumquassel.

"Yours, sir, seems a thoroughly divided family," remarked Sir James, not caring greatly whether he offended this unlikely kind of fellow or not.

"It is that," replied Mr. Morrisson. "I live alone here and concern myself with my Moffatt estate—poor as it is, I find plenty to do—and my only child being carefully educated for the grand marriage that her guardians have in view for her."

"And will you, sir," asked Sir James, "have nothing whatever to do with this same marriage? Surely it will make a little difference to you what manner of son-in-law you find you have?"

"I doubt it will make any difference at all, sir," said Morrisson. "That gallant and myself are not likely to meet often. The lady has been to Drumquassel and expressed her disdain of it and, obliquely, her disdain of me. She is all her mother in pride and narrow-mindedness and ill temper, as I believe. You must not suppose that she lives like a girl at school . . . oh no, she has her own parlour and friends and entertains, and those, the ladies Ladelle, who are set over her, give her a great liberty so that there is not a great match in the two kingdoms but might not woo her if they would."

Sir James believed that his host was exaggerating his daughter's importance; it was curious that he, who had been so sharply interested in this matter of heiresses, had never heard of Miss Grace Morrisson of Edinburgh, who appeared to be being offered almost publicly to the highest bidder.

So he made his farewells without any comment either side as to any future meeting, and took his way with Thomas Pratt, his body-servant, that was all that he could now afford in the way of a retinue, along the rough, broken road through Moffatt towards the capital.

There was some long-ago connection on his mother's side with Scotland, that caused part of his property to lie in the hands of Scottish lawyers, and this was the mundane reason that had brought him to the northern capital that he, knowing nothing of it personally, yet disliked greatly from its reputation.

He was a man easily pleased; he had fully enjoyed his own estate; his vists to Paris and London, until too careless a disposition, too open a hand and too generous a heart, together with an extravagant taste in building, had brought him to a precarious position and he at last realised that unless he could get some sudden and immediate help, all his career would be but, as he said himself, "a tumbledown affair."

He had allowed the matter of his revenue to go on too long. If he had taken it in hand, say, two years sooner, he might have got a place at court, or a colonelcy in the Guards—he had friends and influence; but now his affairs were desperate. He needed money with which to pay importunate creditors, with which to maintain at least something of the state to which he was used, even if he had to stop his building and some of his pleasures.

The ride north had been, however, more than this, more than an attempt to raise funds to retrieve his existence . . . he used to himself no less a word than that, for existence with him meant the means with which to keep up a lordly state, a large hospitality and a noble participation in the sport, amusements and scandals of his class.

No, he and Pratt the body-servant, although they had exchanged no confidence on the matter, the man being well trained to keep his place, had both felt a sense of adventure when they had ridden from the pleasant, warm, familiar south to this dusky and dreary north. They left behind very much that was agreeable, but they escaped much that had been extremely galling and unpleasant—the adventure was as important as the quest.

Sir James had contrived sufficient funds to keep his estate at least paying its own way under his steward, Mr. Swallow, for six months, a long time to allow for a journey to Edinburgh, but his mood was then, as it had been when he came to Drumquassel Castle, restless and adventurous. Nothing had happened in the least out of the way, save that elderly, plain man's talk of his haughty and disagreeable daughter with the large fortune, who entertained lavishly but with a set design, in Edinburgh, nothing to justify that sense of mischief in the air.

"He does not give her a good character," the Englishman thought. "I suppose there's spite and ill will . . . there would be. I wonder how the Spanish marriage went, and when and how the wife died? It's a pretty puzzle in its way, but I don't suppose it's one for me to solve."

* * * *

Sir James put up at the Edinburgh hostelry that was rather beneath his condition, yet something above his purse, for as one never used to spare expense, he had, even with Pratt's careful economies, spent more on the journey than he should have done. He had a few jewels about his person, and he feared that these would go into the safe keeping of an Edinburgh goldsmith before he was able to return to England.

He put off for a day or so the tiresome, and no doubt humiliating, interview in store for him with the Scots lawyers and, as a matter of mere curiosity, rode past the grey palace that lay at the end of the royal mile, and took the turn as directed by Mr. Morrisson, that led him to a genteel-looking house enclosed in its own garden; a house of grey stone with flagged courtyard in front, and at the back as could easily be seen, for the mansion stood at a corner, a small orchard in which grew several large pear trees. The sight of this little plot gave the Englishman a deepening of his sudden sense of nostalgia. In England now the weather would be golden, the air a-sparkle with the last flowers of the year. Here the days were autumn, and winter seemed crawling up from the hills; while the fruit, that in England would have been over-ripe and would have been eaten quickly before it rotted, was still hanging hard and green among the withering leaves. Perhaps Mr. Morrisson of Drumquassel had meant a severe jest when he had spoken of the lusciousness of these pears and suggested that Grace, his daughter, should offer them to her visitor.

It was not until Sir James had passed the house the third time that he rang the bell and asked the manservant who came (for there was no porter) if he might wait upon the ladies Ladelle or Mistress Grace Morrisson. As he gave his name but no credentials he was denied, and with a certain sternness that amused him; for, however serious might be his present plight, Scotland was to him a poor place and the Scots were a sorry crew hardly worth an Englishman's attention.

As he turned away he glanced up at the windows, but there was no reflection here of the ballad that he seemed to remember in his boyhood; flat, square and blank they showed in the grey stone. There was not so much as a drape of lace in any one of them, nor a bird in a cage and no sweet, beckoning face looking down.

* * * *

He had at last to wait upon his lawyers, and found them, as he had expected, forbidding and unsympathetic. They read him a lecture upon his extravagance, pointed out to him that the Edinburgh

13

property which he now wished to mortgage so heavily had been in his family for two centuries and was really intended to be used for the dowry of the unmarried daughters of the Troyes. The young man's petulant jest that there were no unmarried ladies to be provided for, nor like to be, did not soften the lawyers, who, while not exactly denying his right to mortgage or even to sell the property, made some very injurious aspersions upon the imprudence of such conduct.

"You will sell in a bad market, doing so suddenly and without due and cautious survey of the situation. You will get perhaps half what the lands are worth, and the immediate advantage to you will be quite small, because we cannot promise you a large sum."

The younger of them, Tobias Skrine, had at least, however, some definite advice to offer.

"Why do you not," said he, "sell all that is not entailed of your southern property, and come to live upon this Scottish estate? With what you might yet raise . . . "

Sir James Troyes interrupted dryly with the information that half the timber was sold and the place pledged to the Jews. The lawyers declared that they were well aware of this deplorable situation, but still, when all was said and done, a few years' thrift and Lyndley Waters, which was a magnificent property, would begin to pay its way, then to bring in money, and meanwhile he, Sir James, could be living quietly on the Scottish property.

No proposal could have been more disagreeable to the young man; he listened to it merely out of idleness, while he sat silent, cornered by fortune, and also somewhat by the drowsiness or laziness of his

14

own disposition. He was well equipped to lead the life that his father had led before him, and ill equipped to face any sudden turns or quirks of fortune such as this.

Mr. Skrine continued his plea, becoming more warm as he thought his client was listening with some respect, not for a moment guessing the complete indifference with which Sir James was staring out of the window at the narrow, busy street, so he was brought up shortly when Sir James asked, "Do you know anything of a Mistress Grace Morrisson? I heard what seemed to me a rather foolish tale about her. . . ."

The lawyer, who had been declaiming on the merits of retrenchment and the plan of living on the Scotch estate, was stung into silence; but the other answered, civilly enough, that Grace Morrisson was a considerable heiress who, under the eccentric provisions of her mother's will, had her fortune completely separate from that of her father. He went on to outline a story that Sir James supposed was the same as that he had heard from Mr. Morrisson himself. There had been a sudden wedding . . . an unhappy marriage . . . one child. The mother had died heartbroken, it was believed, in the foreign country with the foreign husband whom she so soon disliked, and the mother's relatives had taken the girl and placed her under the care of various tutors and governesses in the capital.

"Why didn't they," asked Sir James, "have her with them? Why did they not let her return to Spain?"

"I believe the father was legally able to prevent that," replied the lawyer, "but I do not know the details of the case, as it has never concerned me. Why, sir, may I ask, do you show this curiosity? Is it your intention to put in for the hand of the heiress? I believe that she is in every way difficult."

Sir James Troyes was in no mood to consider that a woman being difficult would be any great obstacle for him asking for her hand; if she were rich enough, that was.

"What is the amount of her fortune?" he queried.

The lawyers did not know, they believed it was considerable . . . some Madrid bankers were among her guardians . . . everything was done in an economical and yet magnificent fashion. The lady had just come of age . . . several offers for her hand had been refused . . . she lived with three elderly gentlewomen, the ladies Ladelle, in a most correct and precise style, and it was difficult for a stranger to enter the severe-looking house by Holyrood Palace where she resided.

"I've seen it," said Sir James. "I called there—I was asked to do so by her father." He related casually his encounter with Morrisson of Drumquassel. "My reception was by a servant and uncivil."

"We could get you letters of introduction," suggested Mr. Skrine, the younger lawyer, doubtfully.

There was a pause of silence in the commonplace room while the three men looked at one another and the scheme came into being; they decided that he was personable enough, and he decided that they were bold enough to undertake the winning of Grace Morrisson, if this should prove worth while. Not only was Sir James, under his casual exterior, pretty well desperate, but he had this lazy, whimsical turn in his disposition. He had made some efforts to marry the daughters of wealthy esquires and lords in the south, but had always met with a prudent refusal . . . but here, perhaps, had come his way one of those extraordinary chances that sometimes save a man from the penalties of his own follies.

"I wonder," he cried gaily, "she has not been carried off before!"

He laughed. He felt certain of success—it was not only the fortune that attracted him, the girl was no doubt uncommon, and he, extravagant and ostentatious, would like to show to his neighbours, especially to those who had refused him, an exotic beauty.

"We will find out," promised the lawyers, "the precise amount of her fortune. It will not be very easy to do so, and it will take some time. I do not know if it is sufficient for your needs."

So the matter was come at bluntly, without his having declared his part.

"I can stay in Edinburgh for a while," he said, thinking of the jewels that he had in his travelling case. "I can cut some kind of a figure. Of course, when it comes to a settlement all these Spanish grandees, whoever they are, will have to know the condition of my estates and revenues. . . ."

"And I cannot, I confess, see why they should overlook all these disadvantages, Sir James," said Mr. Tannahill, the elder of the lawyers, while the younger remarked slyly, that the young man's sole chance lay in the lady taking a fancy to his person.

Sir James confessed that he was not of such a vanity that he could suppose himself to be more prepossessing than the many ruined men of title and condition who must already have made an attempt to obtain this Spanish gold, but his advisers saw that he

17

was very sure of himself.

* * * *

The Englishman returned to his rooms with an elation at heart which made the alien city, to him dirty, dark and depressing, of more cheerful aspect. It appeared to him as if his destiny was already settled, that his wooing of the lady would not be of so long and austere a nature as the lawyers seemed to think, and that with this foreign money, that seemed to him to have an almost magical character, he would be able to return to the south and to commence again with his building, with his parterres, his walks, alleys, fish-ponds and aviaries. He was nothing of a business man and his fancy leapt from one extreme to another, always with an extravagant turn, and he had already thought of this Spanish fortune as being fabulous, not only in its origin but in its amount. He remembered, with a touch of regret and compassion, the crude mansion and the rough host who had first told him of this treasure, and decided that when he was Mr. Morrisson of Drumquassel's son-in-law, he would pay him all respect.

Sir James had not brought with him any particularly brave appointments, and looking at himself as he had never looked before in the square mirror in his toilet case, he wondered, with the gravity of a man who surveys his sole asset, if he was indeed personable enough to win a capricious, wealthy and spoilt woman. His humour was such that he was amused even at his own scrutiny, yet that was serious enough. A man of twenty-eight, a good athlete, a good companion, a fair Englishman with nothing mean r besotted in his countenance—yet what had he to offer more than many another? She might

18

perhaps be attracted by the thought of the splendid estate that he was laying out? She might be eager that her money should be spent on so noble an enterprise? He knew how to make himself agreeable to women, and his person had always been sufficiently agreeable to be a passport to what good grace he desired from them, but this was different; this was a design on a large scale.

For want of other company-he would not use the few letters of introduction that he had had to acquaintances of aquaintances in Edinburgh—he confided, after his habit, to Thomas Pratt, a tall, florid man whose family had been in the service of the Troyes for several generations.

"I have found, I think, Pratt, an heiress—an uncommon creature to whom I intend to pay my addresses. You must support me as best you can, both by your demeanour and by your assent to any tales that you may hear me tell. You will know full well that I have gone courting heiresses before without luck; but perhaps in this outlandish place I might have a better chance. The creature can scarcely know what true civilisation is—it may be that it will not take much persuasion to induce her to cross the border."

Pratt was sincerely and entirely of his master's opinion. He had seen the house where Grace Morrisson lived. It looked to him almost squalid beside his master's estate; not good enough for the Dower House, very little better than the steward's residence by the mill. He had no doubt that his master would make a sure and certain success, and in the few days they had to wait while the lawyers

arranged the presentation, he did his utmost to fur-
bish up his master's wardrobe, which was scanty
enough but of its kind magnificent.

Sir James Troyes did not by any means consider
himself an adventurer, nor did his servant. Even then
at this period of his story, when he might have
supposed himself to be in a humiliating situation, he
not only held himself proudly but thought of himself
with a good deal of complacency.

* * * *

The presentation of the young English lord, as
the Scots termed it, to Grace Morrisson, was arranged
without very much difficulty, but he was rather
amused at the ceremonies that had to be undergone
before he found himself in the presence of the
heiress. "Poor and proud," he had always termed the
Scots in his mind, and they had shown him evidence,
he thought, of both qualities since he had crossed the
border.

It was with a good deal of curiosity that he
found himself in the presence of the girl who had at
the least an unusual history. She received him with
three stiff gentlewomen standing behind her chair in a
room that was, to his taste, mean. The hangings were
no more than serge, so were the curtains at the long
window that, looking northward, had a bleak aspect.

The girl was handsome, no doubt of that. This
was his first and obvious reflection; but she did not
seem at ease. There was a lowering aspect upon her
handsome face and her hands moved nervously. She
was dressed in a style far too sombre, the Englishman
thought, for her age; dark blue interchangeable silk
with a fine shawl of black lace over it. The three
gentlewomen, Grissel, Lilias and Annis Ladelle, also

wore shawls, of more substantial material, and high-boned bonnets tied under the chin.

Grace Morrisson took a seat and desired the young man to take the chair by the window, so that she was in shade and he was in full light. He felt, for all his well-bred effrontery, a slight dismay at being thus placed in the full scrutiny of a very interested pair of eyes, but carried himself with an air, while she saved him some embarrassment by coming directly to the point; as he was observing that her features—her ears, her figure and hands—were all nicely and neatly formed, she was saying rapidly, as she stared at him out of her full, bright, brown eyes:

"I believe you come as a suitor to my hand, Sir James, upon report of my considerable wealth?"

"Well, madam," he replied, "that is a blunt way to put it, but saves no doubt time and other useful commodities. Perhaps you would like me to tell you that I saw you at an upper window as I was riding past and was so enamoured at your unusual charms that I could not depart from Edinburgh without striving to make myself master of them?"

Her mouth, that was beautifully shaped, lifted in a slight sneer at this insolent compliment.

"I desire no flatteries," she replied. "I am of age now and can settle my affairs for myself. No doubt you consider that I am doing so in an unwomanly fashion, but it matters very little to me what you think."

This was too much for the Englishman, who replied with asperity, "Madam, if we are to be man and wife, it will have to matter to you what I think, even though you be an heiress with a swinging fortune."

"Do you know," she asked disdainfully, "what my fortune amounts to?"

"Not in so many round figures, but I believe it to be considerable."

"I am a very wealthy woman," Grace Morrisson announced. "I have far more money and estates than you would readily believe. It has been a long minority and my funds have been most carefully looked after by worthy guardians. I have had a great many offers from people of title and position. Yours, by the way," she added rapidly, "is somewhat damaged, is it not?"

"It is in temporary lack of repair," admitted Sir James, knowing that this fact would not be by any means hid.

"And what do you offer me in return for the money that will put you in the position you have lost?"

The young lady's statement of the case, in words so much plainer than he had used himself, angered the young man. He decided that it had been no foolish rumour that had described her as a disagreeable, haughty young woman, and that if he took her he would pay highly for her money; but he was by no means prepared to give up this prize that dangled so temptingly almost within his reach. He was inclined to be philosophical on the subject of marriage. After all, how many happy unions did he know of? He need never quarrel with his lady, as he could leave her too much alone to her own devices.

"You put the affair," he said frankly and with a smile that included the silent *duennas,* "on so businesslike a basis that I know not what to say. I am at a loss also to understand why you should even have received me, seeing that I have so little to offer."

Grace Morrisson unfurled from the chain that hung at her side a large chicken-skin fan on which was painted some oriental pergolas and palms. She waved this to and fro and said sharply:

"You might have a good deal to offer; you might come as if in answer to a petition."

"This is all very mysterious to me," replied he. "Shall we have in the lawyers and the advocates, some for you and some for me, so that all can be threshed out in a legal atmosphere?"

Her fine complexion heightened at this sneer, but she stood her ground.

"You know nothing of me, and I know nothing of you, sir. My history has been a peculiar one. I have lived here free and yet in seclusion, seeming marked apart from the other gentlewomen of my age and pretensions. My father, Mr. Morrisson of Drumquassel, I believe you have already seen?"

"By an odd chance, yes," said Sir James. "I was coming northward to look into some poor managements of my own and chanced—yes, I must repeat the word—to come across Castle Drumquassel and to request the hospitality of your father."

"He is a plain man," said Grace Morrisson. "He would have little to offer one like yourself. I see that you are used to soft and caressing ways."

All this seemed to Sir James rather beside the mark and likely to lead to no useful conclusion. Here, plainly, was a girl to whom he could not pay court in the way to which he was used to pay court to a pretty woman, nor a business woman who would come quickly to a closure of the deal. All that she had said so far seemed to him but like a beating about

23

the bush, waiting for the quarry to rise. Being by no means bashful, and conscious that he was the only male in the room, he took the lead and asked her in set terms whether she approved of him as a suitor or not.

"I like you well enough, madam, and what I have heard of your fortune—the settlement shall be as your lawyers decide. I also have something to offer. . . ."

He related to her, with a dry briefness, that was not without its touch of scorn, the splendour of his own place, Lyndley Waters, his name and reputation in the county of Wilts and all the honours and glories that he might hope to attain when he had settled his transient difficulties.

But her answer was, still swirling the fan to and fro, "I have had finer matches than that offered to me."

Again he tried to bring the matter to an end one way or another, for she did not so entrance him that he desired to stand there like a rustic staring at her, unless there was something substantial to be got from this interview.

"Why, then, madam, did you receive me? I beleive that I and my affairs have been thoroughly investigated by your lawyers. The Scots are not backward in money matters . . . you have your own guardians, too."

"There has been no time," said Grace Morrisson, "to communicate with those who are in Spain . . . they have their representative in Edinburgh it is true. . . ." A touch of sadness came into her voice as she added: "Those who knew my mother are dead; those who manage my affairs are more or less strangers—honest and able men, but those who act merely from conscience and not from affection. I am indeed, sir, somewhat of a lonely woman. . . ."

"I marvel, then," he replied, "that you did not years ago accept one of these eager suitors?"

"There were reasons," she answered. "A woman's reasons—light and idle—not to be repeated, indeed forgotten."

"Perhaps, then," said he with a smile that made his comely face appear very attractive, for it suited him best to be gay and light, "there are some of these same feminine—caprices, I should call them sooner than reasons—why you should accept me as your husband?"

"Perhaps there are," admitted Grace Morrisson. "I may as well, I suppose . . ." she gave a half-appealing look to the old woman, Miss Lilias, who stood on her left, "come to the point. I believe I have been too long already, but it is not easy to make an affair that should be one of passion and the heart so dry."

He was sorry for her, instantly, at this note of yielding. She was indeed in a forlorn position with that rude and queer father, in his rough castle, who had washed his hands of her, with foreigners and strangers guarding her large fortune. At that moment he almost wished that he was clear of the whole negotiations. She had, to tell the truth, taken his fancy but little. He admired her with a cold and academic eye, but he would never have crossed the road to make himself her suitor in any sense of the word; but the thought of Lyndley Waters, of his debts, of the earnest need he had to return south triumphantly with money to his name at his bankers, checked what feelings he might have had of natural compassion and disdain of the sordid bargain he was making—sordid it was, yet such as men of his rank made every day of the year.

"I do not wish to press you, madam," he said, "but my affairs will not allow of a long sojourn in Edinburgh. . . ."

"I suppose," she answered cruelly, "you have not even the means to furnish yourself for more than a few days in our capital, poor as it is supposed to be?"

"Put it like that as you will," replied Sir James. "You seem determined to give the most drab aspect to the affair. Will you give me yes or no?"

At that she rose with a certain passion not understood by him and declared, "It is 'Yes.' I will take you for my husband. I agree that the marriage shall be immediate and that you shall take me south as soon as you conveniently can. The settlements must be as my lawyers and guardians desire, but I will undertake that they are not such as will cause you any displeasure. I shall reserve a certain independence, both for my dressing and for my fortune; for the rest, all is yours. . . ."

These words, like most words that have sudden and unexpected good fortune, were hard for the young man to credit.

All his sophisticated wit could scarcely provide him with an answer. He advanced and kissed the lady's hand and thanked her and made some courtly asides, and all the while he was conscious that she looked at him with disdain.

"There is something behind this," he thought. "She has refused better matches than I am—but it is not for me to be questioning when the gold is poured into my lap."

26

Grace Morrisson accepted his forced compliments in the same fashion as they were offered.

"You find this chamber, I suppose, depressing?" she said. "I have lived very abstemiously. . . . I have had very little object in my life. I am inclined, as you perhaps have heard, to be religious. . . ."

He had heard as much and put the matter by, but now it occurred to him that he had been a fool not to guess that perhaps she belonged to the old faith.

"If you're a Papist," he said, "it might be difficult . . ."

She declared with some warmth that she was not, but belonged to the Calvinist religion, and had done so since her early childhood, having been instructed by the minister who had converted her mother from the errors of papistry.

"Well, then," said Sir James cheerfully, "there will be no difficulty over that. I am building a splendid chapel at Lyndley Waters and it shall be very much at your service."

He was pleased with what she had told him. To his mind, religion was very much a woman's business, and the more a woman was absorbed in prayers and good works, the less likely she was to get into mischief. If her being a dull *devotee* was the cause of her high and haughty manners, well, it was as good a reason as he could have hoped to find.

"I suppose that I shall have full liberty for the exercise of my faith," she continued, "which is not that of the Church of England?"

The young man assured her that this should be so, even though at the same time he realised that some difficulties might arise.

"The Church and State are one in England," he

27

said, "and I am bound to support both . . . but if there are any little feminine quips or quibbles in your belief, why, I suppose they may be allowed for."

With that, and without the offer of the least refreshment or further courtesy from the ladies Ladelle, she bade him *adieu* and he left her, feeling that this had been one of the strangest wooings that any man had ever attempted. The flavour of it was not very pleasant on his lips. He paused and looked back at the house of blank grey stone; it seemed no more inviting than it had done when he had first seen it, and to one of his exquisite taste it was depressing. Now, as then, there was nothing at any of the windows . . . she had not come to wave farewell to her betrothed lord. There was no sign of any feminine finery—a bow of ribbon, a bird in a cage. . . .

"Ah well," he put these trifles out of his mind, "when I get her out of Scotland things will be different. . . ."

* * * *

That evening, after a deal of rather perturbed cogitation, Sir James waited on the two lawyers who had undertaken the business on his behalf—Mr. Skrine and Mr. Tannahill. He told them candidly of his interview with the lady, of her distant, unamiable manners, but of her acceptance without argument of his suit. He asked them if it was possible that he had been the object of some girlish whim . . . if he was being made the butt to bring on some more favoured lover . . . for the whole affair, he confessed, seemed strange.

It was Mr. Skrine, the younger and more talkative lawyer, who assured him that they had received from Miss Morrisson's representative her assent to the marriage. "There will be no difficulty about these settlements."

These words had begun to ring like a chime of tiny bells forming a malicious tune in the young man's mind—"no difficulty about the settlements." There was something sinister in the sound. However, he should of course be glad to know as much. What more could he have asked for? The whole adventure was like a fairy tale.

"She don't have to ask her father's consent, I understand?" he demanded, and Mr. Tannahill assured him the wishes of Morrisson of Drumquassel were not in question.

"His daughter visits him now and then in the summertime when the weather is bearable in those rough regions, but he has no say in the disposal of her person or fortune. The representatives of her guardians in Spain have consented, though I must confess reluctantly, to this disposal of her person. You see," added the lawyer with a grin, "they had no choice, she being now of age, and by the provisions of her mother's will, able to choose her own husband."

"I wonder," said Sir James, "why she chose me? There's something behind this . . . she didn't fall in love with me at sight . . . she was determined to have me before ever I set foot in that room."

"It may be so." The lawyers were diffident. These questions of the heart and emotions did not concern them, as they seemed to infer. "We may congratulate you, Sir James, upon a very wealthy marriage. As I told you before, the full account of the lady's revenues, estates and capital is incomplete, but I believe that you will find it to be rather beyond your expectations."

"I hear," remarked Sir James, without replying to this, though it had a pleasant sound in his ears, "that she has always lived much as a recluse, and is what they call in Paris, *devotee*?"

"That is so," agreed Mr. Tannahill smoothly. "The young lady has never cared much for entertainments, nor diversions, though she has now and then entertained various suitors ... but these, I believe, only because they were put forward as suitable by her guardians ... and she has soon dismissed them, and not in a manner, I believe, likely to make them offer themselves again."

"And now, as soon as she is of age and free to do as she will, she chooses me, the first man who comes along. . . ."

The young baronet was doubtful. More and more it seemed to him that there must be some snare behind what seemed so golden a piece of luck, yet what could there be?

"There's nothing against the lady's reputation, I suppose?" he demanded. "Not that you'd tell me if there was."

"I dare swear that we can assure you as much," replied Mr. Tannahill suavely. "You can ask anywhere you wish in the society of the capital, and you will find the lady has lived, as we said just now, more or less the life of a recluse. She is of a learned turn of mind, a good lutenist, learns Latin, begins the Greek, I understand. . . . She has passed her female tutors, and the minister who has assured her salvation has also supervised her studies."

"Who is he?" asked Sir James carelessly.

Mr. Skrine replied in the same indifferent tone, "A Calvinist minister by the name of Nicholas Jerdan, a poor fellow who got himself through college by cleaning the other scholars' shoes . . . one very zealous among the Calvinists."

"Ah, it all sounds dull to the last degree," sighed the Englishman, "but the gold . . . and I daresay I can manage a bigot of a wife. She'll have time enough on her hands for prayers at Lyndley Waters, for I've got business enough of my own to keep me fully occupied. The marriage is not one that is much to my taste, I admit, but I'll take it . . . indeed, I have little choice."

"You would surely," said Mr. Tannahill, tapping his dry quill on the roll of parchment before him, "be a fool to refuse. This lady, you must remember, is but young—only last month did she reach her twenty-first birthday. She has lived a strange life, enclosed with ancient women, carefully if not somewhat unkindly chosen for her by these guardians, who have never seen her and have little concern for her. . . . She is naturally, it would appear, of an austere disposition and seemingly, I think, rendered morose by her own story—the fact that she is so isolated, that she has no family and cannot easily enter into the enjoyments common to youth. She is a beauty, you must admit," added the lawyer tentatively.

"A beauty, I suppose," Sir James frowned as he made the admission. He recalled the figure of Grace Morrisson standing in her gown of shot silk, in her hand the fan painted with pergolas and palms . . . her clear pale complexion . . . her dark hair and full brown eyes. . . . Yes, she was a beauty, no doubt a painter could make her appear such; but she had no lustre, no glow, no light, no flame. He could think of a dozen others who would better her in his regard.

31

"How long," he asked, "must I stay in Edinburgh before all is settled?"

The lawyers thought that a few days would see all completed. There was the ceremony to be thought of; no doubt the lady, as her tastes were so quiet, desired a very private marriage. He, Sir James, had none of his kin in Edinburgh, and she possessed none save her father, who possibly might find it worth his while to travel from Moffatt to the city to see his daughter married to the Englishman—and who possibly might not be at so much trouble.

"There is never," said Mr. Tannahill, "any accounting for the way Morrisson of Drumquassel will behave."

"Well, I'm glad I shall have little of his company," smiled the Englishman. "As he is set up there in that northern eyrie, I suppose there'll be small chance of his coming my way?"

"He might have a fancy to visit the south," admitted Skrine, "but these are matters more for the future. We have to get off our hands an elaborate and intricate business, which we admit has been our chief concern for many years—the safe marriage of this heiress whose situation is so peculiar, and in a way dangerous . . ."

"How dangerous?" interrupted Sir James.

"Well, sir, does it not occur to you that she might be the prey of a fortune-hunter the moment that her person and her money is in her own disposal? That is why we are glad that she has agreed to marry you, even though you may be, as you say yourself, the first person who has offered for her after her twenty-first birthday. Supposing that this girl were to go out into the world . . . she would meet knaves and charlatans—those who would soon flatter her, dismiss her *duennas* and her maids and, with all the tricks that come so easy to a libertine, beguile her to her ruin."

As Sir James walked home through the dark and, to him, dismal streets of Edinburgh, he recalled this speech. How did he know that *he* was not beguiling Grace Morrisson to her ruin—that she, perhaps, was not beguiling him to his own downfall? A loveless marriage—could all the gold in the world compensate for that?

There was a drag on his spirit as he contemplated his return to Lyndley Waters with this proud and gloomy stranger at his side. He was in no mood to woo her to softer ways, but rather inclined to let her do as she would. He had a dozen projects in hand . . . he was full of zeal, of energy, of schemes for the future, of lust for adventures—of her he wanted nothing but her money. And what did she want? Not himself, he believed; even if he had been a finer man than he was, he could hardly have supposed that; her surrender had been too sudden, had had too prepared an air.

She wanted a husband . . . she wanted perhaps to get away from Edinburgh? But then there were others; there were Scots lords who would have willingly taken her dowry to help their ambitions, or she might have contrived to return to her mother's country, where everything was gorgeous, bright and splendid, and there to have made a careful matrimonial choice. She had money enough now to set herself up handsomely, yet she lived there in that grey house with those three grim-featured women in those rooms hung with serge.

He recalled, with a sudden distaste, the hard, unripe pears hanging among the withered leaves on the trees in the small back orchard. That was what she, Grace Morrisson, was like—hard, unripe fruit. Well, he supposed he would have to endure that . . . a woman, young and fair enough to look at, but immature and sour, as mistress of Lyndley Waters. No doubt she would find the chapel, as he had designed it, far too worldly and ornate for her Scots Calvinist taste? Well, there would have to be a struggle over that, for he did not intend to ruin Lyndley Waters as he had planned it, for her sake, however much he might be indebted to her for the rebuilding of it. . . .

He remembered, too, with some uneasiness, that she had reserved to herself some liberty for her person and a portion of her fortune. That meant, he supposed, that she would take a stated income from her revenues that would be entirely in her own control, and that he would not be allowed to interfere with her comings and goings. He would have to see to that . . . not many of his masculine privileges he would forgo.

Sir James told Pratt, when he returned to the room that seemed cheerful after the house that Grace Morrisson inhabited, of the mingled fortunes of the day—the distaste he had felt for the whole matter, the repulsion almost—it was that for the person of Grace Morrisson, yet the huge prize that it all was—a vast fortune thrown into his hands. . . .

The florid face of the manservant did not express that satisfaction that Sir James had hoped to find there, because he had in his heart hoped that he was doing better even than he had supposed he was, but now in the servant's faithful countenance was confirmation of all his own fears.

"You think I've made a bad bargain, Pratt?" he demanded swiftly.

"I think so, Sir James. If I had been you . . ."

"It is an impertinence for you to even think so. Still, Pratt, you know what I am—aye, even when you are singularly impudent. . . ."

"You may think me grossly impudent or not, sir," replied Pratt nervously, "but if I were you I would return over the border as fast as my horse could carry me and face all my debts and entanglements single-handed, if I couldn't find a rich lady to my liking, rather than take such a one as you describe on the pillion behind me."

"It won't be a pillion," mocked Sir James, speaking frivolously on purpose, for his servant's words struck a deeper dread into his uneasy mind. "Oh no, we shall have to have a coach and four, and outriders no doubt, and everything such as a lady of means may fancy. . . ."

"But, sir, look how she lives," cried the servant. "Why should she suddenly step into such splendour? It's likely enough she'll ride pillion, sir, or in a plain carriage without arms—but what matter for that, it is a detail—what concerns you, and what I would say concerns you in a deadly fashion, is the manner of woman that you are taking to wife and the strange way in which she has accepted you."

"I'm not such a fool I didn't notice that," replied Sir James, "but I cannot afford to be nice. Her reputation is good . . . she is a gentlewoman and would be presentable in court . . . a beauty, as I suppose, in any company. She is of good family on both sides—that rude old fellow at Drumquassel is of fine descent. Her fortune . . . well, it's solid enough and vouched for by Scots lawyers, and I am to have it unhampered."

Thomas Pratt was still unpersuaded.

"I say, sir, that it is no use for a man to take a woman like that into his house, even if she bring a gold-mine with her."

"What have I said of her," asked Sir James, trying to make light of the matter, "that should give you such a poor opinion of the lady? A lady like that, you say; what do you know?"

"Quite enough," the servant insisted. "It's not only what you've said, sir—it's what I have seen and heard for myself. She is a hard, stern bigot . . . one who has turned her face from all the pleasures and enjoyments of youth."

"Well, she's young and malleable," Sir James quoted the lawyers. "I intend to take her, Pratt, no matter what you might argue. Indeed," he added, with a casual air he did not feel, "I should be an odd fellow were I to be turned from a matrimonial engagement by the arguments of my body-servant."

* * * *

Sir James waited regularly upon Grace Morrisson and always found her in the same reserved mood. He was never permitted to see her alone—sometimes one of the ancient gentlewomen, usually Miss Lilias, was with her, sometimes an old man, whose name she did not give, but who he presumed to be the pious tutor spoken of by the lawyers, was present.

At times she was a little gracious and would play on the spinet or harp for him and show him some of her pencil drawings or engravings, or read to him some of her Latin translations. All this he endured with equanimity, for the marriage was fixed for a day not so far off, and he hoped to be again at Lyndley Waters before the cold locked the north from the south.

He made some attempts to get behind the mystery of her acceptance of him, but always received a rebuff. She either had no reason for taking him as her husband, or was determined not to disclose it; nor could he come at any intimate conversation with those who guarded her; the utmost that she conceded was this:

"I suppose, sir, that being open to take a husband, and not being of an ambitious disposition, it was perfectly reasonable to accept the first gentleman of rank who presented himself, and so as to be done with all this tedious legal business. I have no doubt that as mistress of your home I shall have as happy a life as I could have expected."

"But why," cried he, exasperated, "an air so dismal, an outlook so gloomy? You are young, fair and rich, and though I confess you have repulsed me with a good deal of bitterness—yes, I can use no less a word—yet I am willing even now," added the kindly, good-humoured fellow, "to help you to a more cheerful view of life."

The lady smiled at him, and he dropped his eyes uneasily; it was not somehow the smile he would have expected to see on the lips of a young gentlewoman.

"I am not," said she, "of a romantic disposition. I have had, while I have lived here in this odd company—well, I have no doubt to most young girls of my age it would seem odd—my own musings—they led me to this, to accept the first gentleman who should offer himself after I was twenty-one years of age."

"But why," asked Sir James, "did you not accept one of those whom your guardians offered to you when you were of tenderer years?"

"They were all of them," she added, "distasteful to me. I will admit this—it is my great wish to get away from Scotland."

In this he was in hearty agreement with her, though he was surprised when he discovered that she did not desire to return immediately to Lyndley Waters as was his earnest wish, but rather to go on the Continent. She asked him if he had a licence for travelling and if they might visit Paris or Italy before they took up their married life in his English home.

To Sir James, already satiated with foreign travel, this request was not acceptable. He was completely selfish and not inclined to indulge the young girl in what was, from her point of view, a completely reasonable desire. He knew well enough that if they took a short tour abroad to all the places that he knew so well, if he introduced her to his friends in Naples, in Rome, in Genoa, in Paris, if he even took her to her mother's native country and showed off her dark beauty in Madrid or Lisbon, she might lose some of her awkwardness and develop a gaiety more congenial to his own dispostion. But his desire to return to Lyndley Waters was stronger than this consideration; so he put her off guilefully.

"Grace, I am perfectly willing to obtain a licence to travel and to take you abroad, but first let me show you the home over which you will be mistress. You cannot, in Edinburgh, procure the appointments necessary for your rank. You cannot, from this outlandish place, make the plans necessary for these journeyings. Let us return to Lyndley Waters," he urged, "and from there I am very much at your service."

She did not reply to these words and he could not gather whether she took them for what they were, merely courtesy, or if she counted on their sincerity.

Sir James thought it curious that his bride, who had lived so dull a life so placidly, should have a desire to travel for amusement, and he questioned the lawyers on this point, asking if they supposed it to be a whim, or if she really had a secret appetite for pleasure?

"If this was so," he added, "she could surely have indulged it before by connivance with her guardians?"

Mr. Tannahill assured him that whatever the lady's reasons were, they were not a wish for anything light or idle.

"That, I think, is not in her disposition. Whatever her object in desiring to go abroad, it would not be for entertainment. You must remember that she is learned—she probably wishes to collect a cabinet of curiosities, to see historic monuments and to meet the most renowned pedants of the day."

On hearing this possibility, which was one that had not occurred to him, Sir James felt intensely relieved that he had put off his future wife's wish to go abroad.

"I shall certainly," he thought to himself, "see, when we do return to Lyndley Waters, that she never leaves it, if her interests are these, so dry, so unbecoming to a woman."

Teased by the subject, the next time he saw Grace he asked her if what the lawyer had suggested was correct, and she agreed at once with an accent of surprise.

"Did you suppose that I wished to frequent ball-rooms, masquerades and gambling halls?" she demanded. "No—I have heard, from my tutors and guardians, of centres of learning, of sights that every cultured person should see. I desire to make myself better acquainted with the Latin tongue, and that can be done only, I believe, in Rome or Bologna."

"My dear," said Sir James, "our dispositions are strangely dissimilar, but once we are married and have come to some sort of an understanding, I shall try to gratify your outlandish wish."

* * * *

The young man was not quite as easy in his mind as these cool words seemed to imply. Having no intimate friend with him (he had made some acquaintance but no more) in Edinburgh, he discussed the matter with Pratt, a man who might be trusted never to overstep the distance between man and master and yet who had the interest of the Troyes truly at heart.

The servant, however, with that shrewdness that his master found so irritating yet so useful, said, "Sir, why do you go over the pros and cons of this match with me, when you are determined to make it?"

This forced Sir James back on to himself. He had to examine his own emotions, and after a little he exclaimed with an accent almost of alarm: "I believe after all that there are certain things that might cause me even now to forgo both the lady and the fortune."

"What, Sir James," asked Pratt, "are those certain things?"

"By Heaven!" said the young man earnestly, "I

do not know. I have a sense of . . ." he paused, for the word that had been forming on his lips had been "evil," yet it was absurd to associate evil with a prudish girl of irreproachable conduct who had been all her life so carefully guarded.

"The marriage has everything against it, sir," urged Pratt, "except the money—and one of your name and person might hope to attain that on less severe terms."

As he spoke he was shaking out his master's coat of saffron velvet that had been folded at the bottom of the portmanteau with some hope that the traveller might obtain introductions to a noble family. As they had driven farther north, this hope had appeared more and more absurd, for both the landscape and the architecture had become so rude that the velvet and the bullion lying at the bottom of the valise were but a mockery.

The young man laughed as he saw the piece of splendour, that had been so carefully tailored under his own eyes and advice, held up in Pratt's careful hands.

"You do not think that Madam Morrisson will like me the better for going a-wooing in that finery, do you?"

"I was not thinking of Madam Morrisson at all," replied Thomas Pratt as he slipped his hand into one of the large, flat pockets and drew out a small case of red gold-flourished leather. "I was thinking of this, sir."

"Ah, romantic," smiled Sir James, but he did not refuse the case, but took it in his palm and snapped it open. It contained the miniature of an auburn-haired young woman considerably flattered, with an azure background of blue sky and fleecy clouds, a light white drapery and a string of monstrous pearls.

This little picture, not very well executed, represented Celia Plaisent. She had been a neighbour of Sir James's all his life. He had played games with her when they were children and partnered her in the dance and at the hunt when they were youth and maiden. She was not, in his opinion, a great beauty. He was by no means enamoured of her, not even to the extent of writing her a paper of verses, but now, looking at this crude and flattering picture of her gay and tender face, he wished that he could have had her as his wife instead of Grace Morrisson.

The servant watched him with sarcasm.

"You'd better turn home and face your difficulties, Sir James, than remain entangled in these northern mysteries. Mistress Plaisent would prove a good wife to you—a good housekeeper for Lyndley Waters. With her, as I, a plain man, see it, will be happiness and prosperity, differences, of course, but more of that measure of smoothness that a common mortal may hope for."

As he paused, his master added lightly:

"Well, I suppose you prophesy that in my arranged marriage the reverse will occur? But why do you speak of these northern mysteries? Everything is plain and above-board."

"That, sir, I deny," replied the Englishman with heat. "We are strangers—in a manner of speaking, foreigners, in Edinburgh. You have not even used the introductions you had, but have gone straight, like a man bewitched, for a match that was put into your mind by a chance stay at a wayside mansion."

Sir James admitted this was true, and for a while

his servant's common-sense words gave him a little pause, but he still boggled at the words "northern mysteries" which sounded in a fashion so grotesque on the lips of matter-of-fact Thomas Pratt.

"Expound to me these mysteries," he demanded at length.

"They are plain to see," demanded the servant, speaking more with the authority of an older man than with the servility of a mere domestic. "These lawyers, they tell you what you want to hear. . . ."

"I am sure of the money," put in Sir James. "I have satisfied myself about that."

"I do not dispute that the money is there," replied Pratt. "That is clear enough—I have made my own enquiries in Edinburgh."

"The devil you have!" exclaimed Sir James. "Well, I suppose you would, in taverns and gossiping at corners . . . though I suppose you find it difficult to understand their barbarous dialect?"

"I certainly do," replied the Englishman disdainfully; "but you must remember, sir, that there are a fair number of Southerners—Border people, and even English—in the city, and I know my way about as is befitting a gentleman's body-servant. You must recall, sir, that we left Lyndley Waters on what might be termed an adventure, and that I consider myself equipped both by way of physical prowess and gift of intrigue for such an exploit as you had in mind."

Sir James laughed loud (and he was glad to have something to laugh at) at this speech, but he was none the less keen to know what was in Pratt's mind. Was there any definite blot, carefully concealed from him by the lawyers, on the fair fame of Grace Morrisson? Thomas Pratt would not admit as much.

He returned firmly to his word "mysteries"—the way the girl lived, the amount of money she had, the indifference her Spanish relatives showed as to her disposal of it, the quickness with which the negotiations had been made; the smoothness of the lawyers and, above all, the hard and unmanageable temper of the young lady herself and her, as it seemed, unaccountable whim—it could be called no more—of marrying the first man who asked her when she was free to dispose of herself and her fortune.

"Consider too, sir," added the servant earnestly, "to what you expose yourself . . . a shrewish and pedantic wife. She may wish to fill Lyndley Waters with philosophers, alchemists—I know not what in the way of busybodies. She has already, at her age, the character of a religious woman; none could be worse."

Sir James agreed. "But I shall be master in my own house," was his consolation.

Pratt was not so sure of the truth of this statement.

"You are of a soft disposition, sir. You will be deeply engaged in your own affairs, and this woman—this foreign woman—will be mistress of Lyndley Waters. What will the neighbouring gentry think of her? Her descent, to say the least of it, is peculiar . . . her demeanour, I expect, will offend many, sir; I do not myself consider the risk one worth taking."

Pratt had a good deal more to say in this train which had the effect of darkening and confusing his master's mind, but not that of making him swerve from his point. He was, he knew, dismayed and uneasy. The match was about as unlikely a one as he could have conceived of, but it was the only one that came his way that was in the least capable of mending his fortunes so that he could continue to rebuild Lyndley Waters.

He stared at the miniature in his hand. Poor, sweet Celia, with the small portion of a third sister . . . a family not wealthy . . . all merry and good-hearted . . . and Plaisent Court . . . a charming place. But what use was that to him with his grandiose ideas?

He recalled that when he had been in Italy on his Italian tour, he had thought of Celia a good deal and with such tenderness and softness that he had almost persuaded himself that he was in love with her and would, on his return, risk a poor marriage. Yes, while he had been travelling with a larger retinue than he could afford through the gay cities of Rome and Naples, attending the gambling houses and the salons of such gentry as were open to him, he had recalled, among that atmosphere of gaudiness and ostentation, the tall figure of the English girl with her pretty auburn hair that was merely looped with a dark bright ribbon, with her kind, steadfast eyes and her conversation that was not brilliant nor witty, but kind and cheerful.

His fancy now went back to those Italian days. He remembered the marble palaces in their garish colours, the Bay of Naples when there had been a great concert on the occasion of the birth of a royal prince, and the sky had been hit by cascades of stars and fountains of artificial fire that rivalled the sultry glow from Vesuvius. Then, as now, he had felt a stranger, rather as if these dark foreigners, in their glittering brocades and street masks with the slits for the sparkling eyes, had despised him as little short of a rustic. He felt that they had known his embarrassment, and he had never got near enough to the core of their society to even form the scheme of selecting a rich wife from among them. Besides, an Italian—a Scot might be tolerated, but not a woman from the continent! Yet he mused still on those days, wantonly and foolishly, for they had nothing to do with his present circumstances.

He recalled the lonely walk that he had taken with one of his friends about the ruins of a Roman fort high above the city and Bay of Naples. The moonlight was so bright that it had seemed to him that it must have been artificial and the trees had stood out against the gleaming pallor of the sky with an intense blackness. In the intermittent glare given forth by the volcano, he had seen the smooth waters of the bay curling in regular wavelets on the shore, and the light skiffs that, even at this hour, passed across them, intent, as he supposed, on some game or pleasure; but to him the scene had been as unfamiliar as it was gloomy.

The arch had cast a black shadow across the road that was dead white in the moonlight, and he recalled, because it had been the first time in his life that he had felt that sensation, a thrill of fear as he had approached it. Like all travellers in southern Italy, he had been warned of the banditti who lurk in lonely places to surprise the stranger, and he had put his hand on his friend's arm, warning him, with an air of lightness, to be ready with his sword or dagger. The other Englishman had assented and agreed that the spot seemed lonely and had an air of terror. "But it is only, as I suppose," he had added carelessly, "our disposition. We have come for the sake of the cool air up from the heated, painted salons of the city, and this quiet of nature is likely to oppress our spirits."

They passed under the arch without incident. Sir James remembered the large tufts of ferns that, growing from the broken masonry, stood out like the plumes of a warrior's helmet against the sky that, lit by the radiance of the moonlight, seemed to sparkle with a thousand atoms of brilliance.

When they had passed the arch they had found themselves, not as they expected on the clear high road, but entangled, as it were, in the ruins of a Roman citadel that was approached by steps from the city below. Here were large, important towers, still strong against the continued, unwearied assaults of time; quarries had been made in them as people required material for building; but the main outline was undefaced—a Roman fort and one of formidable pretensions.

The two Englishmen had leant upon a parapet, moving carefully lest a false step should send them into some underground chamber or other danger. "For who knows," Sir James had said, "that these fools of foreigners may have excavated and left exposed some cavities?"

He recalled his feelings as he had looked out across the bay, when the mountain had sunk into plumes of smoke, the water was silver clear from the moon's glow and might be likened to a burnished platter, for the ripples on it were so small that from this distance they were imperceptible. When Vesuvius sent out curls of gold and scarlet flame, the whole bay was lit up by these same sombre and terrific colours, while the palaces and churches of the city below became momentarily visible in a sulphurous glare.

As Sir James, in his sober northern chamber, dwelt on this scene, he knew, of a sudden, why it had come thus, un-asked, into his memory. . . . It was a symbol of his present situation. He was now, he believed, in some such position as he had been when looking over the ruins of the Roman fort, though then it had been but a play, a wayside adventure, meaning nothing . . . now the position and the scene might be symbolical of his entire future.

Every day was ordinary, filled with the preparations for the marriage between a ruined man with a title and a girl of no particular birth with a large fortune. . . . So on the surface—but there were times when the whole of this commonplace affair seemed lit up by a glow of red and yellow gloom as threatening as had been the plumes of flame from Vesuvius.

"Still," said he aloud, "I must go on and take my destiny." And he returned the red case to Thomas Pratt, adding that it had been given him in childish sport only.

* * * *

It was but five days before his marriage when Sir James waited upon Grace Morrisson with a wedding gift. His credit was not so low now that it was known he was to marry the heiress, and he was now able to raise funds through his Scotch lawyer. He had taken another servant to supplement Pratt, moved to finer lodgings, though he swore that there were none in Edinburgh fit to house a gentleman, and he had paid that morning a visit to Heriot's Row, where he had made choice of a jewel for his unloved bride.

48

He did not intend to spend more than would acquit him of meanness. When he purchased this gift he had in mind his own standing, not the lady's merit, and it was almost with disdain that he made his offering, but by chance he had come upon a stone of a most unusual beauty that the goldsmith had told him had been in his charge for many years. There was a story belonging to it to which Sir James had not listened very attentively. All he had gathered was that it had been brought from Kashmir by a Scot who had deposited it with this particular merchant in return for a loan and never called for it; so it now became the goldsmith's property to sell, which he did to Sir James at a considerably reduced price. It was what was known technically as a male sapphire, Kashmir blue, far paler than Sir James thought such a stone ever could be, and he saw by the quick sparkle in the lady's eye that she recognised the magnificence of the gift that he had bought at so low a price.

The gem was plainly set in a golden circlet and was attached to a very fine gold chain. This lay in a small box of sandal-wood, roughly padded with a loose piece of crimson velvet, the whole enclosed in beaten silver and fastened with a small lock and key.

"This is all that I can offer you as a marriage gift," remarked Sir James casually, "until we return to England," and he smiled to himself to think how true were all the quips that had ever been made of womankind, for now that she held this jewel in her hand, the lady's demeanour was certainly softened.

She held it against her austere gown of a dull grey colour that he much disliked, and then against her neck, which was round, white and pretty enough, and did not even disdain to turn aside and glance at

49

herself in a mirror.

"Yes, my dear, you might be a beauty if you would take a little trouble with yourself," continued Sir James to himself. "I hope, when you get to Lyndley Waters, you will leave aside this sad and sober dress . . . this plain fashion on arranging your hair and, in brief, attire yourself more becoming to your position as my wife." This he added aloud.

This comment, ending with what seemed to the girl a proud reprimand, dulled her pleasure in the stone. She put it aside and replied with her usual coldness:

"I propose to lead my own life whether I am in Scotland or in your home; that is in the marriage contract."

"We will hope," replied Sir James, "that human nature will overcome the clauses of a mere marriage contract. I believe that it usually does so. It is not likely, my dear Grace, that you are of a more unyielding material than any other woman that was ever born."

He thought that she was struggling with herself, that she wished to show temper but decided for some selfish needs of her own to be amiable.

Turning on him her brilliant brown eyes, she forced a smile and asked: "Have you thought further about our journey abroad? It is quite usual for young married couples of our rank—and you insist, Sir James, a good deal upon your rank, if you never mention mine—to take such a holiday."

Her request brought to his mind the sharp memory he had had in the Bay of Naples and the dark ruins of the Roman citadel.

He replied: "I do not know what pleasure you

would take in such foreign cities as I know of, for the places I could take you to are what you would most thoroughly disapprove of ... Rome, Paris, Naples"—the word was just on his lips when she interposed by saying:

"I thought of travelling to Switzerland."

He was astonished by this choice. Switzerland was little visited by people of rank or fashion. What was there to offer but barbarous mountains and rustic villages? He told her as much, expressing his amazement at her suggestion. Yet she was no fool, he knew, and instantly, with a pang of fear—queer, indefinable fear—he felt there was some reason behind her request ... if there was, she would not give it. . . .

"I like mountain scenery. I greatly admire our own hills—one can call them no more. Nothing pleases me better than to ride among our Scottish mountains, but it is not often that that is possible. My father, who should be my companion and guardian on these occasions, is seldom of the temper to accompany me, and I have read that in Switzerland there are mountains of a tremendous height. . . ."

"Of a height so tremendous," replied Sir James, "that none but those trained guides who are natives of the place may attempt them. The ascent is usually made in litters, carriages being taken to pieces and carried thus by mules over the passes. I must confess that I do not consider such a prospect either amusing or profitable. I will not so far deceive you as to pretend that I should look with favour on a journey to Switzerland."

He could not avoid a smile of genuine amusement. The girl was strange enough, why she should add so peculiar a request to her other oddities—but well, there was nothing to do but to smile as at a jest.

The lady's face remained severe.

"I have it near my heart," she insisted. "I intended to put it forward as a proposal to any man that I might marry. It is unfortunate that it is impossible," she added reflectively, "for a woman to travel alone."

"I cannot hold out any hopes of gratifying you," said Sir James. "Tell me something," he added in order to divert her, "of your travels among your native hills. They are steep and lonely enough . . . too much so for my taste."

"There is much to be seen among them," she replied quietly. "In the early morning, when the light strikes athwart the glen and the eagle hovers in the silver mist, one may see perhaps wraiths crossing lonely fords, one may behold the spirit of the water kelpie waiting with his flowing white mane to catch the unwary traveller . . . hobgoblins lurk in the granaries of the lonely farmhouses, and it is possible when passing through some lonely ravine to behold on a distant slope phantom armies . . ."

"So much I have heard," replied Sir James. "Your country is haunted. . . ." He laughed, trying to give this talk an amusing and even foolish air, but the girl's eyes were on him gravely. "In a lonely country, such stories would be likely to arise," he added. "But tell me where you have been and what you have experienced yourself."

"I have nothing that would interest you," she replied. "I once or twice undertook a ride with my father. He can be, when he wishes, good company. Although I favour in my person my mother so much,

I believe it is my father that I resemble in my disposition. . . ."

"I should say that it was," smiled Sir James. "You appear, my lovely Spaniard, to be in your character no more than a Black Cameronian. . . ."

The girl appeared to take this as a compliment and proceeded to relate how on several occasions she and her father, riding with a small retinue through glens that were to all but the natives inaccessible, had come upon the remnants of the Covenanters' gatherings . . . a rude stone building designed perhaps as a place of worship, a ravine haunted only by the fox and the eagle, but that had been obviously cut into steps by human hands, that led them with great difficulty to some shelter, no more than a hole in the bare rock, that could easily be screened by bracken and heather.

"Many a time," mused Grace Morrisson, "have I slept upon the heather—and never slept sweeter. . . ."

"Not, I hope, in those filthy hiding-places," smiled Sir James.

"No," replied the girl gravely, "in the open, wrapped in my thin plaid, with the summer air about me—and when I awoke, the harebell on its delicate stalk close to my face."

"You seem," remarked her future bridegroom, "curiously attached to what you consider your native land, which makes me the more surprised that you are willing to marry a southerner. I should like," he added, speaking of no set purpose, but because the matter slipped into his mind, "to meet this man, Nicholas Jerdan, your former tutor and instructor from whom, as I suspect, you have imbibed many of your opinions and ideas. Is that the name? It was given my by Miss Lilias."

"He is abroad," she answered casually. "He is a learned man and one who is not content to bide long in one place. I believe at the present moment he is at the university of Leyden, where he pursues a course of theology."

Nothing to Sir James could be more dull and depressing than this conversation. If he disliked everything that was to do with divines, especially those of the Scottish denomination, he disliked even more any talk of fairies, ghosts or wraiths. In his view the girl's mind had been disturbed, perhaps even for ever darkened by the people in whose charge she had been left. He felt again a throb of compassion for her. He saw her as a child alone in this grey-fronted house, with those indifferent and far distant Spanish relatives, given over to the grim Calvinists who had been selected by her guardians.

"I wonder," said he, "there was no attempt to make you of your mother's faith?"

"My mother," she replied, and her eyes darkened as she spoke, "was converted to the religion of John Calvin before she died, and it was through her most earnest request that I was left in the charge of Madame Ladelle and her sisters, in whose establishment I now am."

"And your father, is he of such stern inclinations?"

"By no means," replied Grace Morrisson. "But that doesn't alter my own convictions."

"You must consider me," said he, rising and taking up the silver case to which she had returned the sapphire, "as a most light and frivolous fellow . . . you have had no word of serious discourse from me; nor have I been able to talk to you on any subject that would, as I should suppose, be agreeable to you."

She inclined her head and said nothing, as if she did not wish to answer the question; but he would not let the matter be . . . it was but five days from his marriage, and there might be something he could discover that would make that marriage impossible.

"Tell me," he urged, with all the force of his native candour, "once more I ask you, why it is you selected me? If you really think you can have no fondness for my person, no tolerance for my point of view? Remember, I feel it my duty to warn you that if you marry me for some secret reason that has nothing to do with love and tenderness, we are likely, both of us, to be most unhappy. . . ."

As she still did not answer, but sat with drooping head and averted face, he continued:

". . . and you will be the more unhappy of the two. I shall have my sports, my games abroad, my friends, my place at court . . . you will remain at Lyndley Waters that will be in every way alien and distasteful to you." Still the lady did not reply, and he became irritated by her silence. "I think you owe me more courtesy than you use," he complained. "I begin to think either that you are extremely dull . . ."

She looked up at that with a laugh that contradicted his words, "No, I'm not dull. I marry you because I choose to. . . . Is not a woman allowed her caprice? My father will be in Edinburgh to-morrow . . . you can ask him if he knows of any hidden motive why I should choose you. Meanwhile, Sir James, why not be content with your good luck? I believe from what my lawyers told me, that you were but a ruined man when you rode into Edinburgh, and now you have a large fortune . . . cannot you let it go at that?"

She put out her long hand as she spoke and took from him the silver box.

"I am not so indifferent to these splendours as you suppose," she said quietly, and turning the key she took out the pale, glittering disc of fire and held it in the palm of her pale hand. "I have lacked opportunities to go gaily. The ladies who look after me do not encourage the visits of the mantua-maker or the milliner. . . ."

"If you are so strict a Calvinist, you are not allowed to indulge in worldly gear," smiled Sir James with as near an approach to a sneer as his good humour ever permitted him. "Why should you even think of it?"

The lady smiled again. She seemed to be mocking at herself as much as at him, to disdain their bargain.

"Indeed," she said, with some kindness, "I can tell you nothing. We have made a contract . . . let us keep it."

"I should like some pact drawn up between us," he countered, "that goes beyond the articles of our contract and that in some way might safeguard this strange marriage."

Grace Morrisson rose. Her interruption had the air of an insult.

"I have some duties to which I must attend," she said very formally. "No provisions can safeguard this strange marriage."

* * * *

Mr. Morrisson of Drumquassel waited upon Sir James as soon as he arrived in Edinburgh. He made a decent but not a notable appearance in his neat but not fashionable attire, and he had with him one servant, rude but fairly well equipped. Robert Morrisson certainly appeared a different man from the rough fellow who had sat in the light of the log fire and had detailed the story of the Spanish lady and the Scot who had passed beneath her window. Now he was commonplace, matter of fact, exactly like any passer-by whom Sir James might have selected from those who went up and down the Royal Mile.

He did not appear particularly impressed or concerned by the news of his daughter's match with Sir James; he made the conventional remark that it was curious that a mere chance night's hospitality should have led to a marriage. Sir James agreed, and there seemed little more to be said on that score.

It was the Englishman, with his instinct for honesty and candour, who went beyond the articles of his legal agreement in asking Mr. Morrisson flatly if he was content that all this large fortune should be handed over to a stranger, and if he would not himself accept at least some small provision from it?

Mr. Morrisson thanked him without emotion for this generous offer.

"She might easily have fallen into the hands of a scoundrel," said he, "who would have suggested no such thing, and I am grateful to you for your thought—my means, my taste and my dwelling appeared to you no doubt primitive and even disgusting, but to me they are sufficient. I have a small fortune of my own which comes from my land, and I do not desire a pittance—"

Sir James interrupted on that word. "I would not

have said pittance, sir, I would rather you had taken any monies that might have been given to you out of this estate as your due. . . ."

But Mr. Morrisson put all this aside. "I have been," he said, "familiar and, as it were, reconciled to this situation since my wife died. She became a gloomy and religious woman, one in whose company there was little comfort; she directed that her daughter should be taken out of my charge—"

"But how," asked Sir James, "was this possible?"

Mr. Morrisson put the question aside. "There were legal provisions that I made when I married my handsome Spaniard," he sneered. "I was a young man then and proud. . . . Well, there were these provisions made, and Grace was delivered to Madam Ladelle and has been brought up ever since in the house with the little pear orchard in which you found her. I suppose," he added, "those pears are all withered and falling to the ground now? You must make haste and get your wedding over before the winter closes in here in the north. There is very little I need tell you about myself—sometimes I come to Edinburgh to look up a crony or so, sometimes I go on a visit to a neighbouring castle, sometimes I and a servant or two take a ride across the Highlands. . . . Did you see anything of Moffatt, the glens and waterfalls?"

"Your daughter has spoken to me of those same rides. . . . I had understood from them that she broods on the legends of her country, and is full of zeal for the Covenanters."

Mr. Morrisson gave him a quick, wary look.

"You must expect that. I do not think that Grace will be much more of a homely companion than was her mother, but it is well understood that you are marrying her for her money; and I understand, for I have visited the lawyer, that this is a far larger sum than might have been expected."

Sir James admitted as much but without a great deal of shamefacedness. His pride and his complacency helped him here. He really did not feel that the bargain was very unequal; there was his title, his position—above all, the fact that he was English—to set against mere money, and he resolved in his good-humoured heart always to treat the strange girl kindly, even going so far as to speculate, "Perhaps Celia, who is so sweet and gentle, might help there." He knew that it was a dangerous thing to set two women together, yet in this case, with Celia . . .

Mr. Morrisson broke into his musings.

"I have come to Edinburgh only for your wedding; then, though the winter is setting in, I shall return to my castle with a store of books. You did not know, I think, that I was something of a scholar?"

"I understand your daughter is," smiled Sir James. "That is somewhat disconcerting—a learned lady is one of those oddities that no man of breeding knows how to handle."

"Eh, well, have you made all arrangements for your marriage?"

"It has been arranged for St. Giles's Cathedral," replied Sir James, wearied by this insistence on routine detail. "I have left everything to the legal men—that is their business, is it not? I have certain acquaintances, here, by introduction at least, who will serve me for my part, and I understand it is neither your wish, nor that of your daughter, that there should be any festivity? Let the whole affair, then, be as formal, nay, as dull as possible . . . let your daughter select her maids at once and let us return south as soon as maybe. I make no disguise that this is my ardent wish. I should have thought," he added, "that the Reverend Nicholas Jerdan, who has been your daughter's tutor, would have wished to have married us."

"Why, so he would," smiled Mr. Morrisson, "had he been here, but he is abroad on some course of theological study."

"How astonishing," exclaimed Sir James, "the lives of other men appear! I can no more imagine what this fellow must be like, who can spend his days in going from one dreary college to another, to pore over empty points of theology, than he, I suppose, could understand me. Good Heavens, what are these fellows! It seems as if there was no flesh on their bones, no blood in their veins. I am sorry that Grace has been infected with so much—well, I must confess it seems to me little short of—rubbish. . . ."

Mr. Morrisson did not reply. He gave a pull on his long clay pipe, and when he spoke again his remark was at variance with the young man's ironical candour.

"I may be able to find my way south and visit you at your place for which you are prepared to sacrifice so much—Lyndley Waters, is it not called, in the county of Wiltshire?"

Thereupon Sir James civilly invited his future father-in-law to be his guest whenever he would, and it was not till afterwards that he remembered the words "for which you are prepared to sacrifice so much," and considered them, surely, a curious expression for a man to have used about a marriage with his own daughter.

However, Sir James, despite his own indefinable forebodings, the common-sense objections that Thomas Pratt never ceased on any possible occasion to put before him, and even a hint from Mr. Skrine, the younger lawyer, that he would do well to postpone his marriage until he had looked more thoroughly into his own feelings with regard to the lady—continued to press on for an early wedding. The days before this ceremony were heavy on his hands; so far from all that he cared about, from his usual occupations and amusements, disliking the few people to whom he had introductions in Edinburgh, disliking indeed the bleak, northern city, he was driven to that restlessness that often sends people on aimless wanderings. More than once he left his rooms and, wrapped in his winter cloak, made his way out to Arthur's Seat, and, climbing through the rifts of mist, reached that craggy height from which he could look down upon the roofs and spires of Edinburgh.

It was two days before the ceremony fixed to take place in St. Giles's that Sir James thus left his rooms, flinging down with an exclamation of discontent the book that he had been endeavouring to read. Everything that he could do had been done; Thomas Pratt and the lawyers between them had seen to all the practical details. The bridegroom had but to present himself at the altar on a given day and date when Grace Morrisson would be by her father placed in his care as his wife. . . . Well, there let the matter rest. After that he would take up his own life again. He would travel as fast as possible southward. He would see Lyndley Waters once more . . . he would be able eagerly to question his steward, Mr. Swallow, as to the progress of the work in his absence . . . he would be able, and this was the best prospect of all, to pay off the creditors, to engage masons, carpenters and ironworkers again, and to see his splendid home made yet more magnificent by his own taste and exertions.

As he turned to the door the servant made as if to stay him.

"Do you think it wise to go out? It is a strange city and the night's dark, Sir James."

"Who should be at the trouble of interfering with me?" replied the young man hastily. "You try to spoon-feed me, Pratt. Why, I should suppose if anyone had been intending to rob me of my watch and shoe-tags they would have done so by now. Gloomy the city may be, but it seems decently policed."

But the Englishman still urged his master not to go abroad alone.

"Take me with you, sir. I know you intend but a restless wandering in and out of the Wynds, but I would be a silent and perhaps useful companion."

Sir James, however, refused his body-servant's company and went out alone into the cold, dark, northern night. A small oil lamp over every tenth house or so was all the illumination in the city. A fine sprinkle of the first snow was falling, and this seemed to have kept everyone indoors, for the streets, as far as the dim light would permit Sir James to see, were empty. He knew now well enough the fashionable and busy quarters—Greyfriars Church, the Tron Church, St. Giles's Cathedral and the square that contained the grave of John Knox and other such familiar places in the city—as well as he knew the house where Grace Morrisson lived near Holyrood Palace. His own lodgings were near Tolbooth, and he took, after following a usual street for a while, a different turn and set out in a direction that was not well known to him, even by daylight.

He passed several vagabonds wrapped in their cloaks and shawls who begged alms from him, but he paid no attention to them and continued to walk briskly, without a purpose. His surroundings were not very real to him, his mind was more distracted than he would admit, and his fancies dwelt too often for his own comfort on his coming marriage and on the girl whom he was to take home as his wife.

He turned up a long flight of steps that led to one of those small passage streets, to him so unfamiliar, that the Scotch term Wynds. He gave no thought to the possible danger of entering these quarters which he did not doubt were inhabited by low and desperate characters, but he found it difficult to make his way, for the lights were so infrequent and the darkness of the night so dense; so he walked slowly, almost with a stumbling gait, putting out his hand to steady himself by the walls of the houses on one side.

He was startled from his reveries, that were crossed by memories of that view of the Bay of Naples when he had watched the fireworks and then the sombre coming and going of the lights of Vesuvius, by an old woman's voice, who asked him what he did in such a place? He supposed she was but another beggar. Her accent was to him uncouth, but he could by now understand what the inhabitants of Edinburgh said, at least when they spoke of no more than ordinary matters.

63

"If you are begging, my good woman," he replied, "it is useless coming to me. I have but a few pence with me and they are English, not Scots money."

A laugh came out of the darkness, like that of a person who is often misunderstood.

"Would you come into my kitchen and speak with me awhile?" said the voice, or into some such words he interpreted the request made in the Scottish dialect.

He felt a physical need of warm and relief from the icy air. It had been foolish of him not to take Pratt's advice. Better at home in a comfortable room by a large fire with his drink and his book, however tired he was of both, than these aimless wanderings; so he said, with the recklessness that was native to him:

"Why not, my good woman? Do you live near? I cannot even see you, though I believe I discern a smudge of white that might be your cap."

"It is," replied the old woman's voice, "and my door is not two paces away. Will you walk carefully on the left side, for the gutter is full with much refuse? You have been lucky not to have put your foot in it already—and I will open the door to give us some light."

The stranger spoke with a clarity and sense that seemed above her class, also as if she had more reason than the earning of a few coins in her request.

Sir James, accommodating his step to hers, followed her for a few paces until she, as she had promised, pushed open a door that let forth a sharp, yellow light into the street.

The Englishman was then astonished at the

misery of the alley in which he had been walking. It was narrow, cobbled and contained all manner of rubbish that had been flung out of the wretched houses.

With something of a shudder he followed the woman into the room that opened directly on to the street. She shut the door and, he noticed, bolted it. He might have walked into a trap. He thought of that immediately—but he had his short sword and, what he unconsciously relied on more, his considerable physical strength.

The room was extremely mean, and while not kept with a scrupulous cleanliness, by no means as filthy as the alley outside. A large fireplace occupied almost the whole of one wall. Here burned a fire over which hung a pot, grimy with soot and charcoal. In front were two stools and an old settle. The rest of the room was occupied by some poor pieces of furniture, among which Sir James noticed the large, open Bible box.

His first glance, however, was not for his surroundings but for the old woman's person. She appeared to be of about sixty years of age, still active though somewhat bent, and wore the almost indistinguishable garb of the lower classes in Edinburgh, a dun-culoured skirt, a shawl of hues all drab and intermingled, and a tall, white bonnet, soiled and darned, held in place with a dingy greenish ribbon. Her features were weather-beaten and shrewd.

She beckoned him to one of the stools while she took the other herself.

"You're a strange young man to see in my poor room," she smiled, "and I suppose you can understand very little of what I say?"

"I can translate it in my mind into the English," replied Sir James cheerfully. "What do you want with me? I confess that I was weary of myself and in need of some manner of an adventure. I have been now for some weeks in Edinburgh and find it all confoundedly dull."

"That is because you have not seen beneath the surface," she answered. "There is enough excitement . . . love and hate and crime . . . aye, and beauty too, in Edinburgh to satisfy anyone. I suppose a fine young man like you, who has travelled in Rome and Paris and Naples . . ." His flesh pricked slightly that she had used the name of that city, "will find this but a grey, forlorn town, but there are things going on that you wouldn't see, not perhaps if you lived here for some months."

She seemed to him to be speaking slowly, painfully, as if anxious that he should understand everything she said. He noticed behind where she sat was a door that led probably to a stair, and he had his eye on that in case he was surprised by some brawny ruffians in search of his watch or any coins that he might have in his pockets.

The old woman sensed his apprehension and told him with an earnestness that he could hardly mistake, that he need be in no fear and that her intentions were all good.

"I wish to tell you, young man," said she, "you're a stranger to me, and an Englishman at that, but I had a son once who went to sea and never returned again who had something of your likeness, and perhaps it is because of him and because of some whim and perhaps mere Christian charity that I warn you not to marry Grace Morrisson."

This was about the last observation that Sir James had expected, and he could not keep a cloud of alarm from his face. She observed this and added in a tone of quiet triumph:

"You see, you do not really wish for this match yourself; you're forcing yourself to it for the money."

"Did I show as much from my look?" he demanded with a pride covering up his momentary confusion.

"There is no need for you, sir, to try to deceive an old woman who was born in the Highlands and who has something of the second sight."

"I have heard about the Highlanders and your seers and your second sight, and your raving frenzies," smiled Sir James. "I'm afraid in London they make mere tales ... no, hardly that ... we credit them so little we do not amuse ourselves by repeating them."

"You'll hear none of them from me," she replied. "What is, is. What does it matter to you where I come from or what my history was? But perhaps if you knew that, you would give more credit to my warning to leave alone the daughter of Mr. Morrisson of Drumquassel."

"You can hardly suppose that I should break off at two days' notice my marriage with a considerable heiress," said Sir James with an air of pleasant mockery, "on the word of an old dame like yourself whom I met by chance on a cold night in a mean wynd of Edinburgh?"

"You may put it as you will," she answered. "Warnings are but warnings—I know more than you do about this matter, and I give you this warning. I have told you why I give it you. You may not believe any of my reasons—that will not make them the less true."

He was impressed, as people will be by solemn words spoken on an intimate matter by a stranger, and he sat on his stool with his elbow on his knee and his handsome face in his hand and looked at her quizzically.

"You'll have to tell me a little more," he smiled. "The gold's tempting—I need it."

"For vanity," she replied. "For building up a home that perhaps there will be no one to inherit. How will you feel if on your death-bed your splendid place, that you have sacrificed so much to build, has to go to creditors or a stranger?"

This reflection was to him a cold one. He had to put it aside or it would have been unbearable. It was not possible for him to contemplate such a disaster. He gazed into the fire, lifting his brow.

"I suppose at the back of our mind we must all face a prospect of hell," he retorted with an attempt at lightness, "but it must be at the back of our minds, otherwise life would be unendurable."

"But here," said the old woman eagerly, "is a misfortune you can easily avoid. Return to your own country, go to other places to search for an heiress—but do not marry Grace Morrisson. There is a reason that I may not divulge, but that is very potent, that should prevent you, or indeed any man save one . . ." and here she paused.

"Well, who is this one man?" asked Sir James.

"I must not speak of him—he does not come into the story now."

"Bah!" The young man rose. "You are beginning

to mutter like one of those Christmas-time witches who tell tales to amuse fools. How was it that you came upon me so pat?"

"I'd been following you," she said meekly, "a long while. Many a day and on many a night I have followed you—you haven't noticed me, I look like many another old woman—in many places and on many occasions, without the chance to speak to you; but to-night, when your mood was gloomy and you impetuously took this way that led near my own home, I was able to take the chance to give you my warning." She rose with the air of one suddenly fatigued and motioned him towards the door. "Go your way," she said. "No one will attack you, you're safe enough. Ruffians and scoundrels live round here, but they do not risk their necks falling upon solitary and well-known strangers. Turn your face the way you came and you will find yourself in thoroughfares that are familiar to you."

He made one attempt, though he considered this beneath his dignity, to break through her reserve.

"If I were to offer you a bribe," he asked, "would you tell me a little more of what lies behind your foolish talk?"

"No bribe," she replied quietly, "and no threat would make me say any more than I have said," and again, with a gesture that was not without its dignity, she indicated her poor door.

Sir James opened it, threw his cloak closer round his throat and stepped into the darkness of the wynd.

He was not greatly impressed by this adventure, which seemed to have a stage appearance. He was inclined to suspect that Grace Morrisson and those sober yet petulant gentlewomen, the ladies Ladelle, who appeared to be her guardians and her confidantes, were playing tricks upon him out of spite, or with an endeavour to show early in the day their power over his mind and fortunes.

The bleakness of the night and the solitary way that he had to follow to return to his chambers, for he had lost contact with the mainstreet and could but proceed on a winding path until he arrived in familiar ways, helped, however, to make the old woman's words, trivial as they might be, echo in his mind and with a sigh.

* * * *

Sir James was glad with almost a sense of relief to find when he returned that Mr. Widdacombe, one of his London attorneys, had arrived, late and tired, and was waiting for him in front of a large fire carefully mended by Pratt.

The sober Englishman's blunt and honest face, his familiar accent, greatly reassured Sir James that what he was engaged on was no fantastic and perhpas perilous adventure, but a businesslike and sensible transaction.

Mr. Widdacombe was all that was reassuring and comfortable. After the conventional greetings he spoke for fully a quarter of an hour on the extraordinary luck of the chance that had set Sir James in the way of Grace Morrisson, and while he was thus congratulating his client, the young man remained in the hooded chair the other side of the fire, listening with much satisfaction, yet in the depth of his still disturbed mind and soul, wondering why he had ever been perturbed.

He brought these doubts into the light by interrupting the lawyer's harangue.

"Sir, I am grateful to you for thus confirming my own judgment in this marriage establishment, yet I would like to put before you one or two no doubt fanciful objections that have come into my thoughts."

The lawyer stared at him across the candlelit space. He had journeyed post haste from London to assist the son of his old friend and client in making certain of one of the finest prizes in the British marriage market, and he was astonished to hear these words that seemed to imply a certain hesitancy and regret.

"I can assure you, Sir James," he returned quickly, "that we, as is our duty, have made every investigation into the lady's family, status and behaviour."

Sir James put that aside by raising his hand and letting it fall again.

"All that may be known of her I know," he answered, "but the circumstances of her father's marriage. This large dowry left . . ."

It was the lawyer's turn to interrupt, for he felt that now he was on his own ground.

"We have studied the matter, Sir James, I assure you. Mr. Morrisson, when in Madrid, was sufficiently infatuated with the lady who became his wife to permit her fortune to be disposed of, should she predecease him, by her relatives and settled entirely upon her children. He did not wish there to be the least suspicion that he was making this marriage for the sake of any worldly gain."

"Well, it's a strange thing, nevertheless," protested Sir James moodily, "that these strange Spaniards allowed a wandering stranger—I take Mr. Morrisson to never have been of great distinction in air or bearing—to marry an heiress of a noble house with so large a fortune. . . ."

The lawyer was patient with what seemed to him these tiresome debates.

"It is twenty-one years ago," he quietly reminded the young man, "and what human passions and human difficulties led to these decisions is no concern of ours. I believe we may hold it that the lady fell headlong in love with the young Scot, and, being of a very passionate nature and much pampered by her people, they were sooner inclined to allow her to marry a foreigner and to go into a strange land than to thwart her wishes. They were also, as it would seem to me, much encouraged by the young man's refusal to accept any of their wealth. Another point that you must recall, sir, is that this same fortune has greatly increased in the last twenty-one years, and that the dowry Grace Morrisson's mother brought with her to her husband was about a third of what she brings to you."

Sir James then related in a contained and precise voice the sum of his various interviews with the lady . . . the gist of what he had heard about her from the lawyers whom he employed in Edinburgh . . . and touched shortly on Mr. Morrisson himself.

Mr. Widdacombe did not trouble to conceal his impatience with this, as he termed it to himself, dreary talk.

"It is a business matter surely, Sir James, although possibly you have become enamoured with the person of this lady."

"Have I not told you," sighed the young man, sinking farther back into the shadow of the hooded chair, "that she has rebuffed and almost insulted me on every occasion that I have met her, that I consider her ill-bred, haughty and ignorant, and that I feel not only displeasure, but even a certain alarm when I consider the prospect of making her mistress of Lyndley Waters."

The lawyer could but shrug and turn for consolation to the glass of wine that Pratt had so discreetly replenished during his wait for Sir James.

"This is a rude, brutal and rough country," continued the young man, leaning forward so that the glow of the firelight fell over his features.

The lawyer gave him a sharp, sideways look and decided that his face had altered in expression and even it may be in outline since he had last seen it; much of its comeliness appeared effaced. It was beaten upon with the winds and reddened and seemed to the older man to be in some subtle manner coarsened. Mr. Widdacombe sipped his wine, considering the situation cautiously. He genuinely desired the entire good of the young man, whom he liked and admired, not only for his personal qualities, but because he seemed to the middle-class standards of the lawyer to represent much of the grace, beauty, majesty and charm of the English aristocracy to which he, Ralph Widdacombe, was well prepared to pay homage, and from which he was also well prepared to draw his maintenance.

"You might," he admitted at length, with an uneasiness uncommon in his tones, "have made a match more popular among your neighbours and the lady sounds difficult to our common minds—a bigot you say, and of this black religion they have here in the north—it should not be beyond your power to make her change her, perhaps, gloomy faith. . . ."

"I think her fixed in it," put in Sir James, to which the lawyer, with a half sigh, countered:

"A religious wife is sometimes a blessing. Give her her chapel and her chaplain if need be, and her pious friends, and she'll be no trouble to you."

"Perhaps I had looked," smiled the young man wryly, "for something besides a negative quality in my marriage—but I stand here like a fool arguing about a matter on which I have taken my decision."

He then, with a sudden change of subject, casually related the adventure of the night; how the old woman had pulled him in to her mean room as he had been walking along the dark wynd, and how she had warned him against the marriage.

The lawyer laughed with good-humoured contempt.

"They're full of rogueries and superstitions, these people, unlettered and half barbarous as the majority of them are," he replied. "I believe in every village in Scotland you may still find what they term a 'covey of witches' and wise women of all kinds, who will make you any spell you ask for. No doubt you have been marked down as a supposedly wealthy foreigner, and there are those already watching you to endeavour to despoil you by trickery, or the use of some vulgar superstition. . . ."

"You have made a great many words about a little matter," smiled Sir James, "but you have not thrown any ray of light on it for me. This woman did not ask for money—she must have had some difficulty in knowing my person, she must have followed me continuously to have at length come upon this chance of speaking to me alone; but as I am the least superstitious of men, I gave the matter but little heed."

"I do not think you are speaking with sincerity," said Mr. Widdacombe. He rose with a sigh. "Something is troubling you, gnawing at your repose. You have taken, I fear, a dislike to Grace Morrisson. . . ."

"There is nothing that would please anyone," replied the young Englishman with a certain violence, "about that grey house where she lives, the company she keeps, nor the lady herself. But," he added with an increasing harshness, "I have determined on the bargain, and do you, sir, set about what remains as to its details."

With this he turned aside, as if unconscious of the other's presence and stood outlined in the fire glow, a dark figure. None of the small details of his garments nor person were visible to the lawyer. There was merely a shape, with the red light behind it. The lawyer noticed that the candles during their talk had burnt to the sockets of the plain silver sticks over which they were guttering in yellow drops, for a fine wind was blowing through the ill-adjusted shutters.

It was then that the lawyer, a kindly, ordinary man whose values were all worldly and who had never concerned himself with anything that was not material, felt for the first time in his life a sudden stab of frightful doubt as to whether after all the attainment of this world's goods did ensure even commonplace felicity or perhaps even the most ordinary prosperity. He moistened his lips and fingered his glass nervously as he stood there withdrawn into the shadows. One side of his nature was urging him to tell the young man to be done with the whole business, to ride back with him to the south, to face his creditors and the incomplete splendours of Lyndley Waters, and to endeavour by some frank and open means to redeem his fortunes. Yet this project of a warning had scarcely touched the lawyer's mind before it disappeared like thin water flowing into a fierce fire.

Of course here was nothing but moonshine, some fantastic mood on the part of an exiled, lonely and irritated young man. Mr. Widdacombe drained his glass, pursed his lips and affected to be tired and to need to seek his bed.

Sir James made no effort to prolong the conversation, which had been, after all, to him but an aimless whirl of words. He remained encouraged by his fellow countryman's presence, and while he pulled the bell-rope he talked pleasantly enough of Lyndley Waters and of what the last accounts had been from Mr. Swallow, his steward, who had been directed to send his general information as to the place to the London attorneys; Mr. Swallow's news was not so ill. It had been found on adjusting the year's expenses and income that it was possible to continue in a very moderate way—the building of the house, and even the laying out of the garden. The craftsmen employed had shown themselves sensible and willing, rather than lose their entire work, to accept lower wages.

Sir James suddenly became moody at this retrenchment.

"I wish the best of everything," he said sombrely, "the finest architects, painters and gardeners. Well, we can dismiss these inferior men and get the greatest of the day. I'll have that at least out of this marriage. Lyndley Waters shall be second to no house of its size

76

in the British Isles."

To the lawyer this would have been on any other occasion a simple and ordinary boast; he had known many men who had made wealthy marriages, nay, he had known of some who had made as many as three wealthy marriages with the sole purpose of enlarging and beautifying their estates. But now something in this young man's manner again gave the elder man that prickle of fear, of doubt. Why build this grandiose mansion? For what purpose? The work was long, it might be another generation before it was completed. It was more than likely that Sir James Troyes would die, leaving, if he was lucky enough to be still solvent, to his heir the task of laying out those parterres and shrubberies, those mazes and bowling greens . . . of erecting those statues and temples, of putting in place the carvings and tapestries inside the splendid building.

"I suppose," he thought, for though he was an unimaginative man, such fancy as he indulged in was stirred, "these are the young man's dreams made solid. Yet what shall we think of them but that they are foolishness? He would, even at the cost of his liberty, of his self-respect, as it seems, since he is so dubious about the marriage, buy the barren delight of building a house too large and magnificent for him, and in which he is not likely, even with the revenues of Grace Morrisson added to his own, ever to be able to live in such state as he now hopes for."

The lodging manservant, sleepy and unwilling, entered with fresh candles. Sir James went ahead, having taken these lights from the man and dismissed him, up the narrow, winding staircase; Mr. Widda-combe followed. The woodwork was dark from the beeswax of many years; in the gleaming polish the reflections of the two flames mounted steadily.

Sir James showed the lawyer into the room that had been prepared for him. It was next to his own. He paused for a moment at the door to tell the elder man dryly of the sober arrangements for his marriage in St. Giles's Cathedral.

"I suppose the parson who unites you will be this chaplain who, I am informed, is believed to have had such an influence on your lady's character and religion? A certain Nicholas Jerdan, is it not?"

"No," replied Sir James indifferently, "this fanatic—for I take him to be no little else—has tired of his disciple and gone abroad on some errand of bigotry."

* * * *

Sir James Troyes could do no less than offer to wait upon his bride the day before their marriage; before this he had spent his idle time with no more than visits to his lawyers and hers, and a ride five miles from the capital to Cramond Brig, an ancient bridge of stone—three low arches supported by jutting piers—that spanned the River Almond. He went there on a mere caprice, the place never having been as much as a name to him before. The scenery seemed to him flat and ordinary, but the air was fine and he enjoyed being away from the city that was blurred to him by his own dislike.

Sir James pulled up his horse as he reached the bridge, not intending to ride farther, for he had an appointment with his lawyer that evening. There were yet more deeds and settlements to be signed, and the young man himself was not careless as to his own interests. Everything that he put his seal to had been carefully checked by his own judgment first.

He felt this to be a pause in his life. Once he was married, for good or ill, to Grace Morrisson life could never be the same to him. This Scottish journey would run like a scar (the simile came readily into his mind) across his existence. When he had returned to Lyndley Waters it would recur to him with the shape and colour of a dream, as all places visited briefly where some event of emotional merit has occurred return in the likeness of a dream. His existence at Lyndley Waters, he supposed, as he looked ahead, would be resumed; it would differ very little from what his life had been before, under the pressure of his troubles, he had ridden north; but always there would be this memory.

He noted the scene with that earnestness that accompanies preoccupation—the reeds and grasses that grew by the water's edge were dry and bent, the river had the colour of fading leaves and the reflection of the bridge was definite, so that the three arches made three dark spherical shapes. Beyond there was light again, a creeping in of the autumn sunshine on the still water.

As he sat there, his impatient horse now and then jingling the reins with a toss of his head, Sir James observed that another horseman had also paused not far behind him on the road. A chance backward glance discovered this, and that the fellow wore the ordinary Scottish dress of the upper classes; a plaid or shawl was over his dark green jacket and the national bonnet was pulled down over his short, dark hair.

Sir James found the sudden appearance of this stranger only a few yards away disconcerting—as if he, the foreigner and the spied upon, had suddenly been put into a dangerous position.

He turned his horse's head from Cramond Brig immediately and took the homeward road, passing the other man with a full look of appraisal. The fellow gave him but a slight smile in return.

"He knows something about me," the Englishman thought immediately. "I believe he has been following me from the town. Perhaps he, like the old woman, has something to say to me . . ." and he turned in the saddle and called out, "I am Sir James Troyes of Lyndley Waters. Have you come to this lonely place to speak to me?"

The Scot was still silent, though he turned his head quickly and appeared to listen with quick interest to this open challenge.

Not able to endure what seemed to him a flouting of his dignity, Sir James turned back and drew up his animal alongside the other horseman.

"It would pay you best to be frank with me, sir. If you think to put any pretty tricks on me, you will find that in the end of the story you are the loser."

At this the other spoke in a voice that was but lightly touched with a Scots accent and therefore proved him to have been a travelled man or one who had studied at one of the universities.

"I do not know," he remarked, "why two men cannot pause to look at the water at Cramond Brig without one of them losing his temper."

Sir James was honest enough to allow the justice of the rebuke, and he was reassured and in a fashion soothed by discovering that he spoke to a gentleman. He observed, now that he was so close to the other, that all his appointments were rich of handsomely wrought silver, and yellow and purple stones in the

Scottish fashion; that his mount was costly, and that he wore in his bonnet a flashing buckle and a dark plume. There was something indescribable in his person and bearing which reminded Sir James of Grace Morrisson. The cavalier might almost have been her brother; but the Englishman knew the lady to be an only child.

"Your fancies seem to trouble you," continued the Scot. "Why should you be at the pains to tell me who you are? You are of but little importance to me."

"Nor you to me," retorted the Englishman. "But I tell you, I had the impression that I was being followed and spied upon."

"A man's conscience is in an ill way when he is in that fashion tormented," replied the other, and with a genteel air doffing his bonnet (but the gesture was slight), he touched up his horse and passed over the bridge.

Sir James was now the one to watch and, as it were, spy. He paced his horse steadily behind the other to the rise of the bridge and watched him till he was out of sight along the ill-kept road that wound past a lonely stone house into the distance. The Scot did not once look back, and Sir James, with his mood somewhat worsened, made his way to the capital.

He had but a short time to put in after he had reached Edinburgh before his appointment with the lawyers was due, so he rode down Heriot's Row where the goldsmiths' shops hung out their massive signs and the splendid hospital stood as a memorial to George Heriot—his industry, piety and charity.

Sir James, even from horseback, could spy many extraordinary objects of massive silver displayed in the small bow-fronted windows from which but one, or at the utmost two, shutters were jealously drawn back. He would have liked to buy some of these magnificent utensils with which to adorn the new apartments at Lyndley Waters, but he had the prudence to hold his hand and not to pledge a fortune that was not yet his entirely.

As he passed the shop where he had bought, at so cheap a price, the blue jewel for Grace Morrisson, he saw that lady herself leaving the narrow porch and stepping into a plain carriage, emblazoned with an heiress's arms, that waited outside; an equipage well kept but modest to the point of meanness.

This sudden, unexpected sight of the woman who was now so important to him, and who had been so much in his thoughts, almost startled the young man, and yet it was the most natural thing in the world that a lady, two days before her marriage, should be pricing silver.

"She had gear enough of her own, I thought," he muttered.

He had heard the lawyers talk of great chests of goods and plate that would be taken in waggons from the north to the south as part of the dower of Grace Morrisson.

"But it is always the way of women," he spoke as if reassuring himself, "to go about on the least occasion to price this and that. . . ."

He called for a passing lad to hold his horse, dismounted and himself entered the little shop. The interior seemed itself to be made of gold and silver, for a small lamp had just been lit and the orange-coloured light of this was reflected again and again from the articles of precious metals. On the low polished counters stood salt cellars, cases for wine cups and goblets and plain chains of thick links formed of both the precious metals.

The jeweller recognised Sir James immediately—both he and his story were now familiar in Edinburgh—and asked him, with an undisturbed courtesy, how he could further be at his service.

"I saw Grace Morrisson, my bride," replied the young man, "leaving your shop just now. She was in her coach . . . it would have been unseemly for me to have followed her . . . I do not like to make a noise and clatter in the street. I had a wonder, however, if she had come to return the blue stone to you, not liking it?"

"She came with the blue stone, sir, certainly," replied the goldsmith, "but it was only for a little matter of the setting and we were able to adjust it to her wishes at once."

"She should have asked this of me," replied the Englishman, displeased. "Nor should you have touched my purchase without my consent. Are you sure," he asked, with rising bitterness, "that the lady did not come to value my gift?"

The other gave a smile, which was as good as to say, "If you expect me to tell any secrets, my noble sir, you are disappointed."

"It was but an adjustment of the setting, sir," he repeated, with a civility that did not touch on servility. "One supposes, a matter you would leave in the lady's own hands; though it meant adding to the gold—but you will hardly dispute that expense?"

"It is a matter in which I should have expected to be consulted," replied Sir James, noting that she had added to the monetary value of his gift—more gold, eh?

He felt as if he stood in a box of jewels himself, for as the lamp flame strengthened he could distinguish that the precious objects by which he was surrounded were set off and emblazoned by sapphires, rubies, emeralds and turquoise; these gave off sharp and brilliant colours that had at first been indistinguishable in the general blur of golden illumination.

The old jeweller stood erect waiting respectfully; his black skull-cap fitted neatly over his grey hair, his black gown being straight. Sir James had the feeling that this man, like the young Scot whom he had passed by Cramond Brig, was watching him, spying on him, mocking him . . . but he knew, and with a creeping sickness of self-doubt admitted, the danger of allowing such fancies to take possession of his disturbed mind, so left abruptly.

Sir James returned to his rooms and spent the evening in concentrated attention on the details of the articles of his marriage settlement. That had been signed twenty-four hours ago . . . and to-day he had no excuse, and perhaps no wish, to avoid seeing Grace Morrisson herself, but he detested that house where she lived and resolved to make a bid at once for supremacy over the lady by demanding that she should see him in some pleasanter surrounding. So when, unattended, he came to her sombre residence, he demanded, without dismounting from his horse, of the manservant that Madam Grace should come riding with him.

"The day is fair and mild, and surely that is rare enough in your north?" he added, smiling, "and I have heard that she takes pleasure in horsemanship. I shall not dismount but await here for her answer."

The man, who now treated him with more respect than when he first turned him from the door, yet with no great courtesy, promised to take this message to his mistress, and Sir James remained in the narrow courtyard, striking idly with his whip against the thin pilasters of the door.

Again he glanced up at the windows. Again—though in each there was a glimmer of the sun, that appeared now for so short a time each day here—they were blank, and, as it seemed to him, had an empty look.

He soon had his answer, and it was, at least as interpreted by the servant, a gracious one.

Madam Grace would willingly ride. She would not keep Sir James waiting longer than it took her to put on her habit.

Indeed, he kept his horse pacing up and down in front of the house for more than ten minutes, when the lady was on the doorstep in a dark green habit, fashioned in an amazon style, with a masculine cravat held by a great brooch of diamonds. She pulled on her guantlet and slipped her hand through the loop of her whip as her groom brought round her horse.

"I approve your decision," said she, "for a ride abroad. I, too, find this house dreary. . . ."

"I have not said as much," he replied, "nor I think implied it."

"You are very certain of your courtesy," replied Grace Morrisson. "Perhaps you allow people to understand your disdains and affronts more clearly than you suppose."

"Then I am at your mercy and you must chide me," he replied, "if I have been lacking in any civility."

The groom helped her to mount. Sir James saw with approval that she was a good horsewoman, a light weight, straight and easy in the saddle, yet with no apeing airs such as some ladies on horseback employ to attract praise. Here and now there was no question but that she was a beautiful woman, set off in her dark, handsome habit, on her dark, handsome horse that she named Belle, with her hair falling freely under the plumed hat. Not the type of woman, perhaps, that Sir James had imagined as mistress of Lyndley Waters, but one who surely had both spirit and a certain ardour and enthusiasm that might, in the hands of the proper master, be turned into qualities that would illuminate his life.

As they came out upon the high road she asked him where he intended his ride to be.

"Why do you ask me?" he said mischievously, "I am the stranger here. I would suggest we take the road to Cramond Brig."

"You went there yesterday," she countered at once. "Your servant came to wait on me—you remember you sent him? He was to ask if I had any demands to make of you."

"Yes, I remember now that I sent Thomas Pratt, and I suppose he gossiped as to where I was gone and you wondered why I should take a solitary ride instead of coming myself to see you?"

She was not to be drawn, however, into any kind of a cross-questioning or curious conversation.

"You made a random choice yesterday," she replied straightly, "but to-day you do it deliberately. You saw me coming out of the shop where you had purchased the sapphire—I obtained that knowledge also from Thomas Pratt. He saw no harm in giving it—you must not upbraid him."

"I would myself have told you," replied Sir James coldly, "but this trifle, for I take it to be no more, is occupying too much of my attention. I should have been flattered if you had returned it to me for the alterations."

"You would?" she asked, and for the first time since he had known her she laughed pleasantly, as if she were really and in a kindly fashion amused.

"Well, then, what did you have done to the stone? It is of some value and rarity, and I suppose that you must wear it sometimes, therefore there is no need to make a mystery as to what your alteration was."

"Why, I got my cipher placed upon the box," she answered casually. "Did not the old man tell you as much?"

"He told me nothing. I should suppose he is used to secrets." Sir James's lack of candour matched hers—she had not admitted that she had added to the value of the gem.

"Secrets?" Grace echoed the word, still pleasantly but with an undertone that might have been of scorn. "You seem to imagine yourself, sir, of such importance in Edinburgh that everyone is either spying on you or keeping secrets from you. Have you had any peculiar adventures?"

Sir James related to her how an old woman had pulled him into a poor house in Edinburgh and warned him against his marriage.

"That is all," said Grace Morrisson lightly, "in the style of the ancient Scottish superstitions. They can let nothing pass but they must have their wish or their word about it, and I should suppose, pious as your old dame seemed, she wanted a piece of silver in return for her warning. Did it have any effect on you?" the lady added.

He was silent. He was trying to clarify in his own mind what effect all these incidents, so trivial in themselves, were having on him and whether he did not wish even now to break off his marriage, aye, even though the contracts were signed.

They turned their mounts without any further dispute about the matter on to the rough road that led to the River Almond.

Grace Morrisson was the first to start some manner of talk by observing it would be considered odd for them to ride thus alone, without any servants or friends, but that for herself she cared nothing, and she was glad that he had taken this direction for, beyond, Cramond Brig was a place that she often visited.

He asked her if she meant a small stone building, as that was all that he had been able to see from the rise of the bridge.

She replied, "No. It is a disused burial-ground— kept up by the more pious of the Calvinists in memory of some of their brethren who, having been hanged in Edinburgh for their faith, had been, by affectionate hands dedicated to revenge, there placed at peace."

"This is a gloomy fancy for a wedding eve," protested the young man, but the day was so fair—though the sunshine was thin and the sky blue, so far away and so pale—that it could not encourage dreary thoughts.

Indeed the young man's spirits were inclined to rise and he felt himself able to dismiss as mere whimsies of his loneliness such doubts and suspicions as he had held hitherto against his marriage. Why, after all, what cause for concern was there if the lady was religious-minded and could on occasion be pert and proud? He had known other men who had accepted smaller fortunes with larger defects in those who brought them, and to-day she was gracious at least; her attitude was not lover-like, but she was neither flouting him nor disdainful. She even spoke gravely enough of their future together and asked him about his designs for Lyndley Waters.

"I have not plagued you with those," he replied, upon which she told him that she had learned something of her future residence from the lawyers and Thomas Pratt.

At this he felt a little touched, a little ashamed. So she had, behind his back, been forced through strangers and servants to satisfy a natural curiosity that he should have assuaged.

"I hear," she added, "that you will have a very fine chapel, lined with cedar-wood?"

"Nothing, I am afraid, will be to your taste. Nor should I be able to alter it to your requirements."

She looked at him, as if recognising this attempt at mastery.

"I know," she answered, "that I shall be the stranger there as you are the stranger here, but I do not object if your chapel is splendid. It shall be as handsome as my means can make it."

When it came to Lyndley Waters he was always obstinate and "my means" galled him.

"I have the designs, the drawings complete. The altar-piece has been painted, the carvings and the panels of cedar wood are complete. The floor and the pillars are of black and white marble. . . . How curious," he checked himself, "such a description appears in this pale, featureless landscape."

"It must be very rich," said Grace quickly. "I have never seen anything like that—never, never. There are others here also who have known nothing but the dark kirk and the plain meeting-house and the sombre closet."

"Ah," thought Sir James, "not such a Puritan after all, perhaps!"

"You do not, then," he asked aloud, "find any distaste in the thought of a chapel that is almost as much adorned as would be a Papist's praying-place?"

Grace Morrisson did not reply. "I take my fate as I find it, I suppose. I merely said that I have never seen such magnificence. I have heard, too, of your alabaster fountains and the grottoes in the grounds, the stove-houses with the glasses covered up with mats at nights in the winter, where strange fruits and flowers are grown. We have beautiful gardens in Scotland, but I have seen none of them."

"I do not know," remarked the young man thoughtfully, "why you have lived thus enclosed. It seems to me that you have been more forced into your saintly seclusion than have chosen it yourself."

"Can a child of four years of age choose anything?" she asked quietly. "But I am well pleased with what has been taught me."

They had now reached the bridge, and without any comment as to how long their journey should be, or what distance they might go, crossed over it and came out on the road where Sir James had seen the stranger pass out of sight the day before.

"It is only another half-mile," said Grace

Morrisson. "Round the bend of the road. We shall not be unduly late in our return by making this expedition, which is one that I have often made alone. . . ."

"You have a certain freedom, then?" he inquired.

"Alone or with one good guardian, Miss Lilias or Miss Grizzel," she corrected herself. The peasants who were standing in the doorway of the stone house stared after them.

"We must make an uncommon couple in these quiet parts," thought the young man. "We must look to those people like my thought of the chapel at Lyndley Waters looks to me. Well, here she is at her graveyard. . . ."

He saw it, a little off the road to the right hand. . . . There was a matter but of six mounds placed at irregular intervals and carefully tended, with plain, clean headstones.

"There's no one to hold your horse, madam, and yet you say you come alone. . . ."

"Are you trying," she replied, as if her mind were not much on the matter, "to trap me into some confession? There is a tree there to which we may fasten our horses, and a stone beneath it that serves me very well as a mounting-block, and if I do come alone," she repeated, "why should it not be so?"

He took his horse to the tree that she had indicated; a rowan, now bare of all but a small curl of fine leaves and the last of the scarlet berries.

When he had fastened up his own horse, he returned and asked her to dismount, and took her steed to the same place; then, with the two animals secure, they entered the little graveyard that was protected by a rude wall of stones from the highway and the common heath side.

"Do you know anthing about these people?" he asked, suddenly curious on a matter that up to now had not held for him any interest. Curious because there was an oddity, to one of his easy temperament and sumptuous surroundings, in finding in this bare and lonely spot the graves of men who had lived hardly and died violently for the sake of what, to him, whas a grim and disagreeable fanaticism.

She made no reply, and he could see that her interest and her absorption in this lonely spot where she stood were not in any way feigned or even emphasised to impress him.

"Well, why not? She for her convenanting zeal and I for Lyndley Waters."

Sir James lingered a little apart, really unwilling to intrude upon what might, to her, be some sacred office. Perhaps she was bidding farewell to the graves of some notables in her dreary calendar of prim saints.

He was touched by the knowledge that she must know she could hardly hope to return here again. However soft and generous he might consider himself, his kindness to his wife would surely never extend to a visit here again, therefore he could afford to be, on this occasion, tolerant. The more tolerant as she was still further impressed on his senses as rich, dark and splendid, not as something pallid and withered and dedicated to the dead bones of dry fanatics. She might favour her father in her opinions, but certainly she favoured her mother in at least the capacity to assume a grace and a brilliance that were near beauty.

It was of her person, he was thinking, as she moved slowly in and out of the graves, pulling aside here a sprig of ivy that was attaching itself to the stone, rooting up here and there an intruding weed that even so late in the year was struggling to live among the dry grasses—her beauty, and yes, how it might be decked and adorned for the further glorification of Lyndley Waters. He had not, when he had first seen her, considered her as a woman of much more that ordinary comeliness; but now there was a colour in her cheeks and a lustre in her eye and a rich curve on her lips. She might, it was obvious, be roused into something that would be like a flame of splendour and loveliness.

But his absorption in these abstractions was rudely shaken by Grace's sudden action. She pulled from the bosom of her dark habit an object that he immediately recognised, for it flashed with startling intensity in the pale, misty sunlight. It was the Kashmir sapphire that he had given her, and the pale blue fire of it, held for a moment in her hand, seemed to make the whole landscape and the whole day dim and faded.

He wondered that she should bring this out now, and supposed that she had chosen this moment to show him the alteration she had had made in the casing; he saw an added gold knot. He frowned, watching her, however, with doubt and even suspicion for her attention was so obviously far from him.

Then, suddenly, she was on her knees at the side of the grave by which she had been standing, and with a force, surprising in one who appeared not only delicate but slothful, she had driven the jewel into the mould of the grave.

He folded his arms and watched her, temper and

bewilderment darkening his face, but she took no notice of him at all but continued to scrape her hole deeper with the large, flat jewel in the large, flat setting. If she had had any alteration made, it was not one that he could see, beyond the knob of gold for which he would have to pay.

As she dug into the easily yielding earth the suspicion flashed into his mind that she had been there the day before or sent someone else (and he remembered the man on Cramond Brig) to loosen and prepare the soil, for it seemed it was without any difficulty that she had made a large hole in the irregular heap of the grave, and into this she thrust and pushed the jewel with all her force, closing the earth over it again. She remained for a while on her knees, and Sir James spoke.

"Is this action something symbolic, or do you dislike my gift so much that you cast it away on the dead?"

She looked up quickly and he believed that she was really startled by the sound of his voice, that she had forgotten his presence. She rose and shook some fragments of earth and gravel from her wide skirt.

"I never had anything before to give to anyone," she said. "My mother possessed jewels when she died. I have never had them ... save to wear, like this brooch, then to return to Miss Lilias."

"They will be handed to you now, I suppose."

"Yes, and your mother had jewels?—those, too, will be mine, but then it will be too late. I had all I needed, but never money or jewellery. This was my first magnificence, and I gave it to another who never had anything either."

"It is, then, the symbol of some reverence or affection?"

94

He wondered what the date on the stone was . . . his suspicions again darkened his mind and made his expression lowering.

"Who lies there?" he demanded.

She replied immediately, "One who died a hundred years ago. You need trouble yourself with no more than that."

He was vexed that she had, in a way, made a fool of him—making him appear jealous of a rude fanatic hanged a century ago!

"You foolish piece!" he remarked arrogantly. "The jewel is of considerable worth, and you thrust it there to be for ever hidden in the dark, unless, which is likely enough, some strolling vagabond comes upon it."

"How should anyone come upon it?" she demanded, standing erect and looking round the deserted silence that encompassed them, "not unless you tell them of it, and that would be impossible for you to do, for it was your gift to me to do with as I wished, and I have acted honestly by you in allowing you to see to what use I put your jewel."

To this attack, with its air of nobility, he had no easy reply, but he was vexed and stung both by what seemed to him the grotesqueness of her action, by the loss of the jewel and by her complete withdrawal from him and his interests that this act showed.

Now he did not wish to understand her. He put from his mind all attempt to elucidate her motives in doing something that was, humanly speaking, unreasonable and stupid, but he remarked as he walked round the low hedge of stone that separated the little graveyard from the bare heath and the empty road:

"How strange for you to thrust into the grave of

this poor creature, as I suppose he was, done to death a hundred years ago, an ornament that he would surely have despised, for I take it that is of your Calvinists' way of thinking, condemning all that is magnificent—why, therefore, waste upon a wayside grave something which some living person might have treasured?"

She was not at the pains to tell him that he did not come near her meaning. All that she desired to impress upon him was that she had been open and honourable in her dealings.

"That was your gift to me," she repeated, "and that is the use to which I put it."

She took some of the weeds that she had plucked up by their roots and thrust them in on top of the loosened earth.

"They'll take it in charge," she said, "and the nettles and thistles will grow here and the ivy when I am no longer at hand to clear them away. No one will concern themselves with this lonely spot . . . the treasure is safe. . . ."

"Unless I prove a prudent, worldly kind of man," he objected mockingly, "and send Thomas Pratt here to regain it before we left Edinburgh."

"You could not do that." She was on her old defences. "For if you did, you know that I should despise you always."

"But it might be," he argued in his exasperation, "that I would do this without your knowledge?"

"I think you could not," she replied. "It might be in my power to have this graveyard watched."

"It certainly might," reflected Sir James, and his sense of a plot or conspiracy against him, of being spied upon, came again, even here in the pale, misty sunshine that hitherto he had found so reassuring. He knew, both as a man of sense and of honour, that it was indeed impossible for him to disinter the sapphire. She had caught him. It was not worth his while, for the sake of the sum of money the jewel had cost him, to lower his own standard of nicety, and to take back from the dead the gift that had been so fantastically presented to them; nor, as a prudent man of the world, was it worth his while to risk a scandal, an exposure of the whole bizarre incident by sending either Thomas Pratt or any other emissary he might find to fetch the jewel from its gloomy hiding-place.

He thought to himself, "I suppose, madam, you can say for the first round *touche.*"

For the moment he was wise enough to know that in reserve and silence were his best defences.

He brought the horses and she mounted lightly and prettily from the block, thoughtfully, as it were, brushing some earth from her fingers before she pulled on the long riding gloves.

As they returned across the bridge that spanned the River Almond each was silent. Sir James, who by no means lacked obstinacy and a certain strength of character, made his decision and had the courage to keep it. It was not worth his while to risk this marriage by taking any notice of the lady's caprice, detestable and alarming as in many ways it had been. He recognised the danger of allowing her to triumph over him in this their first encounter of wills, but could not do otherwise, save at the risk of losing her and all her fortune together and for ever, and retiring from the Scottish capital discredited and mocked at.

Whatever was behind her action, and, after all, it

was easy for him to convince himself that it was nothing but the caprice of a bigoted girl, it was better for him to overlook it.

The next day Sir James Troyes and Grace Morrisson were married in St. Giles's Cathedral, and shortly after the ceremony, to him gloomy and even melancholic, they departed with a small train to England.

II
ARIA

The cuckoo sat in the old pear tree.
                    Cuckoo!
Raining or snowing, nought cared he.
                    Cuckoo!
Cuckoo, cuckoo, nought cared he.

The cuckoo flew over a house top high.
                    Cuckoo!
"Dear, are you at home, for here am I?
Cuckoo, cuckoo, here am I."

"I dare not open the door to you.
                    Cuckoo!
Perhaps you are not the right cuckoo?
                    Cuckoo!
Cuckoo, cuckoo, the right cuckoo!"

"I am the right cuckoo, the proper one.
                    Cuckoo!
For I am my Father's only son,
                    Cuckoo!
Cuckoo, cuckoo, his only son."

"If you are your Father's only son,
                    Cuckoo!
The bobin pull tightly,
Come through the door lightly,
                    Cuckoo!

"If you are your Father's only son,
                    Cuckoo!
It must be you, the only one,
Cuckoo, cuckoo, my own cuckoo!
                    Cuckoo!"

A YOUNG Englishwoman of a bright and pleasing appearance stood against a background suitable to her breed and grace. Although it was winter, there was no air of desolation about Lyndley Waters. The activity of the workmen who, under the supervision of craftsmen and architects, were rebuilding the Elizabethan house was in itself sufficient to remove all air of gloom from the scene.

Celia Plaisent stood by a column newly brought from Italy, but cracked in the transit, that had been left close to the doorway which, ornate and finely sculptured, glistened fresh and new in the clear sunshine.

Celia was not of a temperament ever to have discerned melancholy in the fall of the seasons. She was one who had few regrets. She accepted such mild sorrows as had hitherto entered her life with resignation, almost as if she had expected them, and turned not unthinkingly but steadily to other things.

Below the parterres that the landscape gardener was having constructed, the Wiltshire landscape, the low chalk downs, rolled into a distance that the thickening mist of afternoon already obscured.

Celia was a frequent visitor to Lyndley Waters. She had the interest of her generation in anything that was new, the interest of a near neighbour in anything that affected James Troyes. She had heard indirectly, for he had not written to her since he had left his home on his northward journey, of his marriage to the Scotch heiress, of their stay in London to purchase new finery for the bride and more furnishings for Lyndley Waters. She had made no comment on news that had been very freely discussed by the young man's neighbours and acquaintances save this, which she repeated, perhaps like a defence when the matter was argued in her presence:

"I suppose that it has long been well known that James would have to make a wealthy match to save his fortunes."

Some commended the young man for what they thought his astute cleverness in securing so large a sum of money, so many estates and revenues, even though with them went an outlandish wife; pursed up their faces and were inclined to doubt if any good would come by bringing a foreigner, a barbarous Scot, to Lyndley Waters.

John Swallow, the steward, who had so carefully kept the accounts, who had so anxiously watched the confusion of his employer's affairs and who had rejoiced so keenly when disaster was headed off, was the only source of information the neighbours had as to the exact happenings in Edinburgh; and he knew, or affected to know, very little. Celia smiled to herself as she saw him coming across the ground, strewn with the new blocks of masonry ready to be fixed in place. Since the marriage there had been a considerable bustle at Lyndley Waters, where the work had been slowed down noticeably during Sir James's northward journey. "Poor Mr. Swallow," thought the girl. "He is coming over to see me quite reluctantly, though generally he likes to talk to me. He is afraid I want to question him about James's affair and his new wife."

Mr. Swallow was a man whose heart was in his work in almost the literal meaning of the word, if the heart be taken to mean the centre of all emotion, for he cared for little save Lyndley Waters and this costly and extravagant scheme of beautifying house and grounds.

Sometimes Celia Plaisent had asked him mischievously what was the sense or what was the good of this great house that seemed so far beyond the pretension of the Troyes, and he had always looked at her a little startled, as if such a query were almost blasphemous. The building to him was an end in itself.

She noticed now and was touched by the hard-bitten business man's look of increased health, the firmer way he trod, the greater boldness there was in his carriage. When it had been a question of fobbing off creditors, of dismissing workmen, of economising here and cutting down there, he had gone steadfastly and yet with an agitated and depressed air.

"It is curious, is it not," he said, saluting Celia with his usual dry courtesy, "that a foreigner's money should go to make this place?"

"I hadn't thought," replied the girl frankly, "that you would so soon touch on that."

"Why not?" replied the steward, as if defiantly. "I know what everyone is thinking. It is a most usual procedure after all."

"And yet," said Celia, "everyone appears to comment on it as if it were something extraordinary. . . ."

"An extraordinary piece of luck," replied Mr. Swallow.

His narrowed, hazel eyes searched over the scene. Several more workmen had come down from London that very day. Yesterday the waggons had arrived with shipments of stone from Holland and Italy that had been laid up at the docks for lack of money to pay the dues on them.

"It will be a splendid palace," remarked Celia with real enthusiasm for the other's enthusiasm. "There will be none like it in the county."

Mr. Swallow looked disappointed at that. She had understated his secret aim. "None like it in England," he wished to have said of Lyndley Waters.

"But I prefer," smiled the girl, knowing his disappointment and humouring it, "my shabby old home. Plaisent, with all its defects in your modern eyes, Mr. Swallow, seems to me adequate enough for all one is like to have in life of pleasure, sorrow and, perhaps, loneliness."

"One would never be lonely here," replied Mr. Swallow with a touch of boasting. "It takes one hundred domestics to staff Lyndley Waters."

She noticed he spoke as if the mansion were already finished.

"Could not one be lonely," she asked, "even with a hundred domestics . . . ? But I hope—one must hope for the sake of James and his young wife—that her fortune and his, when mended, will be sufficient to sustain this splendour. What will James do?" remarked Celia. "Stand for Parliament . . . stay here as a country gentleman and entertain the wits from town . . . ?"

Again Mr. Swallow was baffled. She rebuked herself for tempting him into speculation.

"When are they expected home?" she asked, and he was relieved at the direct question that was so easily answered.

"There are orders for the bonfire, madam, the day after to-morrow; and the silver spending money has been sent by Sir James—generously, for the workpeople's drink. . . ."

"It is to be a festival—a celebration?" Celia's tone was wistful, a little beyond her control. She looked up at the facade of the house; a part of it was gleaming new and magnificent, unlived in; roofed and glazed but unfinished as to sumptuous detail. Parts, too, of the old Jacobean and Tudor mansions that resembled a portion of her own home with the tall, twisted chimney-stacks that were soon to be demolished still stood.

"You're sorry to see that go, I suppose?" said Mr. Swallow, looking aside at her sensitive face; "but the architects complain already of having to leave so much of the old building. They say that their plan is hampered. Observe the five-winged staircase in the Italian style . . . we were fortunate that the steps came over without being broken. This is a dead loss." He put his square-toed shoe against the broken pillar by the hem of Celia's gown. "This sort of thing is a dead loss. Well, the bill for the timber came in to-day. I hope Sir James won't think it heavy—there was a great deal more to be done than he realised when he went away—wainscoting and bannisters and the lining of the chapel. . . ."

"There is always a great deal more to be done in great projects than one supposes at first, is there not?" replied Celia. "That applies to life, too, I suppose. I hope James will be happy here. I am trying to think what it will look like to *her*. . . ."

"What should it look like but a husband's home?" said Mr. Swallow harshly.

"She has lived very retired," said Celia, "you told me so yourself. You said that James had warned you that Grace's"—she brought the word out with a hint of an effort—"Grace's life has been most secluded, and that she has been surrounded with harsh Scotch divines and gentlewomen—one in particular had made a great impression on her mind—and so we must, therefore, indulge her views more," she added with increased warmth, "than we should have indulged her merely as the wife of James."

Mr. Swallow read into these words Celia's resolve (that he knew the girl was capable of carrying through at any cost to herself) to afford the unkown woman who was coming to be the mistress of Lyndley Waters the most glowing of welcomes.

"It will be a change for her," she insisted, tapping her shoe absently on the broken column where the acanthus leaves of the capital curled into the cracked shaft, "and I should say not an easy one because . . ." She checked herself; it was not for her to say before the steward, although no doubt the fact was well enough known to him, "Because there is no love in this marriage, because it is a bargain only. . . ."

"The chapel is to be finished first, and with great care," she asked, "is it not? Can I see it, or shall I disturb your workpeople? You see, this is the last chance I shall have to see Lyndley Waters by myself."

"We had to finish the living apartments first," replied the steward at once, turning towards the house, the young woman walking behind him, carefully making her way between the blocks of stone and marble, "and they are only partially ready. It was a question of the furnishing and all the domestic offices, of the stabling—for all that one must have for life from day to day. Next to that we tried to do what we could to finish the chapel. It is not yet complete, and as Sir James has never employed a chaplain," he added, "we did not see such particular urgency."

"It is for Sir James's wife—for Lady Troyes," said Celia. "We must all understand that."

"She is of that, to us, black and harsh Calvinist faith and I doubt if the chapel will be suited to her taste. . . ."

"But you told me that Sir James wrote she was having her own chaplain."

"Yes, I believe that was in the marriage terms, and reasonable enough. It will keep her from meddling with worse things. It is for him to adjust himself to the situation. I have no doubt that both she and Sir James have sufficient worldly wisdom to pass all off well."

Celia, entering the still incomplete portion of Lyndley Waters, where the tessellated floor of different-coloured woods was laid in place and shining with polish, but where there were neither hangings nor furniture, knew what Mr. Swallow meant, which was that no matter how difficult . . . nay, indeed, sombre or disagreeable the new mistress of Lyndley Waters might be, she must be tolerated for the wealth she brought with her, the wealth that would build the great house, aye, and furnish it, and lay out the gardens.

Celia Plaisent had lived an agreeable life with a family of brothers and sisters who were of tastes similar to her own; the tastes of English gentlefolk who had a small manor in the country, and who went no more than once a year to London, Buxton or Bath, but who found in the yearly routine, enjoyment and pleasure as well as zealous interests. She had long known that her chances of a handsome marriage were small. She was a younger daughter; there were two to be married before her turn came, and her dowry would be small. She had no especial gifts of brilliancy or beauty to balance these disadvantages. Some day, no doubt, her father would contrive a match with some honest fellow, a son of one of his friends, or a young man who might be introduced to him through one of his acquaintances. Mr. Plaisent was not likely to omit something so important as the settling of all his daughters in life. He was an energetic man with an eye to worldly happiness. Celia knew also that she could, if need be, marry Brian Ormerod, and that he was in very respect a finer match than she might have hoped for, but she did not choose, or so far had not chosen, to encourage this likely suitor.

She hesitated now in the splendour that was alien to her modest comeliness and paused. Mr. Swallow looked back at her with some impatience.

"We must pass through these rooms to reach the chapel," he remarked, "but there is nothing to see."

She followed him, but at the entrance to the chapel paused again, almost as if she recoiled, lifting away from the threshold of the chapel the folds of her plain gown of russet cloth.

Mr. Swallow was more interested in the girl than in the chapel. Her human quality seemed to be emphasised by the meaningless magnificence behind her. Although she had given no hint, even by as much as an intonation or a sigh, of her own feelings, Mr. Swallow guessed them, as people will guess, without much ado, the keenest emotions of those with whom they are constantly brought in contact; and for the moment he forgot his joyful task of reconstructing

Lyndley Waters and thought only of the girl.

He knew that she loved Sir James Troyes and had done since as children the two of them had ridden the woods and walked the lanes together. He knew that Sir James had even at one time felt very tenderly towards the pleasant, womanly creature, and that if his revenues had been in a better condition, might have contented himself with marrying her; for the young man had never been of a temperament to expect extravagant passions or much largeness of feeling and experience.

Yes, Celia would have made in every way an agreeable, an efficient and a loyal mistress for Lyndley Waters; but for the old Lyndley Waters, for the house that was like her own house not for this foreign-looking palace that was being reared with such an energy of trouble and expense on English soil.

So the situation for a moment held Mr. Swallow silent and even a little ashamed—as the English lawyer had stood silent and a little ashamed, disturbed out of his worldly calculations, when he had suddenly glanced up and seen as a detached human being the dark outline of Sir James's figure standing in front of the large fireplace where the red flames illuminated the dark room.

Mr. Swallow had not the heart to praise the chapel or even to ask the lady to cross the threshold. He allowed her her own silent preoccupations. She looked more at the place than he had supposed she would, and he recalled with a pang of compassion her own home where, from generation to generation, this and that convenience, had been added, so that the huddle of buildings, so ungainly to the eye of a modern architect, represented the growth of a family—with the odd little rooms, closets and staircases, the added stablings and sheds, the walled garden extended here, altered there. Well, Lyndley Waters had been like that also, and now, because of one young man's caprice—after all it was no more than that—it had nearly gone and was soon to completely go, and instead was this . . .

Mr. Swallow in thinking thus was being a heretic to his own convictions, and because in the girl's look was something soft and tender, her outline, in her plain costume, was that of an English gentlewoman; in her cloak and hood, with the silver lacing inside, her face was lit by a little gleam of brightness, an edging as it were of light.

Celia was twenty-five years of age, but her delicate contours, since early childhood freshened and sweetened by country air, might have been those of a girl of seventeen. Mr. Swallow tried to throw off his momentary—well, was it regret, remorse . . . ? He did not know. At least it caused him to speak gravely:

"There is the chapel . . . the altar-piece is supposed to be by Vandyck. . . ."

"The black and white marbling, I think, is very effective. It is copied from a certain famous church in Rome of which I always forget the name," said Celia sweetly.

He noticed she still did not cross the threshold, but stood in the arched doorway looking within steadily. Her voice, however, was gay, and he admired the strength and loyalty that gave her the power for this dissimulation.

"Yes, the black and white marble and cedar-wood panelling, and handsome gilt candlesticks . . . you must forgive me if I prefer our old parish church . . . but it is all very handsome, no doubt, and in the best of taste." Then she added with a certain force, "Would it not be possible, however, for the light to be less cold? Surely that window faces northward and the shaft of grey that strikes down on to the black and white . . ."

"It will suit the tastes of Lady Troyes, no doubt," said Mr. Swallow, "who is accustomed to the most austere places of worship—indeed, I doubt not that she will exclaim against the great beauty of this chapel. . . ."

"Beauty . . . I don't know," smiled Celia. "I spoke of the light, so grey and cold. It is almost as if a shaft of something hard and solid fell on to the floor, that doesn't appear like a beam of sun, even of distant sun . . . some coloured glass perhaps . . . ?"

"We have not the designs here yet. The glazing is temporary only."

"Well," Celia turned away. He noted that she had not after all entered the chapel. "That is your finest showpiece, I suppose? I have seen your stove-houses and the pavilion with the two statues, and the fall of water that comes so prettily out of the lake. . . ."

"It is a sixty-foot drop," replied Mr. Swallow with pride as they returned through the empty rooms. "Indeed, I agree with you, madam, the manner in which the water . . ."

"Lyndley Waters," smiled Celia.

"Yes, Lyndley Waters falls over the stone steps that have been constructed again after the best Italian model—indeed the pool below is mot ingenious. . . ."

"I am sure that Lady Troyes cannot but admire that. Now you must go about your business, and I am sure that is heavy enough."

Celia gave him a pleasant, smiling dismissal.

"Let me just wander at will among all your curiosities. I will not go into the furnished part, for that would be an intrusion. I must wait till I am invited there by the new mistress."

"We have some things worth seeing there also," said the steward. "I hope you will take notice of them when you enter the Brocatelle room that has been very excellently done, as I consider, and the Volery room which is, perhaps, even more curious. Then I do not believe that you have seen the Cradle Walk since the gardeners completed the entwining of the boughs overhead."

"That, too, I shall leave for Lady Troyes to show me," said Celia. "She will, at first, have few amusements."

The steward agreed in his heart that this course would be in the better taste, although he had a childish anxiety to show off immediately to this pleasant woman, who always had a flattering word as to his work, what he had accomplished in the way of reconstructing Lyndley Waters. But there was, as she reminded him, a great deal to be done, and he went away about the doing of it. . . .

Celia turned away from the house, not looking backwards, and came out into the part of the garden, below the terrace that had recently been rebuilt, that was most familiar to her. Part of this had been laid out again in the inevitable Italian style, with *termini* and square-cut beds and gravel walks, but a part of it remained as Celia had always remembered it—an English rose garden. Would that go also? There were no roses now and no gardeners at work on the beds,

111

but the paths, just wide enough in the old style for three to walk abreast, and the long parterres where the various blooms were set out to advantage, remained the same, and the place was lovely to Celia, though neither leaf nor flower showed and the rose bushes displayed nothing but thorns.

She passed through this garden and came out on Lyndley Waters, the small lake that gave the name to the estate. It lay open to the sky, completely unshaded by trees. The banks were left in a natural state, grown with bramble, willow and those weeds like purple loosestrife that make so brave a display in their season. Water-lilies grew here, too. Celia had never failed, as far as she could remember, to come every year to gather them. Sometimes alone, sometimes with James Troyes, sometimes with other people and once with Brian Ormerod had she gaily taken the boat from the small boathouse, launched it from the little wooden pier and rowed across Lyndley Water to pull up the thick waterflowers from their long, succulent stems—white and pearly pink and yellow.

"Next year," she thought, "I shall not gather any as I suppose—no, certainly I shall not gather any, for if I were asked to do so it would only remind me how different everything was."

* * * *

Celia, when she approached the boathouse, found there was somebody in it—Brian; she had half suspected he would be there. She believed she had seen him on the road as she had come up to Lyndley Waters. Sometimes she was sure he followed her. There he sat in a place that did not belong to him, and that, she thought, was ill suited to him, on the rude bench that ran beside the little inlet where the boat was moored.

"Eh, Celia," he remarked, "is the boathouse going to be rebuilt too? It is old, small and inconvenient."

"What should I know?" said the girl honestly. "I listen to what Mr. Swallow says about all the plans and I forget them again at once."

"Then why do you come here so often?" demanded the young man. "Why do you come here now, into the boathouse where there is nothing agreeable? Oh, I include myself—I know that I do not please you."

"You are moody and difficult," she replied without resentment. "I saw you in the lane . . . I thought I saw you. I had just taken the footway across the fields. . . ."

"Yes, I saw you too. I see you too often, Celia, for my peace of mind. I wanted to speak to you alone. You know that I have said that to you frequently for the past two years."

"Yes, I know a great deal about it," replied Celia. "Let us come out of this boathouse, it is dark. I really don't know why I entered—I suppose it was to see if the old boat was still there. I remember I wrote my name on it once—'The Celia'—that was foolish. It was only a childish prank." She hesitated. "It should come off now, should it not?"

"So that was your purpose? You wanted to see if the name was still there and to efface it if it still was."

Celia did not deny this.

"One doesn't know," she admitted candidly, "with what one has to deal. I think that if I went to my husband's house and saw another woman's name written upon a boat on the pleasure lake I should . . ."

"You would not," he interrupted. "You would neither be jealous, arrogant nor malicious. It is not in you to be anything but kind, Celia." He turned away abruptly. "Of course the name is still there, you know it is. I will if you wish," he added, with an increasing harshness, "take it off for you. She will see, of course, that some word has been scraped away, but she will never know what."

"Thank you," said Celia. "I will wait outside till you have finished and walk home with you, if you will."

"Is that my reward?" he demanded sombrely.

"If you like to think it so."

She did not know why she had no inclination to see him scrape away her name from the boat which she and James had so frequently rowed to pluck the lilies. It seemed merely one of those unnecessary little torments that one might avoid if one would. She peered round now and then to see how the young man was proceeding with his work. He was tall and heavily built, dark, with rather sulky features and, like herself, of no especial good looks, gifts nor charm—the only son of a neighbouring landowner, being trained to run his small but prosperous estates, and trained for nothing else. He was, she knew, an excellent farmer, a kind landlord, an agreeable neighbour. She knew also that he was not for her, though it would have been impossible for her to define the barrier that something in herself had set between herself and this young man who, counting by virtuous ways, was in all superior to James.

She watched his brown and capable fingers

(enlarged and roughened by country life and considerable manual work, for he was a man who was seldom happy without he was doing something with his hands) moving to and fro over the side of the boat his sharp pocket-knife until the painted name had gone and a length of new wood only showed. Then, having completed his work and brushed the shavings that had once been the word "Celia" into the sluggish little backwater of the boathouse, Brian Ormerod came out and joined the waiting girl.

"We are fools, both of us," he said angrily. "Complete fools! Why should people set their hearts, all their desires, on what they may not have when happiness lies within their finger-tip's reach?"

He spoke with an energy that did not, however, affect her at all. Everything he did and said was outside her range. She could do no more than sympathise gently with his emotions that were far deeper than she suspected. She was absorbed, as in a magic circle, in her own feelings and had no more than this detached kindness to give to anyone; but being by nature extremely candid and having no ill thought of anyone in her mind—being indeed incapable of any evil—she did not refuse to discuss with him their several destinies.

"I know what you mean, Brian," she assented as they walked along the bank of Lyndley Waters. "You think that I would have liked— Well, we will not speak the words. I believe you are the only person," she added touchingly, "who has guessed."

He did not reply, knowing well enough that there were others, too, who had read the heart of Celia Plaisent.

Confident, however, that he alone knew where

her feelings lay and that he, by reason of his love for her, was bound to secrecy, she continued: "It is not for me. . . . You see, Brian, James had to marry for the money. I hope, however, that despite it being a bargain and something that seems grim and cold, he will—they will," she stubbornly corrected herself so as to bring in the other woman to her good wishes, "find contentment here."

"Why should they," cried the young man with a touch of impatience, "why should anyone find contentment anywhere!"

"We have always found it," replied Celia, "at Plaisent Manor. Yes, I think you may call our lives contented, Two of my sisters and one of my brothers are happily married. We do not expect great things, but we avoid great tumults."

"James Troyes flies higher," cried Brian Ormerod. "What is the sense of this palace here? Is he so much better than his neighbours that he must house himself so handsomely?"

"In a worldly sense," smiled Celia, "he is better, you know, Brian; his estates are larger, his revenues more considerable. He has the old title and much else that would be tedious for me to repeat to you."

"But he is not justified in building this place," replied the young squire hotly. "I detest it. It seems to me an abomination; all these marbles, heathen statues and strange plants brought with so much cost and trouble from foreign lands. What can be better than a rose garden, a manor house like yours or mine?"

"They do say," Celia laughed, "that the rose was brought to England once. We only think it ours because it has been here so long."

"Maybe." He retained his sombre tone. "You make a jest of it all, Celia. And now there is to be this foreign woman. . . ."

"A Scots woman," protested Celia quickly.

"Fight for her as you will, Celia, you know well enough that she will be like a foreigner here."

"Well, if she is, it will be her story and James's, not ours." Celia turned away from the banks of Lyndley Waters. "We cannot do anything, Brian, except be kind."

"You cannot be anything except kind," he corrected her. "I doubt if it would be in my nature to show any pleasantness towards James Troyes or any of his works or actions."

"I must leave you to wrestle with your own . . ." she did not know how to name them—"jealousies, bitterness" had come to her tongue. She looked at him in candid disarray. "Oh, Brian, I do not know how to speak to you! It does not make me very happy to think of you so set on me when I can never have you."

Encouraged as it seemed by even this slight softening, this turning of her attention towards him, the young man hastened to say:

"Celia, you know there is nothing against it. I would have your father's consent and you would be most warmly received by all my relatives. My estates are unencumbered, they can offer you everything you have ever had—perhaps more."

She shook her head, and he cried out fiercely, "It is true all they say about the wilfulness of women."

"Perhpas," said Celia. "But would you, as the years went by, Brian think of that? As the time passed would you care to see upon your hearth, at the head of your table, in your chamber, a woman who did not love you?"

This was a problem beyond him. He was exasperated that it was put to him for his solution.

He said foolishly, "If James Troyes can endure a loveless marriage, so, I suppose, can I."

"But I do not bring a large fortune with me."

"Nor do I need one, Celia. I need you and you only."

She was touched, but still in that remote fashion, by this emotion that was beyond her and yet slightly disturbed her serenity.

"I can do nothing for you, Brian, and you nothing for me. I suppose we shall see one another at the festival James is giving to welcome her—Grace—home."

"Grace!" echoed the young man in a mock. "That's the last name she should have. She'll bring no grace to Lyndley Waters, nor to the neighbourhood."

"You are wrong in being so prejudiced, so willing to see her as someone detestable," Celia protested, "but how useless for me to argue with you. If you feel in so ill a mood about the matter, Brian, pray do not come. It will not be courteous to permit her to see even one frowning face in the assembly which is supposed to make her new neighbours appear kindly towards her."

"I shall be there," replied Brian. "It is curiosity, perhaps. After all," he added bitterly, "none of us rustic gentlefolk have ever seen a place like this."

He glanced back at the unfinished building that stood on the slope behind them and was outlined—scaffolding poles, facade, half-demolished structure and the finished pavilion—against the pure sky.

"Well, you must do as you wish. I think that if you were courteous, since you dislike the word kind, towards James and his bride, you would also, Brian, be courteous towards me and towards yourself, and so make everything easier for all of us."

With that they were now on the lane that ran by the estate. She paused and said:

"We have walked together far enough. We but repeat and repeat, Brian. When we see one another, let it be as good neighbours and no more."

She crossed the road, pushed open the five-barred gate that led into the neighbouring field, turned and pleasantly waved her hand to him and was gone. Nor did he attempt to follow her. With no more than that he took his way homeward. He had not understood what she had meant by her last words; indeed, he understood very little but his own frustration, his own increasing and passionate bitterness and disappointment.

* * * *

Sir James Troyes and his lady arrived at Lyndley Waters punctual to the hour that he had mentioned to Mr. Swallow, who had allowed for all possible delays at toll-gates and because of the roughness of the road. There had been no accident, and the drive from London had been in every way agreeable. A servant's carriage contained Thomas Pratt and the new lady's maid engaged in London by Grace Troyes; baggage horses and baggage waggon followed. It was but a small retinue, but the steward, ready with the upper servants to receive his master, knew that a more imposing array of goods was to follow as soon as they could be got upon the road.

It was a moment of sharp and painful curiosity on

both sides—it could hardly have been otherwise—when Grace Troyes was handed from the coach. She looked at once, and without any attempt to veil her meaning, about her, and then at the steward and the servants behind him; and they, despite their air of deferential respect, scarcely endeavoured to conceal their keen scrutiny of their new mistress. Each was completely strange to the other; the landscape, the unfinished mansion, the Englishman, John Swallow and his fellow-countrymen and women standing there, easy, cordial in their handsome clothes, most strange to the Scotch woman; and she, with her dark, keen personality, with her rich gown which was so much too pompous and heavy for her years, was completely strange to them.

The men noted her face, its possibilities of beauty, its lines of arrogance and temper, her smile of pride, the glossy lustre of her long, dark locks—a foreigner indeed. The women noted her attire—the quantities of gold lace, the diamonds in her cravat—everything, as they said to themselves, too grand and outlandish; and here was a strange contradiction, for it should have been Lyndley Waters that should have been too grand and outlandish for the woman who had been Grace Morrisson.

They had little time to scrutinise their master, and he had sufficient ease to carry off any situation. He brought his bride into the great hall of the finished pavilion, kissed her on the cheek and bade her welcome to Lyndley Waters, hoped that she was not fatigued after the journey, and asked her pleasure, all with a graceful formality that was yet not without an affectionate touch.

His own people regarded him with approval.

James Troyes had always been popular, save with a very few men such as Brian Ormerod. He had those vices which are so readily condoned and those virtues which are so obviously admired. No one grudged him his fortune or his new mansion save Celia's would-be suitor, and all, with that exception, had wished him well in his choice of a foreign wife.

Mr. Swallow thought now, "He is a comely, pleasant fellow—well-bred, too, and surely incapable of offence. She ought to be able to make him—well, comfortable, but I don't like her look. It seems to me that she is . . ." He could not, even in his mind that was slow and absorbed with business, find the epithet he required for Grace Troyes.

She listened with indifference to her husband's welcoming speech.

"I am not in the least fatigued," she answered, and suddenly laughed and clapped her hands with quite a childish gesture. "Why, it is most admirable, everything! I *will* see it all. Who is to show me?"

"You will not see it all immediately, I suppose?" smiled Sir James. "We must have some refreshment and repose, and you and your new woman—I forget her name . . ."

"Her name is Margaret Cummings," replied Grace Troyes, "but you have a housekeeper here."

She had forestalled a difficult moment. Mrs. Bateman had for long ruled as the *chatelaine* of Lyndley Waters, though always in the capacity of a servant. No female relative had interfered with her since Lady Troyes, the mother of Sir James, had died ten years ago. Now she was to have a new mistress and, as she well knew, "be put in her place"; but she conducted herself with dignity and with resignation—

a stout yet active woman of middle age, in a costume that in Scotland would have been handsome for a gentlewoman, but that here, in the opulent south, was considered as very fitting for her position.

She had her keys in her basket and presented them at once with a ceremonious air, as if she had been the commander of a defeated garrison delivering up the keys of a citadel, to Grace Troyes, who picked them up from the basket, held them up, all glittering clean and shiny, laughed and asked:

"What am I to do with these?"

"Mrs. Bateman will tell you later," said Sir James. "It is not a thing to make a play of, Grace; that is your insignia as mistress of Lyndley Waters, and Mrs. Bateman will tell you what each key unlocks. . . . I suppose you have been instructed," he added lightly, yet with an inward uneasiness, "in the ruling of a great house?"

"That was indeed part of my education," replied Grace Troyes, "but I never thought of a palace like this." She dropped the keys into the basket again. "Keep them, Mrs. Bateman, my good Mrs. Bateman, and show me later on how I am to use them—but perhaps it is you who may continue to use them. I may have other occupations."

Mrs. Bateman withdrew with native dignity. She reserved all judgment as to her new mistress and as to the rights or wrongs of her behaviour. She turned her attention to the new maid; here, at least, would be pliable material, one whom she could understand and who would do her bidding.

* * * *

Grace Troyes, ever since her marriage in St. Giles's Cathedral, had at frequent intervals spoken of the chapel at Lyndley Waters, and her husband, not unwilling to indulge her interest in his grandiose schemes, had shown her drawings, plans and sketches of the work. Now that she was in her new home she wished immediately to see this place, and he again indulged her, reminding himself that if she were once to absorb herself in her religion, he would have the more time for his own pursuits. He was no more in love with her than he had ever been, still a little curious about her, a little piqued perhaps by her changing qualities. She was like shot-silk, now of one hue, now of another. He took her already very much for granted. A difficult woman who might, if the opportunity be given, be imperious; but he did not intend that she should ever have the opportunity.

Mr. Swallow was still in attendance on them and very willingly undertook to show them the chapel. Grace Troyes looked, with a quick, darting glance to right and left, through the rooms she passed through. They did not seem made to live in, she remarked. What would one *do* in such chambers?

Neither of the men deigned to answer this remark directly. Sir James informed his wife that she had her own apartments—the Brocatelle room and others that would be shown her by Mrs. Bateman presently where she might be as enclosed as she liked.

For him—well, if she had a little patience, she would see how he intended to use these chambers, and even as he spoke with this complete self-assurance, he knew perfectly well that he was not at all sure himself. For him, as for John Swallow, the mansion was an end in itself.

When she reached the chapel, Grace Troyes paused, as Celia Plaisent had paused, on the threshold and looked in, keenly scanning the black and white marble floor, the altar with the twisted baroque pillars and the sombre altar-piece painted in hues so dark that the subject was scarcely to be discerned.

"Are you pleased?" asked Sir James. "The window is not yet properly glazed, yet with scarlet and blue glass as was intended it would seem to you, I suppose, to smack of popery?"

"I have not seen anything of popery," replied Grace Troyes. "It is very different from the little chapel we used."

She emphasised the "we," and he wondered if she was thinking of her old chaplain, Nicholas Jerdan. He supposed he would have to put up with the fellow's presence soon. Well, from the first, he must be made to keep his place, and that place would be well out of eye-shot and ear-shot of Sir James Troyes; and he must be taught, too (and that must be not a difficult lesson to learn), that he must not make mischief and, all this understood, no doubt his presence in Lyndley Waters could be tolerated, if, indeed, Grace wished him to come. But it appeared from her next remark that she was referring to the grim gentlewomen, the very names of whom Sir James had scarcely troubled to commit to memory, with whom she had been educated.

"There were the ladies Ladelle," she said, "and sometimes two only. I thought the place very bare and ugly, like those bleak graves, you remember, that we went to see after we had crossed the River Almond."

He did not care for her reminding him of that strange afternoon when she had, in so freakish a manner, thrust his handsome gift into the grave of the Covenanter.

Neither of the men watching Lady Troyes knew what they expected her action to be, but both were aware that what she did do came as an oddly shocking surprise. From the folds of her long and heavy sarsenet cloak she produced a small doll mannequin of a nondescript appearance, wearing a dark cloak and with roughly painted features. So much was to be discerned in the bleak light from the high-set chapel window. Sir James exclaimed with a disgust that he could neither conceal nor suppress, "What do you intend with these trivial toys here, Grace?"

She stepped into the chapel without answering and hung the little figure up, close beside the altar, on a projecting ornament that had been intended for a lamp.

"It is a whim of mine," she said at last. "I suppose one is allowed a few whims."

"I do not think you ever have been," replied her husband sombrely. "Whims? Have you?"

This action had the effect of blighting his good humour and bringing to the surface the uneasiness that did not lie far beneath his assumed cheerfulness.

"Hanging up images, and in a chapel, savours to me more of Papistry than the Calvinists."

"It is something that I consider sacred," smiled Lady Troyes, leaving the chapel after glancing round with what seemed to her husband and Mr. Swallow an avid look, as if she gathered in for her own possession all the chill magnificence of the empty, meaningless place.

"I do not like it," exclaimed Sir James, carried beyond his own intention, for it was not his habit to make much of petty happenings. "It savours more of something . . ."

"Of what?" asked Grace, clear in voice and eye, challenging him straightly.

Mr. Swallow put in awkwardly, "All is but a lady's enthusiasm for some relic of her childhood. Why not, Sir James?" He turned with square honesty to Lady Troyes. "I am the man, madam, who is responsible for Lyndley Waters as you see it now. A great deal of it must appear but a confusion to your ladyship—the workmen are likely to be here, and the architects and gardeners, for some time. I expect it seems an uncouth place for a bride to return to. . . . I have done what I could, with able help from Mrs. Bateman, to procure for you the apartments which you will occupy."

"It is all very different," remarked Lady Troyes, without a look of gratitude or thanks, "to anything I have been accustomed to—I have lived very withdrawn, in a city that is quiet though it be the capital of our kingdom, and my sole diversions have been to ride about my father's estate and perhaps a little deeper into the mountains of Scotland."

Somewhat disconcerted, the steward replied, "There is everything here for your ladyship's amusement and care. The neighbours are eager to make you welcome."

"Why should they be?" she asked. "I must be considered a stranger. No doubt my character and history have been much canvassed. . . ."

"If you speak in that manner, Grace," warned Sir James as they moved away from the chapel, "you will make everything confoundedly difficult. At one moment you are all blunt candour, at the next full of tricks and whims. I should not speak so in front of Mr. Swallow, but that he will be one of the few people who will know of our domestic felicity. I shall be much with him. . . ."

"Lyndley Waters is the passion of your life," continued Lady Troyes. "You must allow other people to have their own obsessions."

"Obsession!" exclaimed the baronet with a touch of anger. "I do not like the word. I am a busy man . . . a magistrate . . . I intend to sit for Parliament . . . I keep my estate myself in good order . . . I visit all my tenantry. I am continually making the most modern improvements . . ."

Grace interrupted him with an air of provoking disinterest.

"We are not concerned, sir," she replied, "or rather I should say, I am not concerned in a list of your accomplishments. I have a trifle of news for you—you use the word trifle so often in connection with me that it comes the more readily to my lips—Mr. Nicholas Jerdan, whom you permitted me to employ as my chaplain, is already on the road to Lyndley Waters."

They had come to a pause by a large purple porphyry vase in the centre of an anti-chamber that the ambitious architect had fitted up very handsomely in the antique style. The windows were not yet glazed and the little peelings from the carpenter's saw lay like fine ladies' curls along the sashes. The wainscoting, too, had not yet been polished. All was new and had a fragrant smell of freshly cut wood, while through the open window blew in the pure and keen air of the English winter day.

"This is a chill place in which to pause," remarked Mr. Swallow between agitation and impatience.

With every word she said, he disliked Grace Troyes the more. He resented her also. He tried, with a sense of justice, to remember that her money alone was making possible the continuance of the work that was his very life. Yet, unreasonable enough, he resented her. His sympathy was entirely with Sir James. Why could not the woman go about her own feminine affairs with Mrs. Bateman, with the new maids from London, with the neighbours who were sure to visit her, and not stand there arguing in her cold voice, with her look that was sometimes fixed and sometimes fiery, about matters that she could not possibly understand? And why the hanging up of the mannequin in the chapel? As a good Protestant, Mr. Swallow had accepted without any scruple the exotic decorations of the chapel, merely because they were the fashion. He had even had a debate, that had come to some warmth, with Mr. Boate, the rector, who had made a protest about the richness of Sir James's appointments in his praying-place . . . it was all a matter for the architects . . . it did not concern religion at all.

John Swallow could worship with equal tranquility either in the homely parish church that Cromwell's soldiers had stripped of every vestige of decoration, or in this gorgeous chapel built by foreign artists and from foreign materials, and typifying, certainly, a foreign faith. But he could not endure that the foreign lady who had come there as a professed Calvinist, a Scot that Mr. Swallow was prepared to detest, should place her mannequin next to the altar, already sacred to Mr. Swallow though not yet consecrated; but Grace Troyes refused to take any heed of his protest.

She was cloaked and hooded still for her journey, and drew over her long, thin hands thick embroidered gloves. They had been one of her extravagant purchases at the Royal Exchange; Sir James had remarked then her instant taste for all that was costly and in a flamboyant taste.

"Why shall I not conclude what I have to say about Mr. Jerdan?" she continued.

"Why, pray conclude," said Sir James.

He contained himself with what Mr. Swallow considered an admirable patience, but his tone was shorter than he usually employed to women.

"He is a good grammarian," remarked Grace Troyes. "He taught me, as I consider, very well."

"A grammarian?" Sir James turned over the expression. "I suppose that is a Scots term for a scholar?"

"It is a Scots term," assented his wife.

"The chaplain's rooms," put in Mr. Swallow, "have not yet been provided for. I waited Sir James's pleasure."

"Now you must wait mine," said Lady Troyes. "It has been permitted me to have so much in my own province—the choice of the chaplain, a certain sum in pin-money, I believe you call it here, that is in my own expenditure . . . and the permission to live my own life even at Lyndley Waters."

"If she continues to speak like that," thought Mr. Swallow, "everything will be impossible. We can only hope that when this fanatic appears she will enclose herself with him in whatever dismal services these Nonconformists favour."

Sir James, tapping his fine fingers on the large prophyry vase that stood inappropriately, it seemed, on the basalt plinth in the centre of the bare room, was willing to be rid of the matter with as little trouble as possible.

"The chambers, I suppose, on the first storey—the *piano nobile,* as I believe the architects call it, next to the chapel are surely those to be reserved for the chaplain."

"Of what do they consist?" asked Grace Troyes.

"Of a luxury, I should think, that a starveling Scot has never seen before," replied Sir James arrogantly.

The discourtesy of these words surprised Mr. Swallow, but he sympathised and rejoiced in them. To smooth over his employer's most uncommon bluntness he began to extol the chaplain's rooms. They were light and airy, already furnished with cases for books. They contained everything that the rather vague conception he had of a religious gentleman's wants might require.

"It was in my thought," remarked Sir James, "to search out some scientific or philosophic man who might find a retreat here and write a treatise that perhaps would do credit to himself and his century."

"And to you and to Lyndley Waters," added Grace with a sudden lightness. "Well, Mr. Jerdan writes . . . he is employed on an essay now. He has published several pamphlets which you would not know of. . . ."

"No," assented her husband with a grave bow, "I should certainly not know of any polemics published in Edinburgh." He turned to his steward almost with his back to his wife. "See that the rooms are furnished. I suppose you may attain sufficient articles to make them habitable even in a short time?"

"Mr. Jerdan," said Lady Troyes, "may be here

within two days."

"Then he can be present at the festival which we must give the neighbours," replied her husband carelessly. "Mrs. Bateman has already seen to that, so you will not have to concern yourself with the food or the dirnk or the accommodation. We must do something for the workmen too, my dear. One has to send them money, you know . . . and they make a bonfire as on Guy Fawkes Day, and drink our healths . . . and it will be expected of you to visit them. . . ."

"I daresay a great deal will be expected of me that I shall not be very willing to perform," but Grace Troyes smiled and her tone was not as harsh as it had been.

It was almost with a gentle air that she talked to Mr. Swallow about the conveniences that might be provided for her chaplain, and the steward found himself touched by her solicitude. "No doubt he is some old penurious fellow whose piety has made a great impression on her youthful mind. He has been, as I suppose, like a father to her and, after all, even if he has bred her disagreeable and cold, he has bred her at least proud and demure." She was, in Mr. Swallow's phrase (one that seemed odd when applied to a personage like Grace Troyes), "an extremely respectable gentlewoman." After all, what more could one want? And with an interest that was not altogether assumed, he told her of the arrangements for making the apartments as comfortable as possible, and "if Mr. Jerdan, by reason of age or infirmity, does not wish to leave them and join the family at meals, there will be no difficulty in having a servant to wait upon him."

Grace Troyes laughed.

"Mr. Jerdan himself will tell you what he requires in that way," she replied. "I thank you for your civility."

"And how long, Grace, are we to stand here?" asked her husband, "in this empty room, by this foolish vase?"

"Foolish!" said Mr. Swallow, eager in defence of anything that appertained to Lyndley Waters. "Why, it was brought with great expense from Italy and is a copy of one to be found in the Villa Trajan."

"I do not know," confessed the baronet, "why it suddenly seemed to be like a folly."

"I think it extremely handsome," put in Grace Troyes. "The colour and the lustre and even the cold smoothness of the touch . . ." She pulled off her glove and eagerly placed her fingers on the lustrous curves of the vase. "I shall spend many days looking at the extraordinary things you have here. You need not concern yourself about me, nor need Mrs. Bateman be in a pass as to what she should tell me about your spice and linen closets, the management of your presses, of your china and plate . . . those matters I have learned, though on a small scale; but this—all this is new to me."

Her attitude astonished and a little confounded her husband.

"You're a puzzle, Grace," he frowned. "I don't know quite how to understand you."

"Likely you'll never understand me," she answered. "Why should you? Perhaps you'll understand me suddenly and at the wrong moment. Never mind . . ."

Mr. Swallow again tried to divert an embarrassing

conversation into safer channels.

"Sir James is pleased, almost overwhelmed, that you, madam, coming from a country where everything, including the faith, is austere and, as we hold, severe and casting a harsh and perhaps bitter judgment on the vanities of this world, should so admire what is, even in England, considered rich and luxurious."

They left the room for a corridor that was being hung with bright tapestries newly imported from the Low Countries. These, in colours of bright blues, pinks and saffrons, depicted a battle between gods and giants. Mr. Swallow did not attract attention to them, for they had been a considerable expense and he wished a more opportune moment in which to confess to his imployer that he had not been able to resist the extravagance of purchasing them, so nicely did they fit the corridor and so handsome—nay, unique, he hoped, were they in themselves. He noted with a slightly shamefaced satisfaction that it was Lady Troyes, not Sir James, who observed them with a sparkling admiration, though she made no comment.

As they reached again the ante-chamber that led to the completed pavilion of Lyndley Waters, Grace Troyes' husband, in a short sentence, tried to put his fortunes as it were to the test.

"Why do you," he asked directly, "care so much for . . . ?" He looked round.

"For all this?" she added quickly. "I understand what you mean. You remember where you found me, you recall my father's house. . . ."

"Yes, I do. I also recall the character I heard of you, as a very pious young woman who lived enclosed. . . ."

"You recall, sir, perhaps, that my mother was Spanish? I suppose in Spain they do not live as they do in Scotland?"

"I don't know." He was still puzzled, and still anxious and even determined—though determination was somewhat foreign to his easy-going nature—to come at an answer to the riddle of Grace Troyes.

"Where did you learn of it? How did you know there were such things?"

"There were books," she said, as if she was as uncertain herself as her husband. "Yes, I got books in which I read of the way the ancient kings of Scotland lived in their palaces at Stirling, at Edinburgh in the castle and in Holyrood Palace. I read of Mary of Scotland when she came from France with the singing boys and girls with lutes. . . ."

"I wonder you were permitted to come at such books," smiled Sir James.

"They were old histories," she replied slyly, "that the closets in our house provided."

"Did not Mr. Jerdan supervise with a somewhat jealous eye these secular readings?" asked Sir James.

"When Mr. Jerdan arrives," she replied, "you will be able to ask him yourself how he conducted my education and question him, if need be, on all these matters."

* * * *

Celia Plaisent, with her father, mother and two of her sisters, attended the festival given by Sir James Troyes to welcome his bride home, to entertain his neighbours and, as was good-humouredly admitted by all, to make a display of what he had accomplished at Lyndley Waters.

"The Spanish gold," as the neighbouring squires called Sir James's newly acquired fortune, had already been spent with no sparing hand. The work in every direction had been pushed forward with energy and zeal. It was quite astonishing to those modest, stay-at-home folk who had been contented so long with what their forebears had left them, only adding now and then some small improvement to their manors or mansion houses, to observe how quickly wealth could, as it were, produce marvels. Even in the bad weather, with the deeply rutted roads, the waggons seemed to come quickly enough from London and the ports, and the stream of pack-horses was continuous. The gardeners, even in this most silent and blossomless time of the year, had arranged a display of foreign flowers in the stove-houses. There was talk of fireworks by the brink of Lyndley Waters itself, and the neighbours, excited, though in a good-natured, almost compassionate way at the thought of the entertainment, hoped that the weather would be fine and the sky clear for this unwonted frivolity.

Grace Troyes had already been seen by Celia and most of her near neighbours. They had come in an informal way—with the easiness of breeding that showed that, though rustic folk, they were of gentle blood and long tradition—to surround with kindness and warm interest the new mistress of Lyndley Waters. She had received them with a complete indifference, baffling both their curiosity and their friendliness.

"She doesn't seem," Celia had remarked to her sisters, "like anyone who has come to stay. Do you know what I mean?—a cut flower in a crystal vase, without either root or blossom. . . ."

"That is fanciful for you, Celia," the other girl had replied. "Grace Troyes is merely out of her place, as any foreigner would be; yet I think there is something odd about her, too."

"The oddness is," Celia had confessed, "that we were told to expect a strict Calvinist, and I suppose that might be what we should call a dissenter—stern and gloomy and turned away from the worldly pleasures and vanities—and instead, we find one who seems to put us in the shade with her extravagant notions, for she *has* extravagant notions," Celia had continued innocently. "She accepts without protest all that James has already accomplished at Lyndley Waters, and wishes even more."

"It is odd indeed," the other one had conceded, and the word had seemed to encircle in their minds the figure of Grace Troyes. "I suppose it is the Spanish blood in her. Do you remember the ballad—'There was a Spanish lady who loved an Englishman' . . . or a Scots gallant, was it?"

"Yes, I remember so much and no more," replied Celia, "and certainly not the end of the story—I suppose they came to no good. Lovers never do in old ballads."

Now Celia stood in the long reception-room of the completed pavilion. It was already full of guests, all people known to her and endeared to her by familiarity, common interests and kindness since her earliest childhood. Yet even these good neighbours in their best attire, cutting, she fondly thought, no ill figure either, could not make the place seem other than alien to Celia Plaisent. Those marble chimney-pieces, with the mosaics of cherries and dark green leaves on the gleaming white . . . that painted ceiling on which the oil still glistened . . . those wainscoted walls of coloured wood . . . the Venetian cord velvet of a yellow colour that Celia had never seen before, hanging at the tall windows . . . the candelabra of crystal. . . . Nay, it was no use of her to run over in her simple mind all the details of the magnificence about her. It was *odd*. What a stupid word for her to keep using in her mind. . . . It did not then, to put the matter plainly, belong to Lyndley Waters, did not belong to England. Did it, she wondered, belong to James Troyes?

Grace Troyes stood by the noble hearth on which burned great logs that had been allowed to glow down to a heart of orange and then sprinkled with what seemed to these Protestants suspiciously like incense, but they supposed it was but some foreign spice, such as musk or bergamot. The lady of the house was attired (this seemed her usual taste) in heavy garments far too stately for her age, and yet they were by no means austere. The dark blue silk gown rippled with light like a midnight sky, when the stars twinkle, filling up what seems a void with transient light, and she wore antique massive clasps of diamonds upon her bosom, on her sleeves and shoes.

The ladies of the company wondered if these were her heritage or had belonged to the late Lady Troyes. The older among them could not remember any such jewels of the former mistress of Lyndley Waters, "but then, you know," they agreed, "such gems could easily be reset." The men were under no such doubt; if James Troyes had possessed jewels like those they would, whether they had been his mother's or no, long since have been sold, turned into foreign marvels or into the wages for workmen to dig up the English sward and to set in there some outlandish piece of rubbish, for so the Wiltshire squires were inclined, always with good nature, to describe the marvels of Lyndley Waters.

No, the men knew that the lady's gems were her own. She must have brought them with her from Scotland, and even their stolid imaginations were quickened by the thoughts of these diamonds and sapphires that seemed of considerable value and that were set in a fashion long past, coming from Spain in their iron-bound strong boxes, lying in the fogbound capital of the north for so long and then suddenly brought to light to gleam here in the new ante-chamber at Lyndley Waters.

There was a concert of music, the musicians having been brought from London, and all the fashionable pieces were played.

Grace Troyes listened, tapped time with her foot and her fan, but seemed to take but little interest in the diversion. Nor did she appear greatly concerned, though she must have known of it, that she was, however politely it might be concealed, the centre of much scrutiny and speculation.

There was no one there, not even the person most nearly concerned, Celia Plaisent, who was able to come to a decision about either her person or her character. Was she beautiful? Was she amiable? Sometimes a turn of her graceful person, a toss back of her long, dark curls, a lift of her rounded chin, and she seemed beauty itself. Sometimes again, especially when she stood pensive, looking brooding at the ground, as if she stared through the black and white marbles, she appeared sallow, ordinary, a dark, heavy woman. Then again, some of her remarks were polished and such as were likely to put everyone at ease, to create an atmosphere of good-will; then, again, she would speak carelessly, as if without any concern for whom she might wound.

"I wonder," thought Celia, "I wonder is there happiness there for him?" Young as she was, she knew how elusive was that—*happiness*, and that we use the word, like we use the word *love*, far too often and far too casually. Is there some kind of contentment for him? she altered her own speculation in her mind. Can he, with this woman, live anything like the life he wants? And then again, "What *does* poor James want? Only Lyndley Waters and money to spend on it?"

Celia had her own dignity, and though unmarried and of no great consequence among the ladies of the neighbourhood, she approached Grace Troyes when most of the other guests had gone with Sir James into the long gallery that was set out, not only with wine and food, but with many of the curiosities that had been sent from abroad to adorn Lyndley Waters.

"You will have seen all these treasures before, madam?" she began without timidity.

"Yes, I have seen them. . . ." Grace Troyes looked at her but seemed not to observe her, the girl thought. "Who are you?" she asked. "You must excuse me if I appear—well, rude. I come, do I not, from a barbarous nation?"

"None of us here have ever thought so," said Celia quietly. "We know very little of Scotland and less of Spain. Why should we despise other countries because of our ignorance?"

"You have been very interested in watching this

house built, I suppose?" asked Lady Troyes.

She unfurled her fan. It was of chicken skin and painted, Celia noted, with a multitude of bright and glittering figures.

"Yes, I have watched it. . . . Our house is but a mile away—the estates, as we say, march."

"You should have married him," said Grace Troyes with a startling candour that defeated its own effect, for it brought no colour to Celia's face; being uttered like that, as a commonplace, as a commonplace it might be accepted.

"No, I should not have married him, madam. I am no heiress. Besides, we had no liking for one another beyond the fondness of childish companions."

"Do you think that he and I have any liking for one another," demanded Grace Troyes, "beyond the liking of two people who try to obtain from one another their heart's desire?"

"I am not bred to such plain speaking," protested Celia. She spoke with what she knew was rebuke.

"Ah, now I can perceive that you are interested both in Lyndley Waters and its master," said Lady Troyes tauntingly. "But what does any of it matter? What does it concern me?"

Celia was confounded. It had been easy to pass the first comment, but this was a direct thrust, and how was it that the foreign lady had been able to deliver it so straightly behind her guard? She did not know how to reply, but stood mute in her yellow and blue sarsenet, with her cloak, that she had so prudently retained, for they were all going down to the water's edge soon to see the fireworks, falling from her pretty, rounded shoulders.

"If you speak like this, Lady Troyes, to every

140

woman in the neighbourhood, they will think you are eccentric," she sighed at last.

"You were the only one to stay behind to speak *to me*—the others only chatted and passed on, staring—and made up their own minds, I suppose."

"I don't think they stared," protested Celia. "They were all very civil and wished you well—and you may believe that we have none of us made up our minds, as you term it, about you, Lady Troyes. I have been the childhood companion of your husband . . ." she repeated.

"Tell me, then," said the other lady, as if she was already weary of this subject, "what you think of this house? Have you seen other such mansions in England?"

"None," replied Celia, "but then I have never been far from home—only now and then to London where, of course, there are many very splendid houses, especially along the river's edge, the Strand and at places like Chelsea or Chiswick; but in the country, no. Here, if you visit us, your neighbours, as I pray you will, you will find that we have much more humble households."

"Sir James has poured all his fortune into this—that must be common knowledge, and now mine must go. I hope he stops before bankruptcy . . ."

"I hope, madam, that you will stop before such—"

"Well, name me my fate," said Grace Troyes, as the other paused. "Before what? I entered into no bond to pretend or to keep silent."

The other woman did not answer, and Grace Troyes crossed the room which the candlelight filled with a fluttering, delicate illumination, and pulled aside the long cut velvet curtain.

"Look there by the lake. They have begun to set off the fireworks. Shall we not go down? I have never seen any fireworks before. I heard someone say that nothing was more costly and more useless—nor more beautiful. Look at them . . . beautiful indeed." She clasped her hands and peered through the glass panes intent on the distant spectacle.

Celia, prompted more by curiosity as to the older woman than to the fireworks, came and stood beside her, and the two of them looked out across the unfinished terraces, parterres and gardens to the banks of Lyndley Waters where the rockets were whizzing into the air, cascading stars and sparkles of light—scarlet, orange and silver. The weather was, after all, perfect. It was dry with a slight frost, and the stars had the brittle glimmer of the artificial fires being sent up from among the leafless willows and the weeds that grew round Lyndley Waters.

"We will go down," said Lady Troyes. "Why did they not come to fetch me?"

"Because you have lingered behind and they expected you to lead the way," said Celia. "Come, let us go together. You must remember that you are the mistress here."

She very much desired to give this foreigner some advice, to tell her to curb her too free tongue, to conform to the decent usages of quiet English people, to pretend certain delicacies, even if she did not feel them. How shocking, for instance, for her to talk of her mercenary marriage!

Celia walked rapidly towards Lady Troyes, hastening her pace. She, too, was interested in the fireworks. Now and then a few rockets had been let off on Guy Fawkes Day when the deliverance of England from popery had been celebrated by a few squires who had sent the drink penny down to their workpeople dancing round the bonfire, and she had always thought the wasteful sight of an extreme loveliness; those flowers of fire appearing, as it seemed, from nowhere into the winter night, disappearing, as it seemed, into nowhere in the winter sky. . . . Yes, they had a poignant radiance, particularly in so far as they typified the brevity of all human joy.

"It is not for me," thought Celia, drawing her hood close round her face as they came out into the air, "to be thus moralising. I wish I felt more at ease in her company. She seems to me as one who is not here save in the body—but I must not dwell on those things either."

They were soon joined by a party of the other guests and servants with torches. The resin flared into the sky in long and untidy flames, but it was necessary to have sufficient light, for the blocks of masonry, the unfinished marbles, the workmen's scaffolding poles and tool-houses, were much in the way, and the sightseers had to take a roundabout route, to arrive at the banks of Lyndley Waters. There the flambeaux were quenched that they might not interfere with the display of the fireworks. These were in the charge of two of the Italian workmen who had come over to set the mosaics and the tessellated floors, and who were experts in this *feu d'artifice* diversion so frequently employed in their own country. Indeed, it was an art in which the Italians were rivalled only by the Hollanders.

They had chosen the flat ground behind the boathouse, and from there were casting their cascades of fire into the night. As the light from the rockets and catherine wheels spread in sparkling disarray into the darkness, it lit up the faces and figures of the spectators with a quick and passing glow; the men, smiling good-humouredly, as if they tolerated an amiable triviality, the women really enthralled, their faces rosy from the frost, their fingers, some bare and glittering with rings and pink from the cold, holding their thick hoods under their chins. A few children had been allowed to be present at this spectacle, and they, warmly enveloped in fur pelisses, stood gaping in front of their elders.

Celia and Grace Troyes found themselves, against the former's will, at the back of the boathouse, close to where the two eager foreigners were making a display of their skill. Celia's wish was to find James and to deliver, as it were, his wife to him, but Grace herself seemed to be under no such impulsion. She was watching the fireworks with avidity. . . . Avidity seemed the word to Celia for her look. It was the look of someone long starved who suddenly pounces upon nourishment.

Now, in the come and go of these unnatural lights, she appeared beautiful again. She wore no hood, but had tied round her head with a careless hand a scarf of scarlet gauze and green wool.

"Some of her clothes," thought Celia, "must have come from Spain with her mother, they are so old-fashioned and different from anything one ever sees in England."

"What is this place?" asked Grace as there was a pause in the display and darkness suddenly settled

144

down on them like something tangible. She touched the boathouse. Celia explained.

"It seems very modest compared to the other magnificence of Lyndley Waters," the new mistress of that property remarked.

Celia did not like this tone of contempt towards something that held for her memories that she would never lose, but it was natural enough Grace should speak like that.

"Oh, they will rebuild it," she replied, "as they rebuild everything else. At present there is nothing there but an old boat. Sir James will have a barge, as I suppose, with lanterns all along the sides. Who knows where his whims may lead him?—and there will be a handsome boathouse to accommodate this rich craft."

"Yes, if I had my way there would be," said Lady Troyes. "Why did he, who cares, as it seems so much for spendthrift ways, keep this ancient shed? I saw it when that last rocket went up . . . it even needs repair."

"Why should it be repaired?" demanded Celia, "since it is so soon to be destroyed?"

A new thought, a curious thought, however, had come into her mind with this remark. "Was there any significance in the fact that the boat and the boathouse that belonged to the past had been preserved to the last—nay, that, perhaps, were not to be destroyed at all?" She could not conceal the radiant joy this gave her; it was peculiar that a remark from Grace Troyes should have put it into her mind.

"Did you ever go in the boat and row upon the lake?" asked Grace out of the darkness thick with fumes.

"Yes, sometimes. We all did—childish sports, you know—to pluck the water-lilies, and sometimes to sail little vessels made of paper. We would make them chase one another as if they were Algerian pirates."

"I never had such games," replied Lady Troyes harshly. "All my childhood I lived enclosed. We had a small garden at the back of our house where there was a pear orchard, but the fruit never seemed to ripen. I walked to and fro there for exercise."

"But you went," said the other girl timidly, for she was both sorry and ashamed in an indefinable way, "sometimes with your father. . . ?"

"Yes, lonely rides mostly to visit graves—the graves of the martyrs. Yet we had our gay times too. Often the lark would sing overhead, and it is pleasant to lie upon the heather and see nothing around you but the valleys and glens. Sometimes there is no cloud at all, and one can view a most distant perspective—a distant perspective . . ." she repeated.

"Let us leave this place—we are too far from the others," urged Celia. "You, of course, will do as you please about the boathouse and the barge . . . you can have now all the diversion that you were denied in your youth. You have spoken very candidly to me, and I will tell you frankly also that I am sorry for you, for your dreary childhood, and that I hope now you will have everything you most desire."

"Perhaps I do more than hope—perhaps I intend it," replied the other, "to have everything I desire."

At this touch of harshness Celia was repelled. She took the other woman by a fold of her thick cloak and drew her firmly towards the circle of sightseers. Now a magnificent display was about to take place. The Italians had fastened their fireworks in position, applying the match to the fuse, and a fountain of flowers of golden fire, and stars of purple and azure flamed, soared into the darkness. Everything was lit up with the utmost clarity, as if the sun had suddenly appeared overhead. Each could see even the least detail of the dress and expression of his neighbour. There was even a certain movement of embarrassment, as there will be among people who in the dark have let themselves go off their guard and then suddenly are caught unawares by a beam of light.

Celia and Lady Troyes moved a little way along the circle behind the first row of sightseers, because Celia's natural courtesy would not allow her to disturb their pleasure by forcing to the front, and the other woman seemed indifferent; but at one point there was a little gap in the crowd, and into this the two women passed naturally.

Lyndley Waters ran in a small creek in front of them. Beyond that was the firework ground, the boathouse they had just left and the circle of Sir James's guests. All this was as clear and precise to them as if it had been on the stage and the unseen landscape and the dark mists of the sky but a drop cloth.

So, on to this stage, as if a principal actor entered, a stranger appeared, moving aside to right and left, though with civil gestures, the other people.

Celia noticed him with a pang of surprise and then realised her own folly. Why should there not be a stranger present?—some friend of James's, or even of his wife's, of whom she knew nothing. But this man had not been present at the entertainment in the pavilion . . . he wore a traveller's attire, and his clothes were of a fine, and even of an extravagant

147

make. So much Celia observed because she thought he might be a servant come with a message from the house; but no, this man stood more like the master of them all, looking upwards at the leaps of fire that mounted higher and higher among the stars, to burst into further drops and gleams of light, and then to disappear; he was young and, in Celia's eye, exceedingly comely.

He pulled off his hat, held it in front of him and seemed absorbed in the whirligig taking place above him, the fireworks disappearing in the sky; of the people about him he was oblivious, but not they of him. There was something in his sudden appearance, in his person, in his air that attracted attention even away from this prodigal amusement offered to Sir James's guests. Not only those who stood nearest to him, but all in the lit circle began to look at him, for he stepped beyond their bounds and approached close to the two Italians so that he was lit from head to foot with a vivid and unnatural light, a glow that picked out even the buttons on his coat, the stitching on his gloves.

Celia could not contain the exclamation, "Who is that just come here as if he were the master of the ceremonies?"

Grace Troyes did not reply. When Celia looked at her, wondering why she was silent, she, too, was speechless at the expression she saw upon the other woman's face that was so sharply picked from the shadows by the lurid light of the fireworks that blazed and crackled within a few feet of the stranger and sent into the dark air their leaping coils of flame.

Celia had never seen a strong passion unbared in a human face before, and she did not know what this was; but it was clear to her that the other woman had forgotten everything about her and was thinking only of the man who, in his careless travelling attire, appeared to be oblivious of everything save the showers of fire in their ice green and lurid scarlet that fell in flakes above him.

There was a sudden darkness, the crowd was eclipsed while preparations were made for the final display. Celia felt cut off from all her companions. It was like watching a spectacle over which the curtain had dropped suddenly and unexpectedly, leaving her in the theatre with all the lamps extinguished. She put out her hand and caught at the cloak of Grace Troyes.

"Did you see that man?" she whispered foolishly, and she felt that she was talking into a void. "A stranger, who behaved so oddly . . ." then her voice fell away.

She could hear the people murmuring, relaxing in the darkness. She could hear the movement, the sound of footsteps as someone came up behind and then passed again . . . the drag of dress and cloak on ground or bush. . . . All her senses seemed acute. The foreign tongue of the fireworkmakers sounded shrilly. There was a smell of gunpowder in the air, and she noticed a cool mist over the lake.

Grace Troyes did not reply, and Celia was sure that she had slipped from her in the darkness. Never had the girl experienced a loneliness like this. She was used to moving about even in the open fields without the light of as much as a star in the pleasant, thrice familiar homelands, and never had she known the sensation of being lost; but now she was lost, standing on the edge of Lyndley Waters, close to the boathouse where she and James Troyes had so often moored the boat after their quest for the water-lilies; lost in her body and in her soul, it seemed to her. She wanted to do something wild, extraordinary—to run, to cry, to call for help; but she stood rigid, true to her long training. All emotion must be immediately suppressed. Besides, what was any of this to do with her?

She wished she had not had that quick stab of foreboding and horror that had convulsed her when she had seen the stranger staring at the bonfire, and then seen the face of Grace Troyes. She thought of a verse that she often sang thoughtlessly, not understanding the meaning of it, to her harpsichord, in the course of an evening's amusement:

Hast thou marked the crocodile's weeping,
Or the fox's sleeping?
Or hast thou viewed the peacock in his pride,
Or the dove by his bride?
O so fickle, O so vain, O so false, so false is she!

The last display was ready. Mr. Swallow's voice gave the signal. The crowd stood back, making a deeper semicircle. The fuse was applied and again the thick, gold brilliancy leapt into the air and again the scene was visible to Celia.

She found that she had moved unconsciously and was now standing against the boathouse. The air was spangled with the fantastic devices of the firework-makers' ingenuity; there were circles and cascades falling, bells expanding, plumes . . . all were reflected through the mist into the water that showed ice green and unnatural. Flower cups of purple and azure appeard in the lake and had an evil look to Celia compared to those fresh, natural lilies that she had pulled from their twisted roots under the deep waters. Like plumage, like shells, like tresses of hair, like branches of coral, the fireworks filled the placid English sky. The crowd, her own neighbours, appeared strange, remote; behind, the faint smoke of the gunpowder mingled with the rising mist.

Grace Troyes was gone as Celia had supposed she would be gone. The stranger, too, had disappeared. Celia remembered that courage was supposed to be in her heritage, hitherto it had never been called upon. "I am not," she thought with self-contempt, "brave at all. Something has happened that frightens me and I cannot face it."

She moved away from the boat-shed, in and out of the crowd. The display was over; several hundreds of pounds of the foreign bride's money had gone in what was no more than half an hour's diversion and excitement. The musicians who had been playing in the distance, though no one had heard their melodies for the crackle and whiz of the fireworks, were already returning to the house. In their reaction after their absorbed attention, everyone began to feel cold and a little disappointed.

Celia spoke to many people whom she knew. They said with mechanical politeness "that the show had been magnificent—nothing like it had ever been seen in their quiet place before." The festival seemed to fade. Some of the parties called up their servants and asked for their coaches or horses; they desired to return to their homes immediately. There was nothing more, they felt, they could do to honour the bride. There was no more, they also felt, to be had in the way of satisfaction for their own curiosity.

"Brian!" cried Celia, snatching at a passer-by. She had never been so pleased to see him. He carried a lantern, and the homely light of it was pleasant after that artifical glare which had produced what now seemed to Celia an unwholesome exaltation of the spirits. The rays fell serenely into the night. "Nothing," thought Celia, "is so beautiful as a lantern," and she remembered many pleasant occasions on which it had been employed . . . walks by lantern light . . . visits to the stable by lantern light. . . .

"Are you lost?" he questioned, "and do you ask me to find you a way?"

"Yes, I think I am lost," replied Celia. "Lost on the banks of Lyndley Waters. The fireworks were not what I expected. . . ."

"You've seen them before?" he asked.

She was glad that he remained close to her. The other people were moving continually with would-be gay words as they passed her, but always moving away, leaving her standing on the trampled ground.

"Well, I suppose they are cloyed with their entertainment," said Brian. "It has hardly been what anyone expected, yet no one could say where the disillusion lay, I suppose."

"Sir, you are more subtle than I thought," she replied. "Something has happened . . . what is it? Who was the stranger?"

He did not answer and she felt that she had said too much. Why should not a stranger have appeared on such a night as this?

She asked again, "Where is James?" and took the man's arm, still gazing for comfort at the rays from the lantern he carried.

"I brought this," he answered obliquely, "for the flambeaux give out so many sparks."

"I, too, prefer a lantern."

"You're shivering. Let us go into the house—or shall I find your father, and would you like to return to Plaisent at once?"

"No." She was sure now of this. "I want to find James."

"I think," said Brian, "you had best leave James alone."

Now she was all anxiety. All her doubts and fears culminated in a trembling whisper.

"Tell me, Brian, what has happened? That man . . . who should he be?"

"Perhaps some poor dissolute wretch who, wandering by to take his bed at the inn, saw the glare and sparkle in the sky and came here out of curiosity."

"I want to know," insisted Celia. "I'll go back to the house."

"One of your presentiments, as I suppose?" asked Brian.

"No." She was not to be delayed in her intention by anything he might say. She knew his light mocks. "I have never pretended to any presentiments—but I saw something to-night. . . ."

He did not ask her what this was, nor did she tell him that it had been the face of Grace Troyes. He helped her to return to the house. It was cold, and she was glad to muffle herself to the chin. With one hand he held the lantern, with the other he guided her past the alabaster shafts, the stone and marble nymphs and fauns that were lying waiting to be placed on their pedestals and which, blind and cold, appeared for a moment and then were gone as the rays of the homely lantern struck them.

They did not see the mansion until they reached it, when it seemed to rise up suddenly out of this darkness that only the lantern rays lit about their feet in a course of widening light.

"They've shuttered the windows," whispered Celia, "and perhaps everything is over and we should indeed go home."

"I think you want to see James," he replied, and they passed up the shallow steps to the terrace where the great carved vases stood awkwardly in a group waiting to be placed along the balustrade.

The door was open and gave at a touch. The hall was lit as before; the candles had been replaced and carefully tended, fresh logs placed on the fire. A few guests still remained. They walked about, looking at this curiosity and that, whispering among themselves. Celia knew what they were discussing.

Where were the three people in whom she was interested?

"We should," she said to Brian, "say goodbye to our host and hostess. Surely we cannot leave James—and Grace"—she forced the word over her tongue—"without our farewells and our good wishes?"

Brian seemed to understand. She could not quite interpret his look; it seemed disdain, perhaps amusement. His face was flayed by the cold. So was hers, she supposed—but what matter for that? Her fingers seemed stiff and useless. She looked about and the room seemed detestable.

"I wish," she muttered, "James had not altered Lyndley Waters."

"Leave James," replied her companion, "to face the destiny he has arranged for himself—but if you wish to see him, well, why not?" and he took the girl's elbow and passed along the rooms—she walking quickly beside him, for his step was so much longer than hers—that had been laid open and adorned for the reception of the wedding guests. In the Brocatelle room were Grace and James.

Celia felt guilty at seeing them. Why? She must wait till she returned home to sort out and interpret her startling thoughts that now were tumbled in her mind like a pack of cards flung down in confusion.

Grace stood by the hearth on which the fire had fallen into embers that glowed among the ashes that were lightly sprayed over the wide marble. Standing beside her husband she said farewell to her guests and thanked them in conventional tones for honouring her homecoming. The passion on her face, that Celia had marked with horror when she had looked at her by the boathouse, had gone; but those smooth features now held no expression at all, and Celia thought that this, perhaps, was as ominous as had been that look of the sleeping furies suddenly aroused . . . at last she had in her mind, put it into words—"The sleeping furies suddenly aroused."

Grace had placed her ermine cape over her handsome gown, the sheen of which was bright in that warm and steady light. She held on her breast a cluster of feathered flowers—an outlandish toy that Celia had not seen before, tinselled and gaudy and something like those adornments that she had read in travellers' books are placed in the bosom of the images of saints in Papist countries.

Now she looked at James who was speaking to

his guests with his usual ease. Perhaps only Celia could detect the flatness in his tones. The man was changed; he was enduring something—perhaps pain, perhaps rage. It was not her place to comfort him. She had seen him. She must be content with that. Grace's glance had singled her out from the people who, half awkwardly, half with an air of curiostiy, were finding their way to the Brocatelle room, admiring the brocade on the walls that was so finely stretched and of so unusual a pattern and that glittered so entertainingly with sparks and threads of gold.

"Will you come and see me again?" asked Grace Troyes.

"Of course—we are neighbours, are we not?"

Celia had nothing but her inbred traditions, her smooth conventionalities to oppose to the eccentricities, as she must term them, of the other. It was not in her own experience to read the faces either of James or of Grace, but surely in the woman was elation, if not rapture; in the man, a leaden greyness that spoke of some bitterness hardly concealed. Celia's modest native integrity, of which she was unconscious, that was very old and English, of the soil, could do no more with the situation. She glanced up at Brian Ormerod, hoping there might be some clue in his look; but there was nothing. He seemed still slightly contemptuous, slightly diverted, like a man who has many comments to make but decides to leave them all unuttered.

"I will take you home, Celia. We can walk, if you please, across the fields. It is not far, the ground is firm after the frost and with the lantern we shall do very well."

156

"You are taking Celia away?" asked James suddenly, turning from the neighbour to whom he had been speaking.

"Yes, everyone is leaving, are they not?"

"The night is still early," said Grace Troyes with a note of mockery.

"Yes ... but the fireworks ... people became exhausted with the cold, with excitement. You must be indulgent to them."

Celia found herself apologising, excusing somehow the failure, the tragedy, perhaps, of the evening. Why should she, who was the most vulnerable of them all, receive these wounds in silence? The quality that had kept her silent—her honesty, her single-mindedness—not urged her to speak, and she did so naturally.

"James, who was that stranger who appeared just before the last display? I suppose he was someone who had come up from the Troyes Arms. Nobody knew him ..."

"And his sudden apparition," put in Brian Ormerod, "was quite startling, as if your magicians— as I suppose we must pretend your Italians are such with their tricks with gunpowder—had suddenly produced a phantom."

James turned squarely. "It was no apparition," he replied in a voice that was without feeling, "but my wife's chaplain newly arrived from Scotland—Mr. Nicholas Jerdan—who chanced to make his appearance in so odd a manner."

"Why was it odd?" smiled Grace Troyes. "He did not know when the festival would be, and of course he was attracted by all that glare in the sky—by the fireworks too; we have not such amusements in Scotland."

157

She did not appear to wish to elude the situation, and Celia marked on her face a flush of indomitable passion.

"Your chaplain?" said Brian. "The neighbourhood will be surprised. No one here—and some of us have travelled a little—imagined a Scottish pastor of that appearance."

"No?" Grace Troyes seemed quite willing to discuss the matter. "You thought perhaps that he would be very old, since he was my tutor? I told you he was a good grammarian."

This comment was absolutely without meaning to Celia. If Brian understood he gave no sign, his glance towards James was, Celia thought, indulgent; yet he held himself remote from all of them.

"Come, Celia. . . . Good-night, James; good-night, Madam Grace . . . " and he had taken her away through the rooms she wished never to see again, across the parterres, the rose garden.

She closed her eyes that she might not see that the lantern revealed nothing but bare stems and thorns and tried to fill the darkness with the huge August roses loosening to their fall in crimson, coral and saffron petals.

"I suppose," she said, "it is no use asking you, Brian, what all this means?"

"All what?" he replied. "Nothing has happened, you know. The new wife has brought her new chaplain—we understood this was to be so, did we not?"

"You're putting me off," said Celia.

"Perhaps it is as well," he replied. "And after all, I know nothing. Leave them to themselves."

They passed the field where a light frost like dew

was revealed by the lantern rays. They saw before them, after quite a little while, the great barn, and then the steep roof and twisted chimneys of Plaisent Manor House.

"It was never intended that you and I should come home together like this," said Celia. "How often you have asked me to walk with you—for a reward, and now I fancy you are doing it—as a penance."

"We walk together because we must. I will not tell you any of my thoughts—I can, if need be, out-silence you."

"I wish I had spoken to him," said Celia. "I wish I had made one quick plea . . ."

"For what?" asked Brian.

"For tolerance . . . for kindness, as I suppose. What will happen when they are alone together?"

"I don't suppose they will be alone together—the new chaplain will make a third to-night."

* * * *

The guests had all gone. The servants had taken away the silver, the soiled cambric and linen napkins, the crystal glasses in which still clung dregs of wine and hardened sugar; everywhere, save in the apartments of the mistress of Lyndley Waters, lamps and candles had been extinguished. The bolts had been put up for the night and the watch-dogs set. The guards, too, had been sent on their duties; there were many valuables necessarily lying about unprotected during the re-building of the house, and every night men patrolled the property.

In the Brocatelle room Grace Troyes sat pulling to pieces, but with no air of agitation, the feathered flowers that Celia had thought so gaudy. She had taken them from her bosom and spread them on her lap. Her ermine cape had slipped to the floor, her long hair hung in small spirals down her shoulders, having been disarrayed from its careful dressing.

Sir James walked up and down with his hands clasped behind the skirts of his full cloak. He wore what was, in a manner, his marriage dress, though these were not the garments that he had donned in Edinburgh—cinnamon velvet, laced with gold and silver, festooned and brocaded with all a London tailor's art. Sir James owed a great deal to his tailor and his hairdresser, but they also owed a great deal to him, for he was a man who set off to the greatest advantage anything that was handsome and fashionable. His face sagged; disappointment, inarticulate passions, gave him a plight of fatigue, almost of exhaustion.

"It would be far better for both of us," he remarked, choosing his words more carefully than ever he had done in his life before, for it was his way to fling them about gaily, as he had flung about his money and his likings, "it were far better for both of us if you were to tell me what your meaning and intention are."

"I have told you," she replied, still tearing to bits the dyed and spangled feathers and speaking without the least emotion, "my meaning. I mean to remain here as your wife, as the mistress of Lyndley Waters. I like pretty well what you have already accomplished in the mansion—I like, I think, the prospect before me. My intention—in what way is that different to my meaning?"

Sir James paused close to her chair.

"Madam, it is one of the hardest things a man

may be asked to do—to come at some clear and honest decision with a woman like you who will trip him up and deceive him . . ."

"I have not deceived you," she replied. "It was understood, it was agreed that I should have my chaplain and my allowance, and I never told you that Nicholas Jerdan was a venerable pastor. What difference should it make to you?"

"He is the man," said James, "whom I saw by the River Almond. I did not like him then, nor the discourse I had with him. He was in secular attire and, I am convinced, following me, yet at the time he was supposed to be abroad—in Geneva so I was afterwards informed. There is deception enough here for me to take umbrage at."

"He returned unexpectedly," said Grace. "He was able to find a ship much sooner than he expected. I myself did not know he was in Edinburgh. Many of our clergy go in wordly attire when it suits them. Are you answered?"

"Answered, but not satisfied. I do not like this man nor intend to have him as a member of my household."

"What have you against him beyond his youth?— and perhaps he has more years than you suppose. His age, I think," she said precisely, "must be thirty-three years."

"I have been misled by my own stupidity," admitted her husband, keeping himself in control but speaking heavily and sombrely. "It never occurred to me that you, living as you were living, with those old women; professing as you did profess the most austere Calvinism, having such a father as Mr. Morrisson of Drumquassel, should also be under the tutelage of a man like Nicholas Jerdan. How was it that this was permitted?"

"That is quite easy to answer." Grace had the delicate, assured air of one who can defeat an opponent by taking the matter superficially. "His father was my tutor, his grandfather had been my father's tutor. The Jerdans and the Morrissons were closely connected."

"I suppose," Sir James, against his own better sense, interrupted, "that it was the grave of a Jerdan into which you thrust my sapphire?"

"Yes—martyrs were among them. What can any of that matter to you? It belongs to me and my story. I told you that this young man was a good grammarian. . . ."

"By which I suppose—an outlandish term to me—" interrupted her husband impatiently, "you mean a good scholar? Yet he does not appear to me like a fellow absorbed in books and abstruse studies."

"You will find that he is," she answered. "He presented himself to you, as I think, courteously. He has his full credentials. You have nothing whatever against him beyond the fact that you saw him once outside Edinburgh and did not like him, and that he is younger than you supposed my chaplain would be. You dare not say," she challenged, "what is in your mind."

This was true. Sir James was too well trained to try to ignore that ugly fact. It was too early for him to venture to come out with what, she put it, was in his mind as to Nicholas Jerdan. If he did so, the unforgettable and the unforgivable would probably pass between them; and he was not a man of direct action nor, indeed, a man who cared greatly for any action at all.

He was tired, too, and had been distracted by the preparations for the feast; by the continual comings and goings of Swallow and the architects and the artificers, and then this bonfire and Grace's chaplain. . . . He knew, his instinct was sure there—that Nicholas Jerdan was more than her chaplain. He was—well, put it like that—her accomplice. But in what? It was true he dared not say. Besides, at the back of his mind was always this caution, her money. "Everything rests on her money. If I let her slide from me I shall lose it all."

Walking up and down he considered the future. It was worse than useless, it was exasperating to try to obtain anything from the woman. She made him feel like a lone soldier who endeavours to force his way through a maze of unknown devices set before him by the enemy. She would go on quibbling and exchanging words and defying him and putting him in the wrong the whole night through. He must think for himself and by himself as to his course of action.

Well, he had got the money in his grip now at last. He must enclose and enclose . . . there were many acres of common land near. It would be easy, with the influence he had, to get permission to add them to his estates. He must sell and re-sell, buy and sell again. His attorneys were good business men. He recalled some excellent advice that they had given him in the past that he had never regarded. Now he would listen to all they had to say. He would lend his name and his signature to their devices to force up rents, to enclose. He would try his hand at making money in the City—it could be done; not by men like himself, but by men like those who advised him.

And what was to be the end of all these nice calculations? Freedom perhaps from Grace and the man whom she had brought to Lyndley Waters.

His apparent acquiescence, his silence would, he assured himself, best defeat whatever her malicious arts might be, so he brought himself to that point of resolution when he could pause in his pacing, turn and lightly kiss her hand, telling her, as any fond husband might have done on such an occasion, that no doubt she was much fatigued, that she had been a superb hostess, neglecting none, offending none, but flattering of many; that she had graced his new and sumptuous mansion as he had hardly ever hoped it would be graced, and that now she must go to her rest with her maid and whatever company she might desire among his female servants.

He saw that she was a little outwitted by this formal speech. She looked sullen. Her mouth as well as her eyes was downcast. He left her, turning at the door to look back. She made an excellent jewel for the Brocatelle room. She was like the Genoese brocade on the wall—foreign, magnificent and in a way not only useless but mischievous in as far as she eclipsed good native qualities. Yes, as the brocade eclipsed the old panelling of English wood, so Grace Troyes had eclipsed—well, women like Celia Plaisent.

* * * *

Sir James did not go immediately to his own chambers. To-night he did not wish even the self-confidence that he obtained from the faithful glances of Thomas Pratt. He was alert; the situation was, after all, more or less in his hands and must, however hateful such a course was to his easy disposition, be boldly confronted. So he took his way

164

alone, for the servants were all abed and Mr. Swallow had gone to his own house the other side of the grounds, to the apartments next to the chapel that he had so casually assigned to the use of the chaplain. There was a light showing through the half-open door, and Sir James entered without knock or scratch.

This was an unconscious assertion of his superiority. Yes, he was superior to the other man in everything, in rank, in breeding, in wealth—Grace's money was his now—and, as he hoped, in intelligence and courage.

As he passed the first room, which was empty, he despised himself for his former dismay. What was there indeed to be alarmed about? He could deal quite satisfactorily with this starveling fellow. In the second room the new chaplain was seated unstrapping a valise that he had on the table before him and taking from it bundles of papers, neatly tied together with silk threads and sealed. He wore his travelling attire save for the cloak that hung over the back of his chair, and the mud on his boots was barely dry. A fire had been kindled on the hearth, but it had flared out with the burning of the first sticks, and the air was cold.

So far the room showed no trace of its new occupant. Everything was as Sir James and Mr. Swallow had arranged it, hastily furnished with odd pieces from the other chambers, with the air of belonging to no one, yet of being both costly and ostentatious.

"I thought," said Sir James directly, "I should see you immediately, sir. I want to know why you played that trick on me?—you remember, when we met on

165

the road by Cramond Brig."

"What trick?" replied the other, at once rising to his feet with no great gesture of respect. "Why was I bound to reveal myself to you then, Sir James? I had returned to Edinburgh unexpectedly, I knew nothing of your plans, nor of those of the lady who is now your wife."

"Maybe not," replied the Englishman, "but I should now like to know something of yours."

"Plans? Why should I have anything so ambitious?" The Scot's smile was thin. "I expect Lady Troyes has told you that my family and hers have long been connected, and I was once an intimate of her father's castle. Indeed, he partially paid for my education, which was beyond what my own parents could afford. A series of accidents left me an orphan before I was able to earn my livelihood, which was ordained to be as a pastor in Scotland; it can be of little interest to you, but in my own country the kirk has a deep meaning. . . ."

"I think you try to put me off," replied the master of Lyndley Waters. "You are not the man whom I expected to see, whom I agreed to take. I supposed that some precise and venerable pedant would be installed here with his theological books and his straw-splitting, and that my wife, who is herself something of a fanatic, would, until she wearied of them, enjoy his ministrations and discussions. For me to maintain at my expense and tolerate in my household a man like yourself must be, as you know, impossible. . . ."

"I should not use that word, sir," replied Nicholas Jerdan. "You have made a contract, I think, with Lady Troyes in which she is allowed her own income, her own chaplain; and there is no specification as to who that chaplain shall be. Moreover, by word of mouth you agreed that Nicholas Jerdan who tutored her in Edinburgh should come to Lyndley Waters . . ."

"I see you have got it all very pat, Mr. Jerdan, and that gives it more and more to me the air of a plot or a conspiracy."

"I think you give yourself," replied the Scot, "far too much importance, Sir James. Do not think that that is an impertinence—but why should you suppose yourself the victim of any plot or conspiracy? And in what way could I disturb your pursuits? My stipend is not princely, my tastes are quiet. I am, though not venerable, a scholar. These are some of my own notes that I am now unpacking; you may find in St. Andrews University the records of my attainments. I have been abroad and seen something of other men, only to find them the same as the men at home—that perhaps was a discovery worth making. It is very late, sir, and I have travelled far and without the luxury that accompanies your journeyings. In brief, I am fatigued and you have had a day of festival. Shall we not take up to-morrow what we might have to say to one another?"

"I have no more to say," scowled Sir James. "I know that some trick has been put upon me. I should like you, for I am a blunt-speaking man, to know that I recognise this deceit. What it precisely is I must not think . . . I shall consider my course of action. I advise you for your own good—and the phrase is flat, sir, and worn with much use, and yet I mean it, every word of it—I advise you for your own good to leave Lyndley Waters. Whatever you may consider your due for my wife's education shall be paid you. You are no doubt a man of some abilities. Employ them, I warn you, elsewhere."

"You speak," replied Mr. Jerdan, "exactly as I had supposed you would speak. I do not compose a reply, believing it useless to argue."

"Yes," agreed Sir James in deep exasperation, "useless to argue, useless to toss words to and fro. . . ." He had found that with his wife. "Yet if we do not use words, what are we to use?" and in his mind he concluded his own sentence, "Other weapons, perhaps?"

"I am here," said Mr. Jerdan, and his air was fatigued, as if he took but a remote interest in the conversation, "as your wife's chaplain, as one who was her tutor."

Again Sir James had the control and courage to end an interview where he could make no headway. He did not regret that he had sought out Nicholas Jerdan. He had at least, in the way of his race, told him his mind, his intentions. Now he gave him a curt good-night.

"I will light you down the stairs," said Mr. Jerdan, and came with the new silver lamp, that an indifferent servant's hand had placed in his apartment, to the door.

The baronet went down without looking back. He could picture only too well, with his fancy's eye, that dark face, that tall, graceful figure standing there glancing at him in careless mockery.

"The man who taught my wife." The words revolved, like the catherine wheels he had lately seen by the lake, in his mind. "And *who* taught her *what?* After all, I know nothing about her. Yes, what did he teach her in that lonely house with the orchard of pears at the back that never ripened. Well, I, too, shall know when and how to strike."

III
VARIATIONS

"On her finger a gay gold ring;
The bridegroom holds up his head like a king!

"Marjorie has married a gentleman,
Who knows when the wedding began?"

CELIA PLAISENT found the sweetness of the evening marred by a melancholy that was foreign to her disposition, but that had not been for some time foreign to her fortunes. The life she led had lost nothing of its former pleasant routine. The jolly, open-headed existence of the daughter of a well-to-do squire belonging to a family where all were occupied in work they understood, were all healthy and amiable, had in nothing changed.

"It is I who have changed," Celia admitted.

She stood by the stile where the first sharp green of spring showed in the hawthorn bushes and the cold white blossoms of the blackthorn that seem to have so little to do with summer were already drifting through dark, thorny stems.

What was happening at Lyndley Waters was unkown to Celia. She had been there once or twice as a guest and seen nothing save what seemd to her like some remarkable pictures; Grace Troyes with a handful of vivid sewing silks on her lap yet idle; Grace Troyes teasing a green and scarlet parrot in an ebony ring lately šent from the West Indian docks . . . Grace in the stove-house admiring the velvet cups and fleshy, trailing branches of some newly-imported creeper . . . Grace always idle yet, as Celia knew, always alert.

She had made no pretence of becoming friendly either with Celia or any other of her neighbours. She allowed formality to become her defence and to hedge her about from a prying into her affairs, though it could not from curiosity. She must be observed when she rode abroad, or took her coach to Winchester to make purchases, or even when she walked in her own grounds. There were too many servants at Lyndley Waters—the architects, the artists, the artisans, the workmen employed there—for her to have much privacy; but by insisting on her aloof, lazy disdain of them all, she had attained what Celia believed was her dearest wish—a spiritual solitude.

Neither had Celia often seen Sir James Troyes. He, too, had been employed, when she had had a glance at him, riding about his estate with Mr. Swallow and the architect, a roll of papers or a portfolio under his arm, or in his pocket, his comely face flayed by the weather and intent on his work.

It was, therefore, with a surprise that somehow was not agreeable, that she saw him approaching now on foot, careless through the mud. The frosts had ceased, at least for a while. The hedges dripped with moisture and the small flinty stones of the Wiltshire soil showed through the damp earth. Celia hoped that this man, of all men in the world the most important to her, would pass her with no more than a salutation; but instead he paused and looked at her keenly.

The girl did not try to evade the occasion. She gathered her forces for some unkown trial of strength, perhaps for some unknown peril.

"Why do you come so seldom to Lyndley

Waters?" he asked her bluntly.

And she, with equal candour, replied, "You know, James, we two should not be enclosed in a cloud of words . . ."

"Words," said the young man heavily, "words—how they trip one up and confuse—and yet dare one trust to a glance or a gesture?"

"One often is obliged to do so. I have waited on Grace several times."

"Did you think her contented?" he asked.

"I could not tell you," replied Celia. "She is in every way different—remote. I think she has a longing for the foreign and the unattainable."

"Different I think she is—different from most honest folk. . . ."

Celia did not like the use of the word "*honest,*" which jarred.

"Because we do not understand her, I suppose we should not judge her," she replied. "But you will force me into a homily and, James, we should not talk about Grace. . . ."

But the young man demanded solemnly of what use were these ancient rules and courtesies when dealing with such a woman as the one that he had married?

"Sometimes she bemuses me into crediting the follies of her native land, where they think that children are changed at birth. I, looking at her now and then unexpectedly, you know, in the half-light—well, I have seen her dancing by herself before the tall mirror that she has had placed in the Brocatelle room . . ."

"You must not speak so," interrupted Celia. "Changelings—there are no such things. These are

171

fairy tales. . . ."

They were silent. She knew that he wanted to talk of Nicholas Jerdan, the chaplain of Lady Troyes who led a secluded life and was only seen occasionally, walking with decorum across the misty fields or along the rutted highways, usually with a book under his arm and his hat pulled over his brows. Such civility as the neighbours and Mr. Boate, and the other resident clergyman, had offered him he had received in an unfriendly manner and put aside.

"You know," cried Sir James suddenly, "that I detest that man she has forced upon me!"

"I suppose you would, but understand that, above all things, I must not make mischief. I must not talk of you or Grace, or this Mr. Jerdan, of whom, after all . . ." she put in the quick plea that had been forming in her soul since the night of the bonfire, "after all, James, we know nothing against either of them. All is surmise and conjecture, and the dislike we have to what is alien to us."

He thanked her dryly for this, said no doubt she considered it as consolation, and he hoped she would leave the matter at that, as she nervously put inside her hood a long curl of her damp brown hair.

"Life goes the same with you, Celia, I suppose?"

"Outwardly," she replied, "but the coming of Grace Troyes to Lyndley Waters has made a great difference to me, and you know it."

"Young Ormerod," he asked, "are you going to marry him?"

"I do not think so," said Celia. "And now you speak of him, I'll tell you that he, too, has a concern in your affairs that somewhat surprises me. He comes frequently to Plaisent Manor, and as he has not asked me for silence, and as he speaks to so many people and I suppose he may repeat it—he talks a great deal of Mr. Jerdan."

"And of my wife too, I suppose?" said James sullenly. "Do you think I am not aware that she is freely canvassed in the neighbourhood? But why, of all men, should young Ormerod be concerned?"

Celia believed she knew. Ormerod could not take his mind off James and James's wife because he could not take his mind off Celia, and because James stood between him and Celia; but this intricate and subtle pattern of likes and dislikes, of revenues and desires, she was by no means prepared to expound to the disturbed and angry young man who stood before her now.

"Are you not at least successful in what you set out to attain?" she asked timidly. "Lyndley Waters becomes a handsome house, everyone admits that—your plans go forward without a hitch. The last time I was there I saw the great advancement that had been made ... the fine ironwork, James, and the statues now set on their pedestals, and those walks already beginning to bud. ... Are you not pleased with seeing your dreams, that were so many scratches on paper, come on to reality?"

He did not reply, and she spoke again quickly of nothing to prevent either of them saying, "What is it all for? What does it mean? Why has this house been built?"

"The man Jerdan must go," he said, ignoring her trivial talk.

"Has he offended you?" asked Celia.

"In no way, he is too careful. His discretion matches his boldness. He knows to a hair's point how far servility will cover insolence. And as for Grace . . ." he added, with a directness that approached coarseness, "I have her watched."

Celia was shocked. Had it come to that? She had not supposed so.

"I should not listen—and I do not mean that as affectation, James. With every word you say you involve me more deeply . . ."

"In my sad affairs?" he finished. "Did you know what happened in Edinburgh, you would understand my uneasiness and my concern. I have been deceived for many months now; since my marriage I have been trying to find out how, but everyone is in a conspiracy to baffle me—her father, the Scotch lawyers, the woman herself and this man. He and she . . ."

"I should not speak of them together," protested Celia firmly. "After all, humanly speaking, it is natural enough that she, living as she has lived, bred as she was bred, should have conceived an admiration for this man, the son of her ancient tutor, Recall that all her mind was bent towards these stories of the persecuted Covenanters. Why not take her to London, James? She will not need a chaplain there. You told me before that she wished to go abroad."

"That was part of the deception," replied the young man. "When she asked me that she believed this fellow to be at Geneva."

Celia had no answer.

"I must go home," she said. "It is getting dark."

"You were never one who feared for the falling of the shadows," he replied. "Walk with me a little way towards Lyndley Waters."

She obeyed, lifting her thick skirt from her thick pattens and walking beside him through the mud that splashed their garments and delayed their steps. When they came to the rise of the road where a tall holly tree was showing the blackish green of winter and the small pale green of spring in the prickly foliage, they saw before them the undulating countryside and, conspicuous in the shadows, the classic facade of Lyndley Waters. It was possible to discern the pavilions, the terraces and the fall of sixty feet of water, of which Sir James had been so proud, glittering faintly now in the rays of the setting sun that for a moment or so parted the luminous clouds.

"It is a splendid place," declared Celia, trying to force enthusiasm into her tone.

It seemed to her as if he said, "It would have been had you been mistress of it," but she knew that he was silent.

A certain scorn for the man and his stupidity, for herself and her fidelity, hardened her. What had he to blame but his own follies, and she but her own weakness? He had married a woman out of hand for her money, knowing little about her as she, out of hand, had given her heart to him, knowing too much about him.

As they neared the great gates where the stone piers had been but recently set in place, crowned with the ostentatious heraldic beasts that held the shields bearing the arms of the Troyes family, they paused and gazed down one of the ancient avenues that had been cleverly contrived to fit into the new landscape at Lyndley Waters lying pallid in the light that was so rapidly fading.

Celia looked across the lake to the boathouse the

other side where she had stood the night of the bonfire. It was impossible for her not to recall the expression she had surprised on the face of Grace Troyes when the glare of the rockets had revealed the stranger standing by the artificers.

"There are two people on the water in the old boat that you and I used to row in," said Sir James.

"Nothing can be more commonplace," replied Celia.

She felt moved, against her own feelings, to accompany him to the border of the lake, In her own words, in which she did not believe herself, "Nothing could be more commonplace" than that she, a kindly neighbour, should walk with him over his grounds. Yet at the same time she was doing what she had just now said she would not do—becoming involved in his sombre fortunes, aye, sombre she felt they must be while they were connected with Grace and Nicholas Jerdan.

In her ignorance and her sympathy, she nervously turned over what he might have been doing during the few months of his married life—spying, making enquiries, trying to put two and two together, he, the alert, the good-natured, easy gentleman, for the first time in his life, with the sense of having been deceived, perhaps trapped, and yet unable to put his finger on anything definite, to find any obvious fault to startle anyone into a confession.

The boat was rowing towards the shore. It contained the two people who had been in the thoughts of Sir James and Celia since they had met—"and long before that, and long before that," thought the girl.

"It is Grace," said Sir James. He paused by the

trailing willows. "And the chaplain."

Celia noted with unnatural precision the silver-yellow catkins on the stunted trees.

"Why do you neglect this part of the grounds?" she asked in a high voice. "The boathouse should be rebuilt handsomely in a baroque style, and you should have a barge to sail upon the water instead of that old boat."

"It would seem unsuitable," he answered, and Celia did not say, "No more unsuitable than your Italian palace in its English landscape."

The boat, rowed by the man in his dark habit with slow strokes of the oars, came to the shore. The rope was thrown round the capstan and Nicholas Jerdan handed Grace Troyes ashore. Her manner was, as usual, passive and yet lively, as if she wore a mask, but a transparent one. She affected no interest in the two standing on the bank, nor did even her glance follow Nicholas Jerdan, who was fastening the boat in the boathouse.

Celia noted that the timbered roof had further rotted with the snows of winter and that the weeds in their dead entanglement had fallen in ugly clusters round the bank that was much trampled, as if the boat was often used.

"It will be pleasanter for you, Grace, when the water-lilies are in bloom," she said.

Lady Troyes did not answer. She wore a cloak of a bright green colour. He dress was unsuitable both for the occasion and for her station. She had, though Celia would not have admitted as much, something of the air of a mountebank, like those ladies of the Italian comedy that the English girl had once seen when visiting London. There was a stiff feather in her small velvet cap and tinsel jewels in her ears. There was beauty in her attire and in her poise and even in the way her long hand needlessly held the clasped hood, worn over the cap, under her chin; but it was a fantastic and alien beauty.

"You know," said Sir James, speaking to his wife as if no one else had been present, "that I am for London tomorrow?"

"I think you told me," she agreed. "What does it matter? I see so little of you here that it will concern me the less whether you are present or not."

"You see very little of me," replied he with an elaborate servility, "becuase I am engaged in the building of this house."

His terms, simple and yet odd, struck painfully on Celia's ear. "The building of this house . . ."

"What foreign niceties may I bring you, Grace?" he asked. "You have your parrot, your boxes of lacquer . . ."

"Oh, I have a long list yet," she interrupted. "If I may not go to town myself, at least I may have some of the pleasures of the town brought to me. But I cannot stand here in the damp considering of it. . . . Good-night, madam."

The indifference of her words were to Celia something worse than a mock. Grace turned away towards the rose garden where the English girl had once been so unthinkingly happy, and so towards the white facade of the house that was glimmering fainter and fainter into the darkness. For a second, like many warning beacons suddenly lit up, the last ray of the sun picked out a reddish light in each of the many windows; then sank and all was dark.

"I shall have to go home without a guide or a

lantern after all," said Celia, "but I know the fields and the way so well, as you said, James."

He did not reply to her. She felt he was in need of her help and her comfort, though he deserved neither, and it was both wrong and dangerous for her to offer them. Yet she was troubled, too, by a sense that this was a moment when all such considerations should be forgotten. As he had complained, words were useless. Her sex, her experience and her timidity were against her; James looked formidable—so much older, so much more important than she was that she became almost afraid of him and his troubles. She shrank from hearing what he might wish to tell her. The nobility of her nature could not arm her against her natural fastidiousness.

She turned away in her thick country clothes that so disguised the delicacy of her youth, and he, she noted swiftly, did not follow. So he, too, was afraid at the moment of what might be said perhaps or what might be done. . . . .

When she reached the stone piers again, Brian Ormerod was waiting for her. She had become used to him so timing his rides and walks that they crossed hers, and this did not trouble her as it once had troubled her. She no longer promised him her companionship as a reward, she no longer indeed concerned herself much about the young man.

"I saw you go in there with James Troyes," he remarked, and there was a steadfastness about his demeanour and a candour about the avowal of his feelings that prevented her from ever finding his interest in her affairs either impertinent or galling. In the state of suspended emotion that she held towards him, she was grateful for his friendship as she might have been grateful for the friendship of a dog.

"James is going up to town," she said, "leaving those two foreigners." She had said more than she intended.

"Those two?" he replied. "The lady and her chaplain?"

"Oh, Brian," she asked, "what do you think it all means?"

"I do not know."

"I would give a good deal to find out, but it is no concern of yours or mine," she reminded him, and she felt that her own words sounded foolish.

"Call it, then, curiosity."

"You do not even like James."

They were walking together down the road, not needing to scan their way, so familiar was it to both of them.

"Like him, no—but there are some situations that interest me, and *you* like him, Celia."

"And would you, because of that, help him should he come to some terrible pass?"

Brian laughed, and she could not read the meaning of that. She was quite unaware as to whether his devotion to her would mean that he would do any service in his power for James Troyes, or whether he concealed a spiteful jealousy that would rejoice in the downfall of his rival.

He would not enter the gates of Plaisent Manor with her; he had to go home and see to his accounts, he said, and he reminded her, as he left her, of something that seemed to the girl alien to all their talk, to their mood.

"James," said he, ""is enclosing and enclosing. He seems to have the land hunger—he is taking the heath, the common land; I hear he is going to build a row of almshouses and to give, every Christmas, blue blankets to the poor. Will these sops suffice? He goes to town to see those friends of his who have influence at court."

"Do not condemn him," pleaded Celia quickly. "He is not a happy man."

Again Brian laughed, as if at something childish.

As he left her and she turned with relief, almost with gladness, towards her cherished home, she thought not of Brian but of James Troyes, of his wife and of Nicholas Jerdan. She wondered if they would all meet when they were together in the large, sumptuous mansion that was still incomplete or whether Grace would sit alone in the Brocatelle room playing with the parrot, the chaplain retreating to the chambers above the chapel where, as he gave out, he was engaged on a learned treatise on some quibbling, straw-splitting point of theology; and James, he would be with Mr. Swallow perhaps, or the architects, checking the accounts, writing in his fine hand marginal notes as to this or that, or examining a new carved wreath to be set above the mantelpiece in the guest-room. Or perhaps they would all be together— and talking of what?

* * * *

Grace Troyes had sent back to London the maid she had engaged when passing through the capital after her marriage. The girl was, her mistress declared, idle and pilfering; she had gone sullenly and with tears. The same end had awaited other women who had tried to take the place of chambermaid to Lady Troyes. The upshot of it was that she desired to be alone; but she knew, although her device so far had been successful and she had at last nothing but the services of the maids who worked under Mrs. Bateman, that she was spied upon at every turn.

On the morning of one day that her husband, with a handsome equipage, went to London, she sat with her hands in her lap in her usual attitude of leisure, considering how she might evade those whom she regarded as her jailers. She was used to such a situation. In the house with the pear orchard she had had to intrigue and use every subterfuge that she could think of to obtain a few moments of liberty. Her marriage had, in a sense, been but a change of prison.

She noted contemptuously that he had left Thomas Pratt behind and taken another body-servant with him to London. Of course he trusted the fellow whom he had known since boyhood. No doubt he trusted Mr. Swallow too, and Mrs. Bateman, who might seem the most ineffective and humble of creatures with her white cap, and her whitish face, and her downcast eyes, and her basket of keys—for Grace Troyes had always tossed them back to her—but who was really, of course, extremely adroit and staunchly loyal in carrying out her master's orders.

Grace Troyes had no more money than she had ever had before. Of all her large fortune there was that small income which she had stipulated, settled on her, and this her husband had prevented her, so far, from handling. Unable to consult with anyone who was in her interest, she had been forced to give in on this point. He had informed her, with those edged accents that he was now used to employ when speaking to her, that she was already pampered and had no need of money. All her wishes were indulged to the point of extravagance—nay, of fantasy—her parrot and her marmoset, her blackboy with the studden collar. Even he, with his taste for the lavish, had determined that she must go no farther with her whims. As for money, even her alms, such as were due from the lady of Lyndley Waters to the gentry and the villagers, were paid by him.

"Money gives one power," thought Grace: "that is why I am never allowed to handle it."

She did not know how a woman placed as she was could have attained much freedom even with money; but she longed for it, to see it glittering through the silk mesh purse, to see a chest of leather, bound with iron, in the corner of her room and to know that it contained *rouleaux* of gold.

Well, she was free of his company—or rather, free of the thought that he was under the same roof as herself; their marriage amounted to little more than that, a common residence. They saw as little of one another as was consistent with his dignity.

She looked out of the window and beheld a day of spring that to her was no more warm and brilliant than the spring days to which she was accustomed in the north, cold, always cold and damp, with mists that might harbour who knew what of spectres and threatening shades, both here and there.

Mrs. Bateman interrupted her lady's sulky idleness by waiting on her, and stood there, a stolid figure with her face that had a locked look, her white cap that rose stiffly like an emblem of office above her thick, faded grey hair, her plump hands that were curdling into the folds of old age, her wicker basket of keys. . . .

Grace Troyes struck swiftly. "You don't come here to ask me what my wishes are during my husband's absence, but to observe my demeanour, Mrs. Bateman—to see how I endure my captivity, to know my occupation—in brief, to spy upon me. . . ."

Mrs. Bateman withstood the shock admirably. She had had several months in which to armour herself against her foreign mistress, as she termed Grace Troyes in her heart.

"You may speak as you please, my lady, and it is my duty to listen. . . . As for your occupation, madam, I never found you had any; and as for spying, I go about my duty as my master sets it. . . ."

"And your duty is to watch me," said Grace. "Why is it he takes so much interest in what I do? Do you not find that ridiculous, Mrs. Bateman—for a man to have such an interest in the actions of a wife to whom he is completely indifferent?"

The housekeeper replied primly:

"My lady, it is for me to take orders from you and to give you an account of what goes on in the household. The establishment is on a very handsome scale and the expenses are large. . . ."

"All reports go to Mr. Swallow," exclaimed Grace Troyes, stamping her foot. "This is but a farce!"

"If you choose to say so!" Mrs. Bateman dropped a brief curtsey. "Sir James bade me wait on you and ask your orders. . . ."

"I never have any," replied Grace wildly. "At least, none that would be obeyed. Supposing I were to ask you, my good old woman, for a bag of gold and a coach with four horses and a portmanteau in which to pack up all my finest clothes—what would you say then? Would you tell them to set the gates wide and let me go to where it is warm and golden, where one can lie on satin all day and do nothing?"

Mrs. Bateman's shrewdness was equal even to this outburst.

"Your ladyship does nothing in Lyndley Waters," she remarked, "and as for the fairy tales, I keep them for the winter evenings when there is nothing else to be done but doze."

Grace did not reply. The contempt on her face was touched with a ferocity that the sober old English woman marked without alarm but very keenly.

* * * *

When she was alone again Grace left her own apartments and wandered aimlessly through those that were completed and furnished; up and down and in and out with no purpose at all, save to stay the workings of her mind by the actions of her body. Then she left these finished rooms and came out into those where the hammers of the workmen and the saws of the carpenters sounded so melodiously in the ears of Mr. Swallow and the architect, who were at their common task of supervising the decorations of the mansion.

During the few months that so much money had been spent on it, Lyndley Waters had advanced handsomely, though it would be several years before it was as complete as the owner and the designer desired it to be. Such places, Mr. Swallow now remarked to the architect, as they stood in the window place, were usually finished by a man's heirs—and then he had wished he had not spoken so frankly, for with such a marriage as this there seemed there might be no heirs, and the whole toil but a mockery since Lyndley Waters would go to a distant relative known to be of austere tastes and little likely to reside in Wiltshire.

Grace overheard the remark. She approached the two men with her light, gliding step and said:

"I consider it the greatest folly to spend so much time and money on building a great house like this. Why, there is even a royal bedroom."

Such mansions," replied the architect uneasily, "are usually given a royal bedroom. It is not necessary that one expects the King to sleep here—it is for any visitor of distinction."

She laughed in his uneasy face. "What does my husband think to do with a palace like this?"

"Well," retorted Mr. Swallow with some asperity, "for one thing, madam, he entertains you very handsomely in it. You are living as few women even of greater rank live in this country."

"I suppose so," she replied.

Mr. Swallow, seeing her in her (as he would call it) quiet mood, like a tigress with its claws sheathed, continued his homily.

"If your ladyship would make the effort to take up your duties to support Sir James in his manifold interests, you would find yourself interested in Lyndley Waters."

"Go on," she smiled, "talk to me—I am used to being preached at."

"As a much older man, and one who has been with your husband since his boyhood, who knew his father before him and his mother, and all the conditions and conventions of this place, perhaps," continued the steward stoutly, "I might give your ladyship some advice. You have lived very much apart from all of us. . . ."

"Oh, no doubt I have given you plenty to talk about from the very fact that I have done nothing at all."

"No," replied he calmly. "You have long ceased to be an object of curiosity. We find you merely a negation. If you care to waste your life in this fashion, we can but be sorry for Sir James."

She lifted her lip at this rebuke and moved away, still with her idle, sauntering air. She had to be on the outlook for a spy, of that she was well aware. In every one of her husband's servants she must suspect a possible watchdog. The only thing to do was to defy them all, to outface them; and what she wished to do was surely not so difficult that she could not achieve it . . . ah, some day!

Malaise and depression clouded her spirits. What should she ask for next to exasperate her husband, to squander her money? A puppet theatre, perhaps, with a chalk-faced clown and a blackamoor and a pale heroine with long, straw-coloured hair? That would be expensive and difficult to obtain. She could easily, however, goad him by saying that all great houses should have such a toy. "Yet what a slow warfare is all this," she thought savagely.

She came into a large room under the centre cupola of the building. The interior of the dome had just been painted with flying figures, who appeared to shower flowers on those standing beneath. The floor was of greenish alabaster, tessellated cleverly by the foreign workmen. The hangings and tapestries were not yet in place; the carvings had been set above the mantelpiece, but the picture which they were going to frame—or was it to be a mirror?—had been left blank.

Grace Troyes shivered even in her trailing clothes of furs and velvet. So much marble required the sun. She understood all these niceties better than they did. She, who had never left Scotland until she had come here! She had read of what alabaster looked like with the sunlight and the shadow of grapes and vine leaves falling upon it; and those long windows, they were not designed to allow a northern gloom to fall through them, but rather for the golden dust of some southern air to enter.

Moving again and quickly she came to the chapel and gave a glance at the little mannequin that she had hung there on her first visit. It was still in its place, and no one, as far as she knew, had commented upon it. They contrived to punish her, frequently, by ignoring her whims. She knew that and fretted at it. They wanted her to know that she was disdained. Mrs. Bateman—how free and insolent the woman had been! If she, the mistress of this place, were suddenly to meet Thomas Pratt he would be no less downright under the guise of a servant's respect, and he was more to be dreaded than Mrs. Bateman, for he had been in Edinburgh and knew perhaps too much for her peace of mind.

Yet to do a thing boldly is sometimes to do it successfully. Caution may defeat its own ends. She ran up the spiral staircase that led from the chapel to the chaplain's room and scratched upon the door.

When Nicholas Jerdan's voice bade her enter, she turned the handle quickly and was in the room and beside his desk before he could speak again.

"Well," she said, "my husband has gone to London."

"And you," he answered at once, "are imprudent."

"Oh, do not argue with me!" she entreated. "Is it not natural that I should visit my chaplain now and then? Let us get out our books of psalms and prayers and recite them together. Let us go down to the chapel if you will and pray. Since we have been so closely watched all the time you've been at Lyndley Waters . . ."

He interrupted her. "It is much more important now that your husband is away."

"I suppose so. It is also important that you and I have one or two matters clearly understood."

She went to the fire that he still kept burning on his hearth. His rooms were lofty and chill, and he spent much of his time at his desk with his piles of manuscript and his stacks of books. He did not leave this position now, but stood by his chair, his appearance at odds with his occupation; although he wore a clerical dress far less rich than his secular attire that passed muster in the eyes of the English for that of a Calvinist minister, yet his open collar, the carelessly tied ribbon at his throat, the loose hair so indifferently buckled back, his glance, his gesture, his poise all belied both his profession and the popular image that the English had formed of a Scotch presbyterian.

Grace Troyes did not look at him but into the flames. She warmed her thin hands that were trembling.

"What good have we done ourselves?" she asked. "I do not see an inch ahead. You have disappointed me."

"I am not going to let you run on and rail, Grace," he replied. "You should know me better than that by now."

189

Then she asked, looking now quickly over her shoulder, "What are you going to let me do? Remember, while we remain inactive others are working against us—that girl Celia Plaisent who loves him, of course, and whom he ought to have married had he not been crazed with the notion of building this foolish house . . ."

"You wouldn't feel it so foolish," replied Nicholas Jerdan, "if you and I were master and mistress of it—indeed, I feel it is very much to your taste."

"Not here," she said impatiently. "Not here. Was it not always understood that we were to go away . . . abroad . . . where we could spend the money—*my* money—as we pleased?"

"I do not know what was understood. Many moods came and went, flickered up and died down. I commend to you prudence. . . ."

"Commend to me prudence!" she retorted hotly. "If I were to be prudent I should sit all day plucking at the tail of my parrot, or caressing my little monkey, or feeding my blackboy with sugar stick. . . . And where would that advance us?"

"Somewhere more desirable, perhaps, than any wilfulness on your part may," he answered sternly.

She sighed with a deep yearning impatience. Her longing was about the room like a miasma, her discontent appeared a tangible thing, though neither had much effect on the young man who stood by his plain, handsome chair and the desk that was too richly ornamented for the pious works that loaded it so heavily.

She began to upbraid him, the words passing her lips very quickly, almost incoherently.

190

"But you promised to do something before this. You said that you knew what to do. I have done my part . . . and day by day goes by and we are still as if we were under a spell . . . bewitched in this detestable place. He has gone to London . . . that is to make a move against us. You know that he has set his lawyers on to me and my affairs."

"His lawyers were on to you and your affairs before your marriage," replied Mr. Jerdan. "Out of self-interest they told him what he wished to hear. They are not likely to disturb him now. Remember, that when he came into your moneys and estates his lawyers had their fees as did yours. It was to everyone's interest to be silent. . . ."

"And now," put in Grace, still with a fretting impatience, "it might be in somebody's interests to speak. Who knows? There are too many in this secret. He told me once, and it shows it was on his mind that he mentioned such a tifle, that some old woman followed him in Edinburgh and pulled him into her room when he was wandering in some wynd—I know not which—and warned him against marrying me."

"You know who that would be?" smiled Nicholas Jerdan. "Some servant who considered that she had been wronged by us? Warned him, did she? Well, I don't suppose there is much to be feared in that."

"And then he saw me coming out of the goldsmith's shop where I had had the sapphire altered . . . the gold added."

"What was the matter for that?" replied Nicholas Jerdan, "when you openly rode with him to put the jewel in my grandfather's grave?"

"Ah, that was a challenge. He could do nothing about it. He could not thwart me there, nor deny me ... I had him on a nice point of what he calls his honour, and that gave me pleasure. ... But to be spied on when coming out of the shop—well, that I detest! Even then I felt he suspected me."

"Any man whould have done so," replied Mr. Jerdan. "The whole affair was so unnatural. But I was quite sure of him ... I had not a moment's anxiety, that was why I followed him that day he rode by chance, as it seemed, toward the River Almond."

"Tell me," she said, "how much money you got for the jewel?"

"I did not sell it, only the knob of gold," he replied carelessly, and putting his hand into his bosom he pulled out the Kashmir sapphire and set it on his desk where, like a lamp, it cast out blue rays that put to shame the thumbed and shabby books, the pages covered with the cramped handwriting.

"You did not sell it?" she exclaimed. "But that was what it was for—to give you money that you might come here."

"Why, I know," he replied with a man's intolerance of a woman's statement of the obvious, "and I found sufficient money in other ways. I had some of what you gave me before—from the diamond. I preferred to keep the sapphire. I should have sold it at a loss and perhaps with some difficulty, even peril. I will keep it until I am able to return it to you."

"And when will that be?" she cried.

She rose and stamped her foot in her pent-up impatience.

"How long are we to live like this?"

He reminded her that they had waited only a matter of months.

"You seem to enjoy," she stormed, "this intricate game you play! Every move that you make, I suppose, is calculated and careful, and there must be, to a man of your disposition, a certain ease and even pleasure in that. But what do you suppose it is to me—it is but idleness. . . ."

"There is no need for you to be idle," he replied. "Play your part a little better . . . be in truth the mistress of Lyndley Waters. Learn housekeeping arts from this Mrs. Bateman, who is your watchdog no doubt; do not so rashly dismiss all the women that they put about you for your service; don't show so openly an aimless extravagance. Behave yourself more as you did when you were in Edinburgh. . . ."

"To what end?" she asked, sulking and pouting. "To what end?"

He did not answer that. He turned to the sapphire and looked at it with a cool consideration that exasperated her.

"Is it not extremely beautiful?" she asked. "Do you not admire it? Are you not grateful to me for the risks and pains I took conveying it to you? Was it not extremely ingenious of me to think of that when it was impossible for us to meet or to communicate? Did I not steal a gem, a little gem of my own, to set you up in finery?"

He answered in conventional terms that she had indeed been admirable in her contrivances, and his coolness further lashed her. She came to the chair whereby he stood, and despite his quick warning that at any moment, under one excuse or another, the door might be opened and one of her husband's household enter, she began to relate how far she had gone in the work that she had come to Lyndley

Waters to perform.

"I," she declared rapidly, "have played my part to admiration, as I think you must confess. I have been, on those things that are most disagreeable to me, prudent and discreet. I have remained secretive, confiding in none, keeping my husband—who, I consider, for all his fine manners nothing less than a dolt—at arms's length, thwarting, too, with my airs of mystery, that girl Celia, who, of course, for his sake is watching me as far as she is able. I have confounded also, I am sure, the gallant who hangs after her—Brian Ormerod. Now I am safely established as the mistress of Lyndley Waters. Indeed," she added, clasping her hands and with a note of appeal, "I believe I have done all that you bade me."

The young man laughed shortly.

"So you think, which shows how a woman may be mistaken, when she follows her own inclinations."

"You answer harshly," replied Grace Troyes.

She beat her foot impatiently on the ground and walked up and down the spruce new room.

"You have spoken plainly," said Nicholas Jerdan, "and so must I." He went to the door and opened it. "We are safer thus. I stand by this door and can see down the spiral staircase . . . if any should by chance come up it, I may change our conversation."

She looked at him sulkily, yet with an appreciation that was deeper than any whim or temper.

"I do not commend your discretion," he replied. "I consider that you have behaved in Lyndley Waters as you behaved in Edinburgh. After all, you made yourself there the clatter of the town. . . ."

"And whose fault was that?" she replied impatiently, but he checked her show of feeling.

What he had to say was of great importance to him, and he was in no mood to tolerate a woman's display of random emotion.

"You need the bridle," he remarked. "I told you so before. You, with your cantrips and illusions—the same fool here as you were there. I have been astonished at your extravagance."

"Did we not come to England to be extravagant, to be sumptuous and splendid?"

"But not in this manner."

"I know, I know," she tried to control herself. "You told me in Edinburgh that we must wait, that we must put people off their guard, that we must behave extremely decorously. Well, I have done it—and it is a matter of months. . . ."

"Months are not long enough," he replied. "We are surrounded by suspicion. It may be there is not enough for anyone to get a handle, but still it is suspicion. We are both watched—and this conversation I consider as dangerous as that which was surprised under the old pear tree."

Grace Troyes could not understand the drift of this conversation, but she believed that it was likely to be something disagreeable. She watched him as he stood by the door, master of her and her fortunes, as he always had been.

"What," she asked cautiously, "did you propose when you came into this plot to come to England with me?"

"Just this," he replied. "To make myself a place in a great man's house."

"Well, are you satisfied with that?" she demanded. "Is your fee sufficient?"

But Nicholas Jerdan was not to be stung by her

sneers. He had a dexterous part to play, and though he did not doubt his ability to play it, he found the work before him sufficiently absorbing to prevent him taking offence at Grace Troyes' insinuations. Besides, he was prepared for them.

"You and I," he remarked, "found ourselves in a position where it might have been a hempen rope for me and a lifelong confinement for you. We extricated ourselves—and now we must, after this spell of due caution, take up our lives again."

"You speak rightly," she cried impetuously. "This is not life here. It is but an existence. I feel no more alive than my marmoset, or parrot, or blackamoor." Then she demanded urgently, "What have you done? You know that I am incapable of business."

"What I have done," replied Mr. Jerdan, "would hardly be interesting to your understanding, Grace. Listen . . . I believe what I have to say will be displeasing. You were much bemused by old chap books and ballads, the sly and droll peddler with his stories, whom we used to admit at the back door and from whom you would buy tags and laces and other trumpery more dangerous. In those almanacs you purchased, Grace, was there no predicition of this moment?"

She could not understand him, and she came, in her agitation, also to the open door, over which he kept a steadfast guard, looking continually down the spiral staircase and speaking in a hushed voice.

"If you would serve me," he whispered, "if you loved me, you would get together all the jewels and money that you could, and deliver them to me here, and I might sell them against our future needs."

"I can get no money, you know that—no more than I could get money in Edinburgh. My small allowance, all that I was able to bargain for, you have already. . . ."

"Those poor pence," replied the young man contemptuously, "went to satisfy some creditors of mine in Scotland. I want large sums of money, Grace, such as the master of Lyndley Waters is able to afford. You must in some manner obtain them from him. Then there are the jewels . . . could you deliver them to me, I think I might contrive to have them copied in pinchbeck and paste? . . ."

He turned away from the door, having satisfied himself that no one was spying on them. His ear was acute, he had long trained himself to live in other people's houses and to mark all that occurred. He was in no great fear of a surprise.

" 'To make a crown a pound young Jaimie went to sea,' " he whistled the old song softly.

"Well, we shall go to sea, shall we not, Nicholas?" whispered Grace. "To Paris . . . to Rome. Why did you tell me that you had gone to Switzerland? I nearly persuaded the Englishman to take me there."

He looked at her quizzically. His attire was careless, yet his air was grand and bold, and she loved him as deeply as she had ever loved him, knowing that there was now and never would be any other for her liking.

"It is well for me," he remarked, "that you believed all those stories I told you in Edinburgh—but now you must be undeceived. There can be no question of Nicholas Jerdan and Grace Troyes going off together on fairy-tale adventures. No, my dear, it is I who must go, and go alone—and it is you who must find the money."

She did not believe him; this seemed to her but so much teasing; she thought he tried to make some proof of her constancy, so she laughed, tossing back her black ringlets, and said:

"We've spoken here a long time. Perhaps it is dangerous. Let us meet in the Cradle Walk as if casually, or row again on the water. . . . How small that lake appears beside our own! I wonder what name once was on the boat, and who scratched it off . . . ?"

"The name was 'Celia,' " replied Nicholas Jerdan, "and she or her gallant, Brian Ormerod, scratched it off. Now come . . . I am growing impatient . . . I have waited, you know, a long time. Recall that it is a year and six months since you came out at twilight and found me under the pear tree, and then your guardian, Miss Lilias and Miss Grissel, surprised us both. . . ."

"A year and a day," sighed Grace in the words of the old ballads.

But he told her sharply she must leave such fond talk.

"I am," he frowned, "for India or Jamaica where a man whose pocket is well-lined does not have his past enquired into, and there I may satisfy. . . ."

He paused on the word, and now she began to stare at him with some alarm, and to recall to him, almost against her will, the lost scenes she held dearest.

"Nicholas, do you not remember those rides round Moffatt . . . the waterfall we called Grey Mare's Tail, the graves of the martyrs hidden in the recesses of the glen . . . the river, open and glittering, and the hills like topaz and amethyst in the sunset . . . and all you told me then about other worlds in which we might be free to live, in which neither God nor devil had a part . . . ?"

"I spoke," he replied, "as the moment befitted. You must not think that I despised or used you . . . the chance came too neatly to my hands. I, like you, half-loved, half-detested that loneliness. . . ."

"I wholly loved it!" she declared with emphasis. "The peaks and summits that seemed to stretch to heaven, the broom and the daisy about one's feet, the village fires, and stars shining out when we were late. . . ."

"We were often late," he remarked gloomily. "I can remember other details—the dry heather that flourishes in barren moorland and bears no fruit, the humble cottage where I spent my childhood with a gandmother who had no thoughts beyond her spinning-wheel and her Bible . . . and the few pounds so painfully scraped that sent me to a college to get my preacher's license. . . ."

"But you had luck," she reminded him eagerly. "You had the luck to receive your father's place as my chaplain. . . ."

"Yes, he had the luck to attract your guardian's attention—a pious man—but I am different. I think of ancestors who perhaps were not chained with the sombre links of a deadly . . ."

He would not further disclose himself. She shivered, thinking that he was about to revile his religion and his God, and then he turned on her sharply and spoke to her as if she was a child.

"That mannequin that you hung up in the

chapel—that was a piece of manifest folly. I have not taken it down or mentioned it, for that would be but to attract attention to it. . . ."

"But it was part of what we were to do," cried Grace. "I told them that you were a great grammarian—they did not know that that meant a magician, that you, if need be, could throw magic over them all. Do you not recollect that we used the circles, the dolls, the wax and earthen images. . . ."

"I thought by now," he replied impatiently, "that you had outgrown such stuff. It is for old wives and children . . . it amused us when we had nothing better to do. Did you suppose that I was coming here to put upon these people, intelligent as they are in their way, ploys that might have beguiled some old fool doddering in a moorland cottage . . . ?"

She grinned at him bitterly.

"You have deceived me," she muttered. "I thought you believed in these things."

"I neither believe nor disbelieve," he replied. "I do not know. All I care about is that I must get away. When I get away, you may play as you please with your games of witchcraft. Remember, Grace, that I am a man utterly discredited . . . at any moment that may be discovered. It was in the interests of all who had to do with the business of your marriage to keep silent, and I was able to take advantage of that; but Sir James is suspicious. It may be that in a few days he will know everything, and before that I must be gone. . . ."

"Did you come to Lyndley Waters," asked Grace, "merely to obtain from me the means to go to Europe?"

Europe. . . . That word contained an enchantment. Were they not both to have gone to Europe, to have dwelt luxuriously and splendidly, forgetting the sombre, misty city . . . the seclusion and prayer, the penitence for sins never committed, the suppressions and longings. . . . She had selected him—she who might have married a prince. . . . That thought rose in her mind, urging her into speech.

"I chose you, Nicholas . . . I would have married you had it been possible."

"It was not possible," he said shortly. "How many words you make. . . . Perhaps one day I shall return, a Nabob, from India or Jamaica, who knows? Perhaps by then Sir James will be dead of an apoplexy, or spitted in a coffee-house brawl—and then you and I . . ."

"I do not want to think of the future any more," replied the girl impatiently. "I want to think of the present. If you go away, I am going with you. . . ."

"Very well," he agreed, carelessly humouring her, "you are going with me—but first we must have the money, you understand. If not the money, the jewels. Where are those once belonging to your husband's mother, and your own mother?"

"They have not been delivered to me," she replied sullenly. "Now and then I am given an ornament to wear. . . . I had some diamonds on, I think, when you saw me by the bonfire. . . . How they glittered! Then they are taken away again by my husband or, when he is too occupied with riding round his estate to view the prospects, by the factor and locked away. . . ."

"If you have any wit you are able to get them," said Mr. Jerdan. "Now I must go to my studies. You may suppose they are as foreign to me as your idleness is to you. . . ."

Grace Troyes went to the open door but did not immediately depart. She found herself in the midst of a conflict she had not expected. There was not only her husband and a girl who loved her husband, and that girl's gallant to outwit—but the very man himself for whom the outwitting was to be done.

"I pined and was solitary," she said, looking back at him. "Such of the men as they sent me I detested—and then you came . . . and why should it not go as we intended?"

"It was spoiled before through your folly," he reminded her. "One could have expected little better from a child. . . . I have been something in the world—to large cities and universities . . . be guided by me. . . ."

"But if you," she argued, "go to these foreign countries and leave me here, what am I to do?"

The question came with curious wistfulness.

Nicholas Jerdan laughed. "There are several courses open to you, my dear. You might win the heart of your English husband, ousting the prim little Celia . . . or you might insist on being taken to town, and there cut a fashionable figure. Or you might—well, I leave it to your feminine ingenuity to think of what else you can do. . . ."

"I shall not get the jewels unless you take me with you," countered Grace suddenly.

She had an instinct that this was a good word on which to leave him, and she fled the chamber in which she had held so long and exhausting a conversation and hurried down the spiral stairs. A new aspect of not only her own affairs, but of human nature, had been opened up to her . . . she could not yet believe that Nicholas Jerdan had merely been using her as a lever to his own fortunes. She thought him humoursome, inclined to tease. Had he not often in Edinburgh been bitter and sarcastic and upbraided her for her follies? What she must do now was to obtain what she could in the way of riches, and then to think of some means whereby she and Nicholas could escape from Lyndley Waters.

Not heeding where she went, she passed the chapel and saw the mannequin hanging up where she had placed it herself on the first day of her arrival at her new home; entering, she tore it down spitefully. She had hoped that Nicholas would have commended her for her cleverness. Instead of that—a rebuke. What had he said about not believing in all the rites they had practised together . . . when she had shown such courage . . . ? Why, she had been prepared to do everything—even to go at midnight and wash a garment where four waters meet . . . even to remain alone at night reading her incantations . . . and now he said it was but chap-book folly and dreaming. . . . Grace Troyes recalled what he called the slight and adroit peddler whom she had crept down to see, with the contrivance of a maid, at the back door of the sombre mansion near Holyrood. Well she could recall the pear trees, always the first to blossom. How they had shone, their frosted clusters against a dun-coloured sky . . . and the maid, also anxious to have the grinding monotony of the pious days broken up, had, giggling, shown her into a closet that smelt of spice where the peddler sat with his pack and his tray of wares. There had been many forbidden things that Grace had bought—charms, and books of prophecy, and sheets of ballads, and little histories of knights and ladies.

Then, when she had been riding on the moor, there had been, under the guidance of Nicholas, visits to old wives who had the rowan tied above their door with scarlet threads and who, when they paused from their spinning or weaving, could tell her many a fearful yet exciting tale. . . . These in her mind were pictures that were impressed one on the other . . . the graves of the martyrs in the lonely glens by Moffatt and her father's house that had been so rudely and incompletely altered from a fortalice to an incommodious dwelling. . . . Always there had been Nicholas. . . . She had taken him to see her father, and the two men had been left alone together while she had gone up to the small bower, as it was termed, where her mother had lived, and turned over the trinkets of little interest to her because they did not glitter or shine, which the Spanish lady had once possessed. While she had fingered a tinselled heart pierced with seven swords, and boxes lined with silver paper lace that gave out an acrid yet pleasant perfume, she had heard the murmur of the voices of the two men talking below, and now and then a shout of laughter from Mr. Morrisson.

He had always seemed in a good humour when she had brought Nicholas to see him, as if he had been on her side against her guardians and her lawyers and all those who cabined her in when she was in Edinburgh.

She took the doll to her room and hid it in her press beneath the folds of the shining silk and satin dresses that she had ordered from London.

* * * *

Nicholas Jerdan was at an uncertain point of his

fortunes. He knew himself to be in fact an adventurer with little assets beyond his own wits. He had done pretty well, he supposed, if he liked to compare his present position with that of himself as a boy, when he had carried the New Testament in a clean napkin behind his grandmother across the moors to the village church and learned the Classic Tongues and Scripture form the corpulent, untidy schoolmaster.

Jerdan had always been ravaged by ambition, but his disposition and his person were not suited to the sole career that had been possible to him. The only son of a minister, for the ministry he was designed; and in those days he had desired nothing better than to cut a figure in the church. To get a parish had been his sole wish, but now he laughed at such mean hopes. He had the roving disposition of his countrymen. There was no feeling in his breast either for his native village or his native land. Poor and born lacking opportunity. . . . Nay, there he was wrong. . . . He sharpened his quill eagerly as he considered how wrong. A precious chance had come his way on the sudden death of his father. He had been, through the silly piety and bias of an old woman towards that gloomy parent, appointed chaplain to Grace Morrisson.

He recalled how carefully he had subdued his own character, even his own appearance; how correct his dress and demeanor had been, how he had looked down and spoken softly when he had gone to interview the old ladies, and how they had been snared, thinking him to be a young man of great piety and learning and one well fitted to, as they put it, "tread in his father's footsteps."

But in that old house by the pear orchard there had only been two people who had been, in his sense of the word, alive—himself and Grace Morrisson, and they had soon come to their pact and their understanding. Neither of them had known the beauties, the joys, the splendours for which they secretly longed. She had half-remembered, half-invented stories to tell that she had heard from her mother, before that poor woman had died of home-sickness in a gloomy land—of the glories of Spain where the sun always shone on the fig and the pomegranate, of marble courts and splashing fountains where behind the slats of green lattices there were easy couches with brocade cushions and agreeable company to make music with mandolins and guitars . . . then there were old women on the moors with their wild stories of the splendours of past days when Linlithgow had shone like a jewel in the north with the pomp and pleasure of kings . . . the chap-books and ballads that they had bought from the wandering peddler . . . and all those tales which need never be written down because they seemed implicit in the heart of youth, had induced them into supposing that they might have some share in the golden dream. They had been thwarted, and yet she believed they had, through his cleverness, extricated themselves; and she had played her part quite well—yes, surely, for an untutored girl, excellently. . . .

She passed out on to the terrace; the distance lay under an aerial haze. In the foreground were still the stonemasons and the gardeners, briskly at their work. Sir James had taken great pains to thin his timber to advantage, so that the trees—the chestnuts, the elms and the planes that had been allowed in his father's time to grow too close to the old mansion and cast too heavy a shadow into the ancient windows—were now, as it were, set back. The old forest had been stayed, the great trees had been here and there dexterously felled so that Grace could look at various pleasant prospects, only during the last few months revealed. Here was a dip into a valley, and a farm set clearly in its fields . . . and there was a glimpse of the rough road, winding between the quickset hedges to the town . . . and there again was a view of a village with the church and the weathercock glittering gold in a chance ray of sunshine that pierced the mists.

Grace had no eye for the beauty of the scene. She was within her own obsession as her husband was within his; he had gone to London, perhaps to find out something about what had happened in Edinburgh before he married her. She, possibly, had very little time to lose, and it was not easy, single-handed, to outwit her husband's household of, to her, not only strangers, but almost foreigners. . . . Mrs. Bateman, now, with her courtly air and her sweeping curtsies, her red shoes with the white ribbon rosettes, her bonnet stiffened with wires, her pale face and her steadfast, watchful eyes . . . she was a formidable figure to Grace Troyes, as was the commonplace Thomas Pratt who, on the surface, was no more than a body-servant, mechanically doing his master's business, but who was, Grace knew, an alert and intelligent human being. They would do their duty, they would be faithful to their master—and as for her, she had no help at all.

She went down into the garden, not forgetting to give a nod of encouragement and a stately word of praise here and there to the men employed by her husband and paid by her money. They took little heed of her, though good-naturedly acknowledging her salutations. Mr. Swallow and the architect had long since considered she was an oddity, though the steward had not altogether conquered a certain uneasiness as to her character and probable conduct. That it was an unsuccessful marriage he knew. He had expected as much, and he consoled himself—for he needed consolation in the misfortunes of Sir James that struck him nearly—with the consideration that without her, Lyndley Waters would never have been built, and now it was being built with a rapidity and splendour that he scarcely could have hoped for, even a few years ago when the Troyes fortunes had not been so damaged.

He continually looked with relish at the new facade of the house that shone new and whitish in the early spring day. How brilliant and fresh glittered the cupola and the weather-vane over the stables . . . how magnificent were the iron gates now in place and being, by patient artisans, carefully gilded . . . how splendid were the views, the vistas that the taste of Sir James had put, as it were, at the disposal of anyone who cared to walk on the terrace of Lyndley Waters; and he admired, with a warm glow of pleasure, the prospects seen between the openings in the trees that Grace had viewed with so cold an eye.

She walked disconsolate through the rose garden. The little vivid green leaves appearing near the thick pink thorns did not attract her attention, nor did the freshly turned earth with its pleasant smell. Indeed, she rather disliked this modest retreat. She preferred Lyndley Waters itself, although it seemed but a small tarn to her compared to those sheets of water that she had known near Moffatt. Yet it had been the scene of the bonfire, a night of excitement, of adventure, when Nicholas Jerdan had appeared suddenly illuminated by the artificial flowers of fire, by the showers of falling sparks surrounded by the blur of the agitated and disturbed faces of her husband's neighbours.

"I believe," she thought with pleasure, "they were afraid it was the devil suddenly set among them."

When she came out by the water, she saw that there was another already there. Brian Ormerod was standing by the boathouse staring, as it seemed in an idle and purposeless fashion, at the unrippled surface. Grace frowned, regarding him with suspicion. She instinctively knew him to be a man much occupied in all the pursuits of an English country gentleman. She knew, too, that he was no particular friend of her husband's . . . she wondered why he had come there. . . . "No particular friend of her husband's. . . ." perhaps she had been mistaken and he, too, had been sent to spy on her. His presence gave a point to her restless and unhappy mood.

Holding up her dark green skirt from her pale yellow leather shoes that were becoming muddied, she walked round the uneven banks of the lake to challenge this foreigner, who might also be an enemy.

He watched her approach. As he did not wear his hat he had no salutation to make beyond a brief inclination of his head.

"He wants to speak to me," thought Grace. She was very much on the alert.

His first words were conventional.

"It must be lonely for you, Lady Troyes, when your husband is in town. James should not leave you so soon after the marriage. Do you not find something disturbing, even desolate, in all this new splendour that is being erected . . . ?" and he indicated the facade and the roof of the mansion visible on the rising ground.

Grace had long since learned how to conceal her secrets with frankness, so it was with an air of candour that she replied, "It doesn't really interest me at all. I like my own apartments—the Brocatelle room—oh, and other curiosities; but I have become weary of looking at them. I, too, wish to go to London. I hope James will soon take me."

"There is no reason why he should not make a show of the beauty whom he has brought from the north."

"You play with me," said Grace. "Everyone here plays with me. I cannot understand why you are here to-day, or what concern you take in me."

"It is curiosity perhaps," replied the gentleman coolly. "When a strange drama is enacted on one's doorstep, one turns one's head to gaze. . . ."

"Strange drama. . . ." She was a little taken aback by that. She had never been to a theatre in her life, but she had read of shows and masks in those forbidden books that she and Nicholas Jerdan had read seated together on the open moorland with the harebells growing at their side, or at dusk under the pear trees in the orchard of that gloomy house where she had been reared.

"You are much bewildered and put about, Lady Troyes," he continued. "I think you are set in a plot that has gone beyond your control. I am compas-

sionate towards you . . . I am even more compassionate towards someone else who is involved in your
story. . . ."

Grace was still suspicious, but she liked to talk
about herself. She had been keeping the mask on for
a long while. It was easy to allow it to slip just a little
way—enough, perhaps, to show a gleam in her eyes, if
not a smile on her lips. She put her hand nervously to
her long locks.

"You and I have never spoken alone together. I
know nothing about you, except that you are
courting Celia Plaisent. . . ."

"I was," he replied, "but let us take that as a tale
that is told. Celia will accept nothing from me—not as
much as a kindness." Then he added abruptly,
"Would you?"

"What?" she asked. "A kindness? Yes, I would
take that from anybody," and she decided quickly as
she spoke, "I'll see what he has to offer. I'll see if I
can use him."

He looked at her as if he had discovered her
devices and found them trivial.

"I would like to help you, but you must not
mistake me. I want to help you because others are
concerned."

"This is a strange talk," said the lady. "We are not
even friendly, and if I am to have advice on my
outlandish manners or my haughtiness, surely it
should come from one of the good matrons who so
often look at me out of narrowed eyes."

"It is nothing to do with your airs or your
whims," replied Brian Ormerod, "and it is nothing, I
think, that another woman could tell you as well as I
can." He considered her thoughtfully. "I believe I

waste my breath, but here is the advice—send Nicholas Jerdan back to Scotland . . . try to behave as if this were your home . . . look to Sir James—he is neither so foolish nor so manageable as you think him. . . ."

She would have willingly had a descant on this theme; long suppressed as she had been, she was eager to discuss, though in veiled terms, her own peculiar position. But the young man had said all that he considered safe to say and left her abruptly.

Then, when she was alone by Lyndley Waters, Grace, whose mind was always full of hidden fantasies that easily touched on alarm, felt a chill of fear. This had been a deliberate warning from one who seemed both worldy-wise and friendly. She remembered the barely contained impatience and anger of Nicholas. Perhaps they *had* played this game long enough . . . perhaps more *was* known about them than she realised. . . .

She returned quickly to the house, but remembered her discretion when she saw Mr. Swallow with a measuring yard in his hand turning to look at her. It was uncommon for her to so hasten her pace. At a slower gait she entered the unfinished mansion.

* * * *

Brian Ormerod was not the only person who had felt a swift and almost desperate concern in the departure of James Troyes for London. Celia Plaisent deliberately chose the lane where now the lush spring weeds were filling the ditches and the knots of primroses were beginning to show under the damp moss, the lane where she knew Brian must pass on his daily round of his estate. He would be on horseback, so she had taken her little cob out of the stable and mounted that; she was in no gay-laced Amazon suit such as Grace wore, but in her usual murray-coloured cloth with the cloak and hood loosely clasped round her neck.

He came punctually, as if to a tryst, and did not seem surprised to see her there. He was not a man who cared much about debates or deliberation, and Celia's candour also made her come directly to the point, so within two minutes of their greeting they were talking, as only those who understand one another can talk, of Grace and James.

"I spoke to her," said the young man. "I met her mooning by Lyndley Waters. She is, I think, what her own people would call daft. I met some Scots in London once—they are queer, you know, not like us at all."

"She is more Spanish than Scotch."

"I know nothing of the Spanish," retorted Brian drily. "After all, here we deal with a woman, one who is wild and born with, or bred with at least, new-fangled notions . . . and then forced to live, as she was, with those three old women in Edinburgh. Well, I told her to get rid of that dangerous fellow. He is up to mischief, but no one can find anything against him."

Celia said, "That should have been James's work. He will detest you for interfering. . . ."

"Perhaps I detest him for interfering."

"If you mean between you and me," said the girl quickly, "your dislike is without a foundation, for I never would have married you, Brian, even if James had not been there."

"Oh, that cannot be debated," he replied. "Say, then, I have an affection for James . . . I've known

213

him since my boyhood . . . he's a neighbour. He knows nothing of that fellow—he confessed as much himself—he suspects that he is in the web of some conspiracy, and so do I. Why did he go to London and leave them both together, even though I am sure she is very carefully watched—especially by Madam Bateman and Thomas Pratt?"

These bold words struck to the dark heart of the matter in a manner that startled Celia.

"You must not think of her—of Grace and the Scotch parson together!"

"Why not?" asked the young man bluntly. "They are of an age, of a nation—they have plotted together—cannot you imagine it? I am not given to fantasies myself, but I can see them in that old house with the three old women. They were so besotted with tales of his piety as a student, and when his father died they, blind and silly as I take them to have been, brought him to fill the old man's place. And were not he and the girl, for she was no more—she is little more now, Celia—at once natural allies? On the surface there would be their dreary religion, and underneath, who knows what in the name of schemes! Perhaps she wished to marry him. . . ."

"Your fancy flies far," said Celia, biting her underlip and staring into the hedge.

The dear and familiar English landscape seemed tarnished, blotted over with shapes of foreign horror.

"They could not have married," said Brian Ormerod. "She would never have attained her guardians' consent to that. She might possibly have waited till she was of age, but even then it would have been very difficult for her to have obtained, ignorant and kept a prisoner as she was, a hold on her fortune."

"You think that he . . . ?" Celia did not know what she thought herself and checked her baffled question.

"I think he is a starveling Scots adventurer," said Brian Ormerod. "I doubt if he has a passion or even a fancy for Grace, but he has some hold over her, and she, as I should say . . ." and here it was the young man who checked. "Well, we will leave it at that, Celia. But I am going to London to tell James to come home; and do you, if you would do us all a kindness, and in the name of honour, go as often as you can to Lyndley Waters and keep Grace Troyes company."

The young man put forward this plan as if it had been carefully thought out and was to be without question boldly, adopted, but it gave Celia a throb of terror.

"You must not interfere," she insisted.

She put out her hand earnestly and touched his sleeve, not noticing that she did so though, but this gesture meant much to him.

"James will never endure it. There will be anger and quarrelling and some disaster brought on all of us. It is no affair of ours. . . . Perhaps, too, she will take your advice and send Nicholas Jerdan away."

"I do not think so," replied Brian, "but I could do no less than offer it and, say what you will, Celia, I can do no less than go to London. By the time I find James he will probably have discovered much of what I have only guessed, of what I believe he has already guessed, for one may be quite certain that he will have set agents on to finding out something more

215

about Mr. Nicholas Jerdan. Now I must go my rounds, Celia. I'll not ask your company—I daresay you'd give it, but to-day I wish to be alone."

"It is as you decide, Brian. It is always as the men decide."

She turned the head of her cob back along the way she had come, through the lanes that were fresh, damp and full of young sprouting green and the first pallid flowers. Yes, it was always as the men decided . . . and this reflection gave her a fleeting sympathy with Grace Troyes who had been from the first snared and netted, and who had no choice, as it seemed, but to become a conspirator, if she were to have anything of what she had longed for. Celia knew—as she rode along the muddy road on her rough cob that still had his winter unclipped coat, she in her frieze without an ornament—she knew what Grace had longed for in the bleak, northern mansion; all that glittered or shone, all that was splendid and beautiful—and love, of course. Nothing but that. She might have prayed and sat with her Bible or her psalter on her knee . . . she might have behaved so decorously that she pleased her guardians and all who observed her comings and goings in Edinburgh city, but underneath she had wanted everything that was different.

Celia knew this by some intuition of the feminine mind, for she herself had no such longings for what was brilliant and adventurous and strange; Celia was for a warm, household affection and a protected hearth and gaiety and the pleasant duties, the routine that held up the spirit like props.

* * * *

Grace Troyes had to wait three days before she

could engage the sole attention of Nicholas Jerdan. During that time she was constantly under the civil and decorous supervison of the housekeeper and her husband's body-servant, and they, she knew, were but, as it were, the leaders of a band of spies, for surely everyone in that household—everyone who even came and went like Mr. Swallow and the London architect—were watching her, and with curiosity, if not with superstition, and would be very willing to repeat the least oddity in her behaviour. But on the third day when, having slept a little and thought much, she went in a desperate mood into the Volery room, she found Nicholas Jerdan standing there as if waiting for her, with a large leather book with brass clasps in his hand. The Volery room was so named because, by a conceit of the French artist who had been employed to decorate Lyndley Waters, it was painted with birds of all kinds and hues. Their plumage, wings, tails and crests covered the walls in a pattern of cascades and stars, in scarlet and crimson and blue, not unlike the fireworks that had lit the lake when Nicholas Jerdan had first come to the home of Grace Troyes. Between the birds were alien blooms with spiked centres and tasselled leaves.

The apartment had taken Grace's fancy, and she had often come there during the first weeks of her residence at Lyndley Waters, but of late it had seemed to her no more than a drop curtain. This splendour was like a nut without a kernel. It lacked all the life and love that should have made it enjoyable.

"Well," she murmured at last, "you are slow at contrivance."

"And you," said he, "are most impatient and indiscreet."

She would not submit to this reproach but violently told him that it was he who was playing the simpleton in delaying so long the next step in their adventure, and she repeated to him rapidly the warning that had been given her by Brian Ormerod.

Whether Nicholas Jerdan was impressed by this or not she could not tell. His lean, dark and comely face revealed nothing. He opened the book he held and placed it on an ormolu desk as yet unused that stood in the window-place.

"If anyone comes upon us," he gave his orders, placing a gilt chair for her, "I am expounding to you this obscure passage. . . . Have you heard from Sir James since he went to London?"

"No. He would have to be swift and loving to have sent to me already," she replied bitterly. "He has employed messengers, of course, and they have gone to Scotland to find out more about you."

"Is there anyone in Scotland who will tell him about me?" pondered Mr. Jerdan.

"All those who were in combine to be silent till I was married might speak now," she answered. "At least those who knew—the lawyers and the old ladies and the nurse they turned away because she spoke too freely. She was a witch, I think an old witch wife, and always threatened to undo me. . . ."

"We are not," Mr. Jerdan reminded her, "discussing chap-books or ballads now, or listening to the peddler. This is our own world in which we move and where we must deal with one another and with these foreigners, not a region of fairy . . ."

"But you," she answered sullenly, "were willing enough to go with me into the region of fairy . . ."

"When it served my turn," he told her bluntly.

This brought to a head all her suppressed ardours, impatience and misery.

"What have you done?" she demanded. "Have I left everything in your hands only to find you have been indolent or have betrayed me?"

He considered her—her curious face, her alert figure, her rich dress, too gaudy and extravagant for the occasion; up to now he had known how to handle her . . . he must not lose his skill in that art.

"I have made every plan," he assured her. "You must trust me. Though I appear to do nothing, I work hard. Now there is something for you to do. . . ."

He was glancing constantly at the door that he had left open. It was a long time since Nicholas Jerdan had spoken aloud and confidently in an apartment where the door was shut. A serving maid passed . . . one of Mrs. Bateman's spies, of course . . . but what could she report save that she had seen Lady Troyes peering over a learned and no doubt pious book with her chaplain standing behind her—not near enough even to touch the carvings of her chair.

"But you understand that now we have created this—I will not say confidence, in view of what this man Ormerod told you—but this atmosphere of—security—let us put it like that . . . you are the mistress here, I am in a respectable post and nobody has dared to challenge us openly—now I agree with you, Grace, it is time we did something. You are for Paris and I am for the Indies. Well, we will dispute that when we are free of Lyndley Waters."

She said, "I wish we could get Lyndley Waters, you and I; were it free of James Troyes and all his friends, we, you and I, could make something of it."

He shook his head. "An idle life. I am not born to ride about an estate viewing the prospects and discussing with architects and carpenters..." He checked himself, thinking it perhaps unwise to allow Grace to know what his designs and wishes really were. "I have got work for you," he continued in his old tone of authority that never had she refused to obey. "You must follow your husband to London. You must assert yourself... there must be no more of this drowsy idleness. You will take with you, if you please, Mrs. Bateman, and any one of the spies she chooses to take with her—take Thomas Pratt as an outrider, anything you wish. . . . What you will have to do will be perfectly decorous." He looked at her over her shoulder, smiling suddenly. "You will tell your husband that you wish to be presented at St. James's—that is your right, though I suppose you have not guessed it. You will demand from him an establishment in his town house—he has one, as I know, in Queen's Square. When you are settled there, you will ask for your mother's jewels, for his mother's jewels... for everything you can get that may be turned into money; and then, when you have successfully played this part, I shall come to London and we shall meet again."

"You want us, then, to part?" That seemed all of his talk that she had understood. "But last time it was intolerable when they sent you away and you pretended you were in Switzerland—had gone to Geneva. . . ."

"It was the wisest thing to do," he replied. "I do not regret it. And it is the wisest thing now for me to remain here at Lyndley Waters. I can play my part in the country as you must in the town. I shall walk in the fields, the brooding student . . . I shall complain of the papist decoration of their guady chapel, merely to vex them and give them something to agitate their placid minds. For the rest, my life will be above reproach, and if I am asked why Lady Troyes does not take her chaplain with her, I shall reply that there would be nothing for a Scotch pastor to do amid the frivolities of the genteel London world, and I shall even leave a hint," he added sarcastically, "that you are becoming too worldly for my approbation, and that I consider returning to the north to continue my studies at the University of St. Andrews."

Grace listened to his voice, to her the most pleasant sound in the world, but gave small heed to his exact words. He had asked so much of her since she had given herself and all she possessed entirely to his direction, and she had been so obedient, not finding irksome for a long while anything he bade her do. Now there was this . . . it meant a separation. It also meant excitement and the employment of those arts that she was conscious of possessing—duplicity and guile. These might be overcast often by her ignorance and her wild temperament, but she believed that she could use them for him.

"I'll do it," she promised suddenly.

"It is the only way," he replied. "If we remain here like this, you will never put a finger on a farthing, and my stipend, though your lord no doubt thinks it handsome, will scarcely serve my purpose."

"How," she demanded, "shall I communicate with you?"

He had, it seemed, thought out even that small but difficult point.

"I know a Scot—a Mr. Dallowe, who keeps a small

print shop by St. Paul's. It is a respectable place where you may go to look at a new edition or a new engraving—a bookseller as well, you understand; a man who, by industry and by application, has become a figure of some importance in London though his beginnings were nothing. To him I shall address my letters. The name on them will be his, but in the corner, underneath the franking stamp, will be written the initial of your name—G."

"And I may do the same by you?"

He replied that she might, but did not seem to care greatly whether he received any communications from her or not.

"Yes, this man Dallowe sends me parcels of books now and then and he can send me letters from you in between the covers; but I look to you to be so quick and clever in your work that there will not be much need for letters to pass between us. Now, if you please, I will leave you; and do not endeavour to see me alone again. It is far too dangerous. This house may be all that is goodly and splendid on the surface, but for you and me it is as if the cellars were stacked with barrels of gunpowder, and there were half a dozen ready with fuses to light them."

When she was alone, Grace took her face in her hands and tried to concentrate all her energies on what had been proposed. She did not wish to leave Nicholas Jerdan. All her emotional and spiritual life was fed by the occasional sight of him she had, by the knowledge of the fact that he was her secret ally, separated by all the etiquette and ceremony of her husband's house, yet still near and, at need, to be called upon.

Yet, on the other hand, here was action. Lazy and

idle as she was, she could be energetic in her own interests; and, moreover, it pleased her to be able actively to cheat and despoil James Troyes, whom she hated. It would be agreeable, too, to so outwit Mrs. Bateman and those others of her husband's spies who were constantly watching her and who were so sure of having the upper hand.

She made no delay, but that afternoon had the housekeeper brought into her presence—still a formidable figure, Madam Bateman, with her hooped skirts and her starched apron, and her wired headdress, and her keys hanging at her waist, and her flabby, pasty face with the lips pursed and the eyes glittering in the pouches of whitish flesh; but Grace Troyes was not afraid. She was only surprised that she had not herself thought of the plan that Nicholas Jerdan had suggested to her.

"I am going to London, Mrs. Bateman. I find it very dull here . . . I have no knowledge of architecture, I cannot employ myself like my lord does with all these mechanics from London. . . . The ladies of the neighbourhood regard me as a foreigner, and what have we to talk of who know nothing of one another?" Then she added, knowing how it would vex her listener, "And when Sir James is away the gentlemen do not call, so there is no one with whom I may talk sensibly."

"The neighbouring ladies are not all fools, madam," replied Mrs. Bateman. "If your ladyship would only accustom yourself to the ways and manners of England. . . ."

"That is exactly what I propose to do," interrupted Lady Troyes. "I intend to go to London. My husband must open the town mansion for me . . . I shall be presented at St. James's and learn to mingle with his quality and mine. . . ."

She saw by the tightening of Mrs. Bateman's already taut lips, by the quick lowering of her puffy lids, that this was an unexpected move, but the housekeeper stood firmly to the shock.

"You would have to have your husband's authority for that, my lady,' she replied stubbornly.

"Why?" said Grace. "I think there is no occasion. Besides, how do you know that I have not got it, Mrs. Bateman? He may have sent me a letter every day for all you know—or do you spy on me so closely that you are aware of what is in the mail-bag?"

"Mr. Swallow has the keys of the mail-bag," said Mrs. Bateman sulkily, "and I don't know what your ladyship means by the use of the word 'spy.' "

"But I think you do—. And you can come to London with me, if you will, and continue your work there and watch me in my city brilliance—for I shall be brilliant, Mrs. Bateman. I shall have more clothes, and I shall ask my husband for the jewels that are mine—my mother's jewels, and his mother's jewels, all of which, I think, are in some strongroom in town. And Thomas Prattt may come also," she added maliciously, "if he wishes. I should think my lord misses his body-servant. . . ."

Mrs. Bateman was baffled. She had not heard anything from her master since he had left Lyndley Waters. Both she and Thomas Pratt knew instinctively how Sir James would disdain either to ask for or to receive without demand reports on his wife's behaviour. The watchdogs were to do their work and be dumb. Therefore it was possible that what the errant lady said was true.

"And is your reverend chaplain, Mr. Jerdan, to accompany you, my lady?"

"No," said Grace, feeling like a gambler that sets on the table the card that wins the game. "He is somewhat disgusted with England. He finds Lyndley Waters somewhat of a Papist flavour. He dislikes the chapel . . . I supposed he would. It is very likely that he will return to Scotland—and soon. The rector, Mr. Boate, and he have been at many theological disputations with little advantage to either. Mr. Jerdan is a very scholarly man and might rise high. No, he certainly will not go with me to London, and it is quite possible that before I return here he will have departed for the north."

Mrs. Bateman had no more to say. She was not satisfied, but she was silenced, and after a brief, secretive and half-ashamed consultation with Mr. Swallow and Thomas Pratt, she obeyed the unexpected and startling orders of her mistress and made preparations for the journey to town.

IV
FINALE

"Through open doors the dogs come ben."

JAMES TROYES had made no ado about opening his London mansion. Lyndley Waters being his obsession, he had taken no interest in the town property but set up himself and his two servants in apartments. There he established a connection immediately with a man whom he believed he could trust in this particular emergency. This was one Keete, who had been for a time his secretary. He had first known him when Robert Keete had accompanied him on his youthful travels as the tutor's assistant.

Sir James had long forgotten this man who was, in his way, something of an oddity, learned enough to earn a few pounds as corrector of classic books for the press, too restless to remain long in one employment, enterprising enough to seek for and to be entrusted with curious commissions.

Sir James, who spared no time or money when his mind was set on a design, soon had this fellow at his apartments and had disclosed to him what he wanted of him. It meant, to the baronet's annoyance, saying rather more than he liked to disclose about his own affairs, and Keete was shrewd, a man to put two and two together; otherwise he would not have been worth employing. Still, the traditions of his class were so strong with the young man that he rapped out what he had to say with annoyance and brevity.

"Look you, Keete, I remember you as adroit and useful—one who could undertake such business as a gentleman might not wish to have known abroad...."

Keete, who was middle-aged and of a nondescript appearance, was used to such preambles that concealed the shyness, perhaps the shame, with which dubious transactions were broached. He waited patiently till the baronet, walking up and down the hired room furnished by the cold taste of the upholsterer, had rid himself of all his scruples. Then he, Keete, put down on his tablets what it was he was supposed to do, what he was to be well paid for doing.

He was to travel northward—he did not relish that, too early in the year, it would be comfortless and rough travelling; he would put down his expenses at a high figure. Well, then, the errand? The pay once settled. . . . He was to go to Edinburgh by Moffatt and Peebles. He was, if possible, to stop at the house or castle of Mr. Morrisson of Drumquassel.

"It is," said Sir James with an accent of dislike, "one of those fortalices where they have built the house from the old stones of the ancient castle. Nothing that we should consider to be more than an antique ruin, yet there, passing very well for a residence of one of the lesser gentry. . . ."

Mr. Keete, posing as a traveller, a scholar or clergyman on his way to one of the universities—"anything you will," instructed Sir James impatiently—was to learn what he could of Mr. Morrisson, "and it will be difficult. They have what they term clansmen; everyone down there will be in his interest, but do not delay long; if you can discover nothing there, or very little, proceed to Edinburgh." He gave him the names of his lawyers. "Go to these men and deliver them this letter, but do not trust them . . . I think they have already deceived me."

"That is likely enough; being men of the law, they probably hoodwinked you, Sir James, for your own good. We have all been pleased to hear that so fine a match was obtained for you in Edinburgh."

"So fine a match . . ." repeated the baronet sombrely. "Well, that has nothing to do with the case. You are then, with what wits you may possess, for I fear I can give you but small clues, to find out what you can of Mr. Nicholas Jerdan, who is, at present, my wife's chaplain at Lyndley Waters."

Mr. Keete prepared to take down particulars of this stranger, but Sir James knew very little of the man who had been uppermost in his thoughts for a long time now. He came of an old Covenanting family, though himself now in the Kirk of Scotland, yet he came from . . . black Cameronians, who had mostly suffered for their indomitable faith . . . some of them were buried in the valleys near Moffatt . . . one, at least, in a small disused graveyard outside Edinburgh, near the River Almond and the small village of Cramond. The young man's father, the first Jerdan to leave the Dissenters, had also been chaplain in the odd establishment where the three ancient gentlewomen Ladelle guarded Grace Morrisson. On old Jerdan's death, this son had taken his place, through some infatuation on the part of the ladies, who bore a great attachment to his family.

"That is all I know," declared Sir James, speaking as if to an invisible crowd of listeners more than to the paid investigator who sat before him. "That is all I know of the fellow. . . ."

"Tell me something of his looks, manners and attainments," Mr. Keete suggested. "These details help one."

"He is well enough in his person," the baronet admitted. "Has no look whatever of a pastor and, when I saw him first, wore a secular dress. He was supposed to have gone to Geneva, where I believe he has relatives among the exiles there, but instead, remained somehow concealed in Edinburgh."

Mr. Keete looked up sharply. He was not as a rule greatly interested or concerned in the various pieces of work he was asked to do, but here seemed something that to his acute mind and his clear vision—always the mind and vision of the spectator—might afford matter for some malicious amusement.

"I believe," added Sir James, bringing out the confession with difficulty, "there was a plot to keep a great deal of this fellow's history from me. He may be a scoundrel; he may in some way have disgraced himself. You must go to St. Andrews if need be, where, I believe, he studied in the University."

"This will cost a considerable sum of money," remarked Mr. Keete, stubbing his quill on the tablets and then proceeding in a leisurely fashion to sharpen it with his pocket knife.

"It matters very little what it costs as long as I obtain the information. Only in this manner can I obtain it. Such friends and acquaintances as I am supposed to have in Scotland will never reveal anything. I know," Sir James added, "you expect a fee before you start."

"Certainly, sir," smiled Robert Keete. "It is a tedious business—it takes me north before the weather be well set—and I had some work to do in London, the publishers keep me fairly well employed . . . there is always a book to correct, a manuscript to translate, a dedication to throw together. . . ."

Sir James put all this by with a backward movement of his hand. He was disgusted with himself that he had to employ Keete and so far open his private affairs to him. He felt even now, when the matter had been completed, a sense of shock—as if he had in some way fallen from his own standards. This was more degrading than riding desperately with Thomas Pratt northward, a man on the verge of bankruptcy, to see what money he could raise from his Scottish lawyers. In this feeling of vexation with himself he dismissed Keete, telling him that fuller instructions—written names and so forth, and a draft covering at least his initial expenses—should be sent to his apartment. But Mr. Keete had not been farther than the door when there was a sound of a commotion on the stair.

Thomas Pratt, against all etiquette, preceded the party who were alighting from the coaches that blocked the narrow street. He gave his master a few quick words.

"It is her ladyship, sir . . . she would come up to town . . . Mrs. Bateman is with her . . . Mr. Jerdan remains behind at Lyndley Waters."

Having thus, as he thought, done his duty and given his master the pith of the matter, Thomas Pratt slipped back into the shadows of the stairway and was decorously at his post.

Grace Troyes had not travelled with economy. She had used her authority as mistress of her husband's house during his absence to come by relay in the finest of the family Mulberry carriages, with outriders and a baggage waggon; and this equipage was now drawn up outside the plain, flat-faced house where her husband lodged.

Nothing could have been more vexatious to Sir James; he at once suspected mischief, but, as was always the case with his wife, did not know where the mischief might be—at least they had been separated. . . . The first half of evening, that he had learned from the country boys to call the owl light, had fallen, and in these London rooms, with the tall, narrow windows, the shadows had descended thickly while he had been bargaining with Keete.

Sir James dragged at the bell pull, and when the perturbed man-servant of the lodgings, who was agitated by this sudden arrival of so many strangers, appeared, asked for a candle. The man brought this from a closet while asking his orders.

"Leave all to me."

With that Sir James picked up the candle and went to the head of the stairs and looked down. She was there standing in the small vestibule. His light, wavering down the shining oak panelling, faintly distinguished her figure; he looked at her with distaste. She was dishevelled by her travel, as if she had come post-haste—her hair falling on to a cloak of vivid green colour, her hands ungloved, her petticoats lifted, her tinsel shoes unsuitable for journeying; she appeared older than he remembered her. . . . What emotion, what thoughts, what apprehension had hollowed and darkened her visage? Behind her was Mrs. Bateman, and Thomas Pratt was already in his place again, and there were two other women whom he had long remembered at Lyndley Waters. He remained at the head of the stairs, allowing her to come up to meet him, which she did as soon as her bright, roving glance had seen the man who held the candle aloft.

"What caprice is this?" he asked.

"Caprice? I thought I should please you. I have been so sullen and idle, and now I am determined to take my part as your wife. I went to your mansion, where Thomas Pratt tells me you live, but it was shut up and only two servants there, who directed me here."

"It can soon be opened. You must return there—there is no accommodation here. . . ."

She looked from him to Robert Keete who, like a spectator at a play, was standing aside, his hand on his breast, holding the handle of the door.

"Why do you stay here?" she demanded.

"I am only in town to settle a few affairs, and it is not worth the expense to open that large house in Queen's Square . . ."

"Your affairs . . . ?" She looked still at Robert Keete. "Is this another architect—another painter for Lyndley Waters, or do you employ him on some quite different commission?"

He did not answer her, bowed a dismissal to Mr. Keete, who went reluctantly down the stairs feeling that he was being shut out from some quite interesting drama, but consoling himself with the reflection that if he was at all successful in his investigations in Edinburgh he would be able, even though it was at the cost of some time and fatigue, to discover for himself the tangle in which Sir James Troyes, his outlandish wife, and the chaplain, Nicholas Jerdan, were involved.

* * * *

Sir James did indeed find it extremely difficult to deal with this situation. Never had the woman who was his wife seemed more remote from him than she did now; in her own house she had been at least part of a curious scene that was not without its fascination; at Lyndley Waters she had been at least the mistress of his grandiose home. Here, she stood like a stranger in these lodgings that were unfamiliar to him—and like a hostile stranger, too.

He had never reckoned on her venturing to follow him to London. Indeed, although he had had in Scotland some experience of her boldness, he was far too easy-going and far too dull of masculine complacence to suspect that she would ever make an independent movement or even gesture. But there she was, seated in the elbow-chair, looking at him harshly with her demands—at once so ordinary and yet so childish—still trembling on her lips, for she repeated them again and again like someone who has learned a lesson by heart.

"I want to take my proper place as Lady Troyes. . . . I want to go to St. James's. . . . I want to have money to go to these shops and the play . . . and those jewels. . . ."

He tried, with the evasion that is the readiest weapon of his type, to put off the issue and to reduce the moment to commonplace.

"You should not have come," he said. "It was stupid and in a way ill-mannered; when I am abroad my wife does not give orders in Lyndley Waters."

"Who does?" she asked,

"I do—I send, from wherever I am, messengers—London is not so far."

He felt himself to be talking incoherently, but he was strengthened by the sound of his own voice.

"If I wished you in London I would send for you. . . ."

"Not your wishes but mine," she cried, rising and twisting her gloves, that she had pulled off her long hands, together.

"Why are you in such an agitation?" he asked. "I cannot speak to you now. You must go with all your train"—he remembered, and it was a comforting recollection, that she had Mrs. Bateman and Thomas Pratt with her—"to the house in Queen's Square and find what comfort you can."

"You will not come too?" she asked.

"No, I shall remain here—I have a great deal of business on hand."

"I suppose," she remarked bitterly, "that you have these Jew moneylenders to deal with, whom you are silencing with my dowry. . . ."

Sir James looked at her very sharply. "You did not think of that yourself," he said; but he did not dare think of the man who had put sentences such as this in Grace Troyes' mind.

He freared an open and dismal rebellion; he half suspected that the lady might have to be carried into the coach; but she went with no show of dignity, but rather with an air of defeat, and he allowed her to go, comforted to see that Mrs. Bateman, whose face was still more pale and unwholesome than usual through fatigue, was on one side of her, and on the other was seated a female maid whom he remembered during his mother's reign at Lyndley Waters.

He made a gesture to Thomas Pratt to come up and speak to him; not that he could canvass his wife's conduct with a servant, but if there was anything serious to say, Thomas Pratt would find a means of saying it; but the man was quiet and respectful. He gave his master an account, as far as his knowledge

234

availed him, of the progress of the building of Lyndley Waters.

"Yes, that . . ." said Sir James eagerly. "I must not forget that—that is the reason at the bottom of everything. All else that occurs is—but so many trifles." Then he added sharply, "You saw Mr. Keete just now. Do you remember him, Pratt? He went with us to the continent. . . ."

Pratt duly remembered without comment.

"Well, I've sent him to Edinburgh. . . . I want to find out something about this Mr. Jerdan. Neither you, nor any of the servants, nor Mr. Swallow have anything to object to in his behaviour?"

Thomas Pratt answered truthfully that the young Scot had behaved in a manner that estranged everyone but could not be termed objectionable.

"He insults no one, sir, and goes his own ways. He seems to be indeed a learned scholar and spends many hours in his own room. He has made not one acquaintance, much less a friend. I believe he has raised some complaint about the decoration of the chapel. . . ."

"He is as out of place in Lyndley Waters," declared Sir James with increasing anger, "as a Bible in a jewel casket. I must somehow get rid of him, and I think, Pratt, Keete will discover in Edinburgh the means whereby I may send him about his business."

Then master and servant looked at one another keenly. Pratt had, as a matter of course, moved quietly about the room and lit the candles on the great branch on the side table, and gathered the fire together on the alabaster hearth and pulled the curtains so that the room was neat and cheerful. Now, as man to man, they faced on another, and Sir

James asked the question bluntly:

"What do you think of him?"

He did not put into words the fact that Pratt had been spying for some days, if not weeks, very skilfully both on Grace Troyes and her chaplain, but his tone seemed to imply, "Well, you ought to know, you've had him under observation."

"Sir, I think he is an adventurer," said the servant. "One that will take any opportunity that comes to hand. I think he has some remarkable qualities—such as control, sir, and sharp wits and an amiable address when he chooses. I believe that under all this he is rash, wild and ignorant of the world, and that in coming to Lyndley Waters he has gambled a large hazard."

Sir James could not push the subject further because to do so would involve the discussion of Grace.

"What will this man do, think you, Pratt, when he is alone at Lyndley Waters—?"

But Pratt put his finger delicately on the word "alone." Jerdan was surrounded by his employer's creatures. They, too, would be watching him—if not as assiduously as Pratt himself, at least with considerable sharpness and even malice. The Scot was bitterly disliked on many counts, some obvious, some obscure . . . he was not "alone."

Sir James made no comment. When he had said "alone" he had unconsciously referred to the parting between his wife and her chaplain.

"You will stay here with me, Pratt. I must return to Lyndley Waters soon—my wife will go with me. This is but a prank on her part such as one may expect in a silly young woman. My place is not in

236

London, but at Lyndley Waters."

The tone of his voice as he uttered the words were like a chorus to his obsession. He could not forbear going to a drawer in his desk and pulling out, for the servant's admiration, further sketches and drawings for the adornment of his magnificent seat. With a hand that was not quite steady, and with sentences that were blurred with excitement, he pointed out this and that design—a statue here a fountain there. . . an improvement in the pavilion by the bowling green . . . a new set of tapestries or of pictures for this corridor or that chamber. . . .

Pratt thought, "It is like a madness—a fury. At this rate he will be ruined again. I wonder if even the Spanish money will cover all this expense; and he is talking to keep his mind off worse things."

* * * *

Grace Troyes had no sense of triumph as she entered the desolate mansion in Queen's Square. The furniture was covered in holland, the great chandeliers concealed behind bags of muslin; the caretakers expressed, as far as they dared, their vexation at this sudden invasion of their quiet life. It was not usual for the gentry to move about without sending messengers ahead of them. All the people employed by James Troyes had lived an easy life, both during his mother's reign and his own early years—and their dislike to this new and foreign mistress was, therefore, naturally keen. Those already installed in the London mansion and those she had brought from Lyndley Waters combined to make her feel, in everything, alien.

She could not like the place, although it contained much of what she had always desired—

237

splendid furnishing and an air of gracious opulence. . . . But the hangings were not on the walls nor on the beds, shutters alone screened the windows. Although it was spring, the air was both close and cold, and she was suddenly sick with fatigue and in a way with disappointment. She wished that Nicholas Jerdan had not ordered her to London. She wished that he had done what he had promised to do when they were in Edinburgh—taken her away at once with what spoils they might acquire. She knew very little of the world, she had no knowledge of how far money would go, of the ways and means of obtaining more. Her ideas of freedom, as of magnificence, were half of a fairy-tale order since they had come from the chap-books and ballads of the peddler, and the wild tales that old Elspeth had whispered to her by the fire of a winter evening or when they were seated together in fair weather under the pear trees in the little orchard at the back of the Edinburgh mansion.

Her own lack of experience occurred to her uneasily. She felt that she moved in a void and, without the support of that dark and formidable personality on which she had for the last three years leaned, she was in a way lost.

She turned away her husband's servants, refusing even their offices in the way of comfort. No, she would have no fire in her room. . . . No, it was unnecessary to put the curtains on the tester to-night. . . . She took what food they gave her sullenly and without thinking of it, then sat alone in the half-furnished bedroom, her black hair fallen to her waist, her travelling cloak on the chair behind her, her tinsel shoes gleaming in the light of the unsnuffed candles that fell fitfully across her brooding face.

Sombre and confused memories crossed her mind that was more in a dreaming than a thoughtful state. Everything was so strange; had she but one friend, one confidante, something might be accomplished. Even to find her way to the print shop that he had mentioned would be difficult—an adventure. Grace Troyes was used to difficulties and adventures, but they had not been on these lines. She knew how to creep out of the house in the half-light without disturbing her guardians, how to find her way across the Moffatt glens and into those remote and gloomy recesses where the graves of the martyrs lay. . . . She knew, when in her own country, how to play many tricks. She had been clever, for instance, over the sapphire that she had found the means to give, together with gold, and to give, with a gesture and a challenge that must have smitten her prospective husband, to the penniless Nicholas Jerdan. But what to do here and how to do it? She had even lost faith for a little while at least—she hoped it was for a little while—in her own powers, in those spells and incantations which she believed, or had believed, would some time or other bring her fortune.

From the bottom of her valise that she suddenly unstrapped with nervous energy she drew the mannequin she had hung in the chapel at Lyndley Waters, an old tattered book, some pieces of chalk and various oddments and rubbish. How futile and stupid they looked now laid on the floor in this formal bedroom! Elspeth had taught her how to work spells long ago. Trembling, she had tried to do the same . . . she believed that strange results had occurred, but these were always confused in her memory. . . . Yet there had been that great triumph when, after sitting all night with Elspeth by the fire that was no more than one or two coals, and listening to her unearthly tales and performing the rites that the old woman bade her perform, there had arrived at that detestable house, Nicholas Jerdan—the lover whom Elspeth had predicted. . . . But now Grace was at a loss what to do next and how to do it. . . .

All night she sat alone, sunk with fatigue yet unable to sleep . . . arranging and rearranging her poor store of magic properties until she heard a scratch upon her door and knew that again she must play her part in the commonplace world. A silken kerchief that had lain ready soon covered all her paraphernalia.

* * * *

It had taken Brian Ormerod, who did nothing impulsively, a few days to so settle his affairs that he was free to come to London. He worked on a deliberate plan after due consideration, and his mood was cool as his purpose was inflexible.

He arrived in London spruce and composed and, being a man who cared nothing for show, put up at the substantial inn, the Black Bear, where the coach from Winchester stopped. To him the whole affair was a question of saving or possibly of winning Celia. This meant almost the same thing to him. She must be saved from any entanglement with James Troyes, and in doing so he believed he would win her for himself. If, so the sensible and determined young man had argued, Grace Troyes, through some extravagance or folly, was cast off by her husband, then he would turn to Celia Plaisent for comfort, and Celia would accept James at any time on any terms. So much Brian Ormerod grimly accepted, but Celia would never—and this was the sole exception in her infatuation—interfere between man and wife; and could Grace be kept but somehow in her place, then Celia would, sooner or later, marry him, Brian Ormerod.

With a plan so clear cut, a nature so resolute and such cool moral courage that some people thought amounted to effrontery, Brian Ormerod did not find his course difficult.

He had not often been to London; the country gentleman detested both politics and town pleasure; and he looked upon the scene about him—the narrow streets, the crowded houses, the swarming people— with considerable distaste, but he lost no time in any manner of reflection, but made his way directly to the lodging occupied by Sir James Troyes, the address of which he had obtained from Mr. Swallow. But Sir James was abroad—Thomas Pratt also. The servants who were in residence had nothing to tell the visitor, and so he found unexpectedly, and to his great annoyance, the day on his hands.

Yet he was not long at a loss and only for a short time rebuffed. He learned from the servants the likely places where Sir James would be and went to them methodically. The first was the studio of the artist who was preparing the canvases for the grand staircase at Lyndley Waters; but Sir James was not there.

The second was a wood-carver on Ludgate Hill who had a large workshop where he employed many men to make for the houses of the great those delicate swags and garlands of carved flowers then so fashionable. But Sir James was not there either, nor at the fashionable coffee-house that he frequented.

Brian Ormerod went to a more substantial tavern for his own meal, dined and drank after his wont, and again set out through the streets, whose squalor was only faintly touched by the spring sunshine, to discover Sir James Troyes. One haunt of that gentleman usually contained someone who could direct him to the next, and Mr. Ormerod's quest came to an end suddenly in a gambling hall off the Strand, that was run at a considerable profit by one of the prominent noblemen whose palaces nearby stood on the river's edge, the gardens sloping pleasantly down to the banks of the Thames. Ormerod found no difficulty in entering this place of entertainment where country gentlemen were especially welcome; but he was not of the type that the professional gamblers hoped to find among the rustics. Shrewd and worldly-wise, he knew exactly the nature of the place and had no intention of losing one penny piece. He did not even think it would be necessary to sit down and play, and for a while it was not noticed that he was taking no part in the gambling, for everyone, both at the large centre and the small tables round the wall, were absorbed in their own throws and cards or wearily asleep after hours of juggling with chance.

"I think," thought Brian, "James did not use to come to such places," and he saw him, as the reflection came into his head, by the fireplace that was piled with cold ashes; the baronet had the air of a man who has not slept all night; his hands were stuck in his great flat pockets, his leg thrust out before him. His head was resting in an idle manner on the back of his chair. The light was artificial, candle and lamp—the salon had no windows; but it was not only this glare that gave an ugly pallor to Sir James's features, the other man considered; no, he was fatigued, distraught, beside himself.

Standing before him, cool, well-dressed and fresh, Brian said, "You did not expect to see me here, Sir James. I have had to pursue you through the mazes of London."

The baronet looked at him sullenly with an unbelieving stare, and then was on his feet, asking if there was bad news of Lyndley Waters.

"Can you think of nothing else but that mansion?" retorted the other good-humouredly. "Come, let us get out of this place—the air is stale and foul, and as for the company . . ." He glanced round it, took the other man's arm and turned him so that he, too, was forced to glance round it . . . "I did not think you were used to keep such—"

"I do not know why I came here," muttered the other. "I've lost a little—not much. I stopped in time, thinking of Lyndley Waters."

"You'd best return there," advised Brian in a voice that was for his companion only, yet that was distinct and clear.

"My wife's come to London," said James, so deep in his own perplexities that he had forgotten how he disliked Brian Ormerod and even failed to consider how odd it was that he should have come to find him . . . at some trouble.

"Yes, I know—I heard before I left. I suppose it is natural enough. . . . I want to speak to you about that fellow Jerdan."

"Everyone," whispered Sir James with his fingers to his lips, "seems to want to speak to me about him. How did he ever come into my household? What do

243

you know about him?"

"Nothing," replied the other frankly. "Let us leave this den—a coffee-house is better, or there is a room in your town mansion perhaps. . . ."

"My wife lives there," said Sir James, yawning and stretching, "but I never go near the place. I'm still in my lodgings. Why are you so concerned in my affairs?"

By now Brian had guided the other man out of the gambling hall. The evening dusk was closing in on the streets. As they walked between the high houses it was as if they walked between towering cliffs that blocked out the sky and the light.

Brian had little knowledge of London, but he knew that towards Westminster there were fields, and so proceeded in that direction, cutting through dark alleys and more pleasantly laid-out streets till they came to the flat meadows where the grass was growing for the haysel. There was a stile there, some thorn bushes and a few sheep grazing. It was not like the countryside to either of the men, since it seemed soiled by the smoke of the town, and too many citizens were walking along the paths or lolling by the gates taking their evening ease. But for all the urban air, it was a place in which they might with some comfort converse.

James was the first to put the situation into words.

"I left my hat and cane behind at the gambling house," he began. "It's no matter . . . I must get my affairs in order. . . ."

"You will not do so by moping in places like that. Come directly to the point," and to his surprise the young baronet did so, with surly fury.

"You want me to throw out the Scot? You think he is going to make mischief betwen me and my wife, and your motive is that you're still hoping for the hand of Celia Plaisent?"

Ormerod felt the tables turned and reddened. He was all for bluntness, but this was more than he had expected, yet in a way it was welcome too.

"Say that is so," he replied stoutly, "What do you intend to do? The man, I can assure you, is nothing of what he seems."

"And you are not my friend," said James sadly.

"Sir, I am your friend in a sense—why not? I do not want to see you brought to some disgrace or ruined by that queer fellow from the north."

"There is certainly a plot or a conspiracy," sighed the baronet, thrusting his hands into his pockets again and hunching his shoulders. "I'm not in the mood to tell you that—you should not have interfered in my affairs. . . . I suppose the whole countryside is chattering over that?"

"We talk, of course, as you would talk. Do you think it was worth it, James, even for the Spanish gold?"

"What do you advise me to do?" the question came with a humility that Sir James did not often show.

"Tame her, school her. She's young . . . she's innocent. . . . She may be wilful and something under the influence of this fellow, but you are the master. Where is she now?"

"Oh, she's safe enough in my house. It is useless for me to talk to her. She has a way with words which will lead you from the core of the matter into mere quizzes."

"Take no heed of her words. Do what you have to do, *as the master*. Send that Scot packing and take her back to Lyndley Waters. Why, remember the thousands you have spent on it—. More than any of us guess, I daresay. Remember the timber that has been cut down . . . the farms that have been mortgaged . . . the pain and toil to hire those craftsmen . . ."

Sir James interrupted, thrust his toe into the soft earth by the hawthorn tree where they stood.

"Why, you speak as if you liked and admired the place, and you've always hated it—thought it marred your own landscape—and now you want me back there. . . ."

"Well, sir, you yourself expounded my motive," said Brian. "I suppose as man to man I have the right to want you. We've been neighbours and companions as children and as boys. . . . You got this maggot in your head of building that Italian palace there . . . why not? I suppose you've every right to do that, as I have to wish to live content on the acres my father left me; and since it has come to plain speaking, I do intend Celia Plaisent to be my wife, and she is fixed in her childish liking for you. Now listen—" Brian took the other man's arm again and they walked up and down slowly as men will when thoughtful, "now listen, James. Here is one of your own blood, as I say, a near neighbour speaking to you. I do not know what cantrips that young rascal may be up to, it is possible he is quite harmless—but be rid of him, he has a core of mischief."

"Do you remember Robert Keete?" muttered James heavily. "He went with me to the continent. Well, I have sent him to Edinburgh to make

246

enquiries. . . ."

Brian lifted his brows; he had not thought that Sir James's suspicions had gone so far; he disapproved of this proceeding.

"It will take too long," he objected impatiently. "By the time Keete has gone to the north and back, why, all the trouble may have been not only begun but ended."

Prudent as he was, he saw that he had come to the end of his argument with James Troyes. A word more and that young man in his disturbed mood might take offence; Brian had established, at least, a semblance of confidence between them; Better to leave it at that.

James seemed absorbed in his own affairs to such an extent that he did not even ask if Brian had come to London especially to see him. Better leave him in his ignorance. . . . Brian was uncommonly satisfied that the matter had been so plainly put before them, even though it did mean breaking all etiquette in mentioning Celia Plaisent.

As they walked toward the town, Brian learned, from chance and broken remarks that his companion made, that Lady Troyes was living an aimless life in London, some ladies of his acquaintance had called on her and she had given them an uncourtly welcome. What the particular grievance was—for he believed there was one—between husband and wife Brian Ormerod could not discover; but since his one object was to bring them together, he led Sir James by divers routes to Queen's Square, and there, under the oil lamp that had just been lit above the corner house, paused and took him by the shoulder and said with all the force of his resolute nature:

247

"Do not live this kind of life, Sir James. Do not drift into idleness and neglect of what you once held most choice. See how these two people—the Spanish lady—let us call her that; it is a less offence—and this Scot—have already divorced you from what you cared for most . . . Lyndley Waters."

Sir James replied sullenly, "But I could not have continued to build Lyndley Waters without—" he laughed, "shall we say the Spanish money—it is the less offence . . . ?"

"Contrive to use the Spanish money and to control the Spanish lady—give no cause for talk or scandal, and send Nicholas Jerdan back to Scotland without waiting for Robert Keete's report."

With that he pressed the other man's hand and then turned away briskly.

Sir James stood for a moment hesitant; he was stung, ashamed and yet, in a way, exhilarated. It was perfectly true that he had allowed himself to sink into a void of idleness, making excuse that he was waiting for Robert Keete's return. But of course Brian was right. He must not for a moment allow the reins to slacken. He must show her that he was master.

He looked across the square, where the trees only slightly obscured the hard line of the houses, at his own mansion; a place that he had lived in but rarely, and that he did not in any way care for. But it was his own property. His father had bought it, his mother had furnished it, and there Grace—the stranger—was living in splendour, even though it was a perverse and hidden splendour. He had seen only yesterday some of her bills. She went indolently in *his* carriage with *his* servants—certainly with *his* spies too—every day to the shops, to the exchange, and bought this and that for no purpose. It was time that this dangerous drifting, both on his part and hers, were checked, he felt something of the other man's cool determination as he crossed the square and turned the key in the door of his own house.

Grace was taken by surprise. She sat by an unshuttered window with a large book on her knee, and she was carelessly turning the pages and not glancing down at the print. On the small table behind her, where there was a tangle of embroidery silks, her husband noticed a letter, unsealed, unfranked, and written in a scholarly, cramped hand.

She did not rise when he entered, but he saw that he had disturbed her, by her flush, her aslant glance. Assuming the air of a master, he jerked the bell pull and called the servants, and soon all was in a bustle with lights and rearranging of the rooms.

"You're coming back to Lyndley Waters," he announced. "You have had your visit to town and bought, one would suppose, what finery you need. It has got to end, you know, my dear, both the buying of the trumpery and idling away the hours. To-morrow," he added briskly, "I must visit the wood-carvers and the painters—I do not know what lull there has been on my activities. . . ."

He had not meant to say that, and she took advantage of it.

"You were thinking about me and Nicholas Jerdan, I suppose," she said. "When are you going to give me those jewels? If you think of me as a child, treat me like a child and give me toys."

He did not give much serious consideration to the question of the jewels. They were at his bankers, waiting to be valued. How slow all these people were ... the assessors had not yet sent in their report. ... As for his mother's gems, such of them as were worth much had already been pledged to pay for the building of Lyndley Waters. They might be redeemed now, but he would have to count the cost. It did not occur to him that she had any definite object in asking for money, or the value of money. He saw her only a spoiled impatient, indolent and possibly under the domination of Nicholas Jerdan. But this was a matter he would not pursue, even though Brian Ormerod had spoken plainly enough. James Troyes refused to believe that Grace was in any conspiracy against him. Others might be—he was almost sure that the chaplain was—but Grace was merely a fool. Yes, for all her stately airs and fragments of ancient learning so unbecoming and so useless in a woman, he believed her to be not only ignorant and inexperienced, but—well, perhaps a fool was not the right word. ... So as this was going through his mind he turned and held a candle up where she sat in the window. ... Was she halfwitted, mad ... ? Had he got a bewitched woman for his wife? The candlelight was on one side of her face and the last of the London daylight on the other, so that she was in a strange reflection of dimmed gold and silver. Her gown was as usual uncommon, in his opinion tawdry. She had an exhausted look.

"I want to tell you a story," she said. "It might explain something to you. ..."

"I don't wish any explanations," he replied, setting down the candle.

He was making an endeavour to render everything ordinary, commonplace. Ormerod seemed able to do that in two words, but he, James Troyes, was too easily tinged with—what was it?—the sense of unseen, unheard forces beating about him, on his track perhaps.

"Have you heard from your father?" he asked heavily. He looked at the letter on the work-table. "Is that from him?"

"Oh yes, that is from my beloved father," smiled Grace, and took it up and put it in her bosom. "He lives the same life at Drumquassel. He never liked me, you know—I think he never liked my relatives for keeping him to his bargain and leaving him in his poverty while all that money was hoarded for me. . . ."

"No man would like it," replied Sir James shortly. "It was a foolish bargain—I wonder your father made it. . . ."

"But how agreeable a bargain for you!" she mocked.

He paused in front of her and reminded her with a good deal of passion that she was not to continue to flout him with her dowry.

"I have heard of other women who have done that. They bring their husbands a few pieces of gold and there is never an end of it . . . it must be always cast up in his face. Whatever the business was between you and me, between your lawyers and my lawyers, I should say it was fairly conducted. You had as good as you gave."

But Grace Troyes denied that. "I could have married anyone whom I chose—a prince perhaps . . . yes, a Spanish grandee. . . ."

"Well, why did you not?" he asked, without any particular meaning in the words; but when they had rung in his own ear like an echo, and he had heard his own voice saying, "Why did you not?" he was brought up with a horrid amazement, as if he had suddenly glimpsed the reason.

As he stood rigid, looking at her, she began to tell her tale and he could not stop her. In brief and carelessly selected sentences, she told him what perhaps had been long and often in her mind. One of those ancient stories begotten in heaven, in fairyland or on earth . . . no one knows how . . . that haunt the lonely hearths and the deserted moorlands of countries where the people have long memories and flat purses, where pleasure may not be bought; it must be taken by such means as this, and old, distorted stories used to distract the mind.

Grace Troyes had had this amusement, and this only, where more fashionable women had had the play, the cards, the gossip and lighted rooms, the hundred and one scandals and tender intimacies of the great world.

"We used to call it," she said, "the story of the jottery-man. . . ."

"Why must you tell it to me?" he demanded, and yet even as he spoke he felt a certain fascination about the woman and anything she might say. He realised then, as he had never realised in his comfortable life before, that hate has its ties as well as love, and that between hate and love there may be but a slight difference.

Grace Troyes seemed careless as to her audience; she curled her fingers into her palm and put her hand against her cheek.

"There was a lady in my own country—I should say in my father's country—but it was a ghostly and mysterious land, as difficult to find one's way across as an uncharted sea. . . . She was married to a clod. He was the laird—dull, stupid and heavy, and as she fretted at her unhappiness, he mocked at her. She became bad-tempered and gave him excuse for his jeers in her furies and rages. The villagers thought that she was a witch, and so did the servants. . . ."

Sir James interrupted. "Grace, we only bemuse ourselves with fairy tales. . . ."

But his wife had risen and was telling her story with force of feeling that showed she considered it important.

"I tell you that the lady went into transports of rage. She broke the china and the glass, and on one occasion thrust her hand through the window. . . ."

"Well, if it was in Scotland it would have had no glass in it," he interrupted carelessly.

But Grace continued, only looking at him the more intently under her scowling brows.

"The lady ill-treated her maids. It was believed that she poisoned some of them in the messes of porridge. In particular there was one, Jessie, whom the laird had smiled at. You see, what was infuriating her was her contempt of her husband. . . . She hated all women who were happier than she was, and so in the neighbourhood there was no one so much disliked and feared, and no one perhaps so unhappy. . . . Then one day came the jotteryman. . . ."

Sir James asked what was a jotteryman, and Grace replied that he was what in England they termed a handyman. This man, she said, was of mysterious origin and strange appearance. Everyone shrank from him, believing him to be a goblin or a fairy. The lady herself was terrified at the sight of him, and for the first time in her life turned to her husband for protection, begging that the jotteryman might be turned away; but he would not go and the laird would not endeavour to make him. He only laghed at his lady's alarms.

"Now my story begins," said Grace, clasping her hands together. "This woman of whom everyone was afraid had met someone of whom she was afraid herself. The tale—and I remember how often old Elspeth used to relate it when we could get away from my guardians by ourselves—says how she was fascinated by her hatred of this creature. She began to live for nothing but to destroy him—she wanted that—to destroy him. . . ."

"A valiant lady," sneered Sir James.

"Ah, but she was strong and bold, and the jotteryman was small and deformed. Once when they were fighting, she hurled a missile that killed by mistake one of the few servants she favoured. In another struggle, all the crockery on the dresser was broken, and there again, in our poor country, you must remember how important we consider china and glass. . . . Now, she thought, was her chance—she could be rid of the jotteryman, for this smashing of the china was a great loss. But he jeered—'it was my lady sho broke the chaney herself.'

"Then she poisoned his drink, but her spaniel drank it by mistake and the dog died. She tried to murder him at night when he was sleeping, but mistook the bed and murdered her only son.

"By now she was completely mad. While she was raving the jotteryman went away. When she recovered, nothing would do but she, despite all restraint, must follow him, and this she contrived to do—but the goblin brought her back, wounded, beaten and stripped. . . . He did not want her, you see. He delivered her to her people.

"Now," cried Grace, "note the turn of the tale. It is clear that she did not follow the jotteryman in a desire for vengeance, but because she loved him."

"What interest can I take in this fantasy," said Sir James, "when so many practical matters press upon me?"

But Grace was absorbed in her story, as the lady in the fairy tale had been absorbed in the jotteryman.

"He bound her with withes of grass and left the place again—but she twisted herself free and followed him and found him in one of those lonely glens where I used to ride—where the graves of the martyrs are—and there he killed her, and her kinsmen, coming up, buried her mangled body on the moorside in a grave that was not, as you may suppose, hallowed. She was mad—she had destroyed herself. The jotteryman was not seen again."

"So I should suppose," sighed her husband wearily, and yet not by any means at ease.

"He never existed," said Grace.

"I suppose not," repeated Sir James, "since all is a fairy tale. Is this the kind of nonsense on which you have fed yourself? I do not wonder if, between that and your gloomy religion, you are not half-crazed yourself."

"He never existed," repeated Grace. "He was her own creation. She thought about him until he was there. They say that as she moved there were screams and shouts and claps of thunder, and that the members of this afflicted household exclaimed frequently, 'God's presence be about us.' It is an old story, but I often think of it. . . . I can tell you another. . . ."

"I have no ears to hear, no attention to give you," he put in impatiently, "I want to come to some practical understanding with you." He emphasised the word "practical." "You keep clamouring to me for the jewels—for money—for a presentation at court. . . ."

"Only because they mean freedom," said Grace. "But listen to my other story. . . . There was another lady, who lived in a lonely fortalice, and she, too, was unhappily married. She had one child, and after his birth whe withdrew completely from her husband. She was very pious, as I am. She resided in a separate part of the lonely castle and devoted herself to prayer and religiious meditation. She, like the other lady, hated her husband and was fanatically religious. She was allowed to have a clergyman, a chaplain or preacher; he was her spiritual guide and support against the husband. When her second child was born, he was brought up in seclusion by the mother and the preacher, quite apart from the elder boy. He was sent to St. Andrews as a student, without being told anything of the family history; but while he was at the University he learned of his elder brother. He learned that his parents and he preacher were dead, and that the elder brother had inherited the estates and was handsome, amiable and popular.

"When he left the University with but a few pence in his pocket, with the design of becoming a preacher himself, he at once sought out his elder brother and had a sight of him in the streets of Edinburgh when he came out of an inn.

"Now he became, as the lady had become with

the jotteryman, seized by a fascination of hatred. . . ."

"I wish, Grace, you would not talk to me so often on these frantastic themes," protested Sir James heavily.

He was fatigued body and soul, yet the word "fascination" might have applied to him, too, since he seemed incapable of leaving the room, but must sit at the handsome desk listening to her, and now and then watching her through his fingers as she walked up and down the polished boards and the Persian tapestries.

"The younger brother, you see, was shut out of the estates—out of everything that he really wanted. He pretended, even to himself, to be religious. But he wanted everything the other had—the gaiety, and the liberty, and the money to spend—and visits to the fine cities, and the jewels and the lovers. . . . And he began to torment the elder, who had everything, although his brother tried to be generous and friendly, Ah, I will not tell you the shifts he employed—they were very elaborate and ingenious, and they were always successful, like the efforts of the jotteryman.

"Sometimes they met, and the elder brother pleaded and argued with him; tried to avoid him—always in vain. And the bright and generous youth was gradually overwhelmed by this persecution.

"Now the younger brother, whom we will call the fanatic, had found a friend—a personage whom he called the Prince. To him he went for advice as to how to torment his elder, and to the Prince he rendered homage. This boy—he was, even when he came to his end, young—first ruined and then murdered his elder brother and then, the crisis of his hate being reached, realised who the Prince was—no other than, you may have guessed, the Devil. The youth then destroyed himself, but without regret or remorse—still in black bitterness."

"I see no more in this than a tangle of supersititon. When, in the name of common sense, Grace, are you going to talk to me reasonably?"

Grace did not give any answer to this; lifting her lip as she replied:

"Of course, the young student, no more than the young man, ever existed, so old Elspeth would fell us."

"What was he, then?" asked Sir James, with more curiosity than he dared to show.

"He was the woman's hatred of her husband, the jotteryman; and as for the other story, there was one youth, not two; that part of him poisoned by the evil mother destroyed his better side, and the hatred between these three people—husband and wife and the innocent boy sacrified to their fury—produced at last the prince of incarnate evil, who destroys them all."

"That is what you would hear on those wild moors where there is nothing but the eagle and the falcon, dense woods, the fruitless heather and the destructive thistle," said Sir James. "Would to God I had never left the pleasant south for your blighted north! I forbid you, Grace, ever to tell me such myths again. They teach one nothing. The open recesses of the human heart and mind that were better left in the dark. But what am I doing?—preaching?—and that was never my role. Come now, you mjust return to

Lyndley Waters. There shall be no money or jewels or presentation at court for you," and he knew that what he was about to say was of great importance, and in a sense he shrank from saying it; to get together what he termed his common sense he added, "Nicholas Jerdan must go—it has become a scandal—even my neighbours are speaking to me about it. . . ."

"Celia Plaisent, I suppose?" exclaimed Grace. "Why should Celia mingle in my affairs?"

"You do not understand how English gentle-women are bred."

"I know what women are," she answered contemptuously. "What does their breeding matter? Celia would find some way or means to convey to you what she felt—oh, it would be disguised, as all the love and hatred was disguised in the two tales I have just told you. She would swear she was thinking only of my honour and your peace of mind, but he real meaning would be—"

"Stop!" said James. "I am in no mood to hear this blunt and, as I think, untruthful talk. It leads you on a false track also. Celia never had a mind to be mistress of Lyndley Waters. . . ."

"And there you lie," said Grace Troyes. "You could have had her any time you asked her, but her dowry was not sufficient. You wanted my money to build your house—and what was your house to be built for?—to make a dwelling-place for hatred?"

He had no answer to that. His weariness increased until it was over him like a leaden cloak. He had built his house because of pride, ambition and gaiety of spirit, and a humour to see his friends entertained nobly, and to be a shining figure among all who knew him; and now, as this dark stranger who bore his name so fiercely reminded him, it seemed indeed as if Lyndley Waters had been built but to house hatred—the hatred that was between him and Grace ... the hatred that was between him and Nicholas Jerdan, and pherps the hatred of Nicholas Jerdan for all of them.

She continued probing with her insight that was at once childlike and, to him, devilish, into his heart and the hearts of his friends.

"And this Brian ... why does he try to save you from the Scots preacher and your outlandish wife? Because he hopes that somehow we shall come together and be united, at least outwardly, and then he will have his chance to win Celia, on whom he has set his heart in the obstinate English way—not with any strong and headlong passion, but with a stubborn determination."

James admitted that this was true, but it had but little bearing on his practical troubles. He found, for the first time in his life, that it was more difficult to deal with someone who gave him this wild candour than with those who preserved the conventions. Though they were confined together in this small, ordinary room, yet they were in everything else so far apart that it seemed as if an abyss, filled with all the winds of eternity, was betwen them. He tried to keep to commonplace matters.

"You and I are married, and there is no excuse for breaking that marriage. I allowed you this preacher, but I consider that his behaviour and yours have freed me of my bond, and he shall leave Lyndley Waters. I have sent to Scotland to make enquiries of him and his behaviour—I believe that in much I have been deceived."

"You have sent someone so far, and while the weather is still foul, to discover something about Nicholas Jerdan? Well, you have wasted your pains, and if you think I will return to Lyndley Waters and be your wife there—why, surely you do not think of it. . . . I don't belong there. . . ."

"Why, that is clear enough," he admitted. "But where is your station? In that old house at Edinburgh with the pear trees in the garden . . . ? On those lonely moors where the graves of those you call the martyrs lie . . . ? Perhaps in that wretched farmhouse by the River Almond . . . ?"

"Where," put in Grace quickly, as if she remembered something delightful, "I thrust your gift into the mould of the covenanter's grave. No, I don't belong in any of those places, but somewhere . . ."

She checked herself, not, he believed, because she wished to hide anything form him, but becuase she did not know herself where she belonged. "She is mazed," he thought, "and confused and half-crazed with old stories and this dour religion."

"Will you give me the jewels?" she demanded.

She seemed exhausted now and had sunk down to a chair of brocade with arms, and was clutching the fringes of it nervously.

He decided he would placate her now; why had not he thought of it before? He must have been distraught—it was the easiest way—like throwing meat to a panther in a cage.

"I'll give you the jewels," he promised, and left the room abruptly.

* * * *

When Nicholas Jerdan found himself alone—that is to say, without his employer or his employer's wife—at Lyndley Waters, he had ample peace in which to reflect on his future course of action. So far he had contrived everything according to his plans; but these plans were whimsically built, on no solid foundation, and therefore shifting with his mood and his circumstance. His intentions were not definite even to himself. He let each day bring its own mischief. He was tormented by dreams that had a startling reality, and by noontide meditations that often shook him in his resolutions. But all these inner disturbances and to and fro calculations he concealed beneath that exterior that everyone found formidable.

There was nothing for him to do, since no one in Lyndley Waters required his religious care; everyone went to Mr. Boate at the village church, and the chapel where Grace had hung the mannequin was deserted.

Lately he had put aside the work on which he had been engaged, and engaged not without relish, for he was a fine scholar and one part of his mind was quite absorbed in the hard and barren work necessary to the understanding of the more obscure classic, or, as he would have termed them, pagan writers. He was much alone. Mr. Swallow avoided him. The upper servant, who was in the place of Mrs. Bateman, gave him but the slightest attention. He was well looked after, there was no cause for complaint, but solitude ringed him about as definitely as if a circle had been drawn round him.

He was a stranger, he knew, and an accursed stranger as well. They suspected him not only of an alien, repulsive faith, but even, probably, of dark practices. The English peasantry at least were as superstitious as the Scottish, he knew that he would find it very easy to frighten them.

As the days passed in this stagnant monotony and there were no letters either from Grace or her lord or from certain friends of his whom he had in Scotland and who were watching his interest, a slow impatience surged behind his outward composure. He had learned that composure when very young, having early seen that this was the only armour that one, poor and without influence, might with convenience wear in a world where all the prizes went to those who did not need them.

He knew that Brian Ormerod had gone to London, and he could guess the reason; there were many gentry still in the neighbourhood. In his solitary walks we would see them riding along the lanes or across the fields. When he passed their gates he would see them pleasantly engaged with one another's company, along the well-kept drives to the well-lighted houses. He was never asked to share either their amusements or their work. No man could have been more set apart; and he began to fret, despite his great control.

He supposed that his hold over Grace was complete. He *knew* it was—but if he had miscalculated on her wits . . . It was the end of April and the weather softer than any weather he had ever known. There had been fair days enough in Scotland, and he had visited in the north gardens where parterres of flowers, anxiously tended, grew luxuriously; but he had never known a sun like this, and it gave him a foretaste of those suns under whose powerful rays he longed to bask—somewhere in the South or the east. . . . He had his adventurous dreams, "the dreams, I suppose," he admitted savagely to himself, "that come to every starveling Scot . . ." to go to the Indies, to Jamaica—to try his fortune, to taste this adventure and that, to see how other men lived who had never been trammelled as he had been trammelled, to bring out of this hard, dry husk of his apprenticeship some splendid, gaudy flower of success.

That he could do much with Grace Troyes he did not know. The moment would come when all his cleverness would be of no avail, when his schemes would be but like a spider's thread in his hands. He had been aware of that from the first; the strange girl could be no more than a stepping-stone to his ultimate fortunes. He would have to go away—far away—and change his name and lie about his history and be careful; and if this pause went on too long, even that would not be possible.

He was more afraid of Brian Ormerod than he was of Sir James Troyes; more afraid of that man's quiet passion for Celia than of James Troyes' exuberant passion for his house. He had known from the first about Celia and James and Brian. It was his business to observe such things, and these people were all candid, and to him simple. He had known whose name it was had been scratched from the old boat and why the boathouse had not been rebuilt.

He stood on this particular day towards the end of April, when the air was of a luminous blue, and watched the thrice-familiar scene; the gardeners and the wokmen and Mr. Swallow and the architect going about from one group to another with their air of happy absorption . . . the Cradle Walk—how trivial a thing it seemed and what care was being put into it.

He turned his head to observe with a cynical smile the labours of the gardeners who, thinking of nothing but their task, were twisting together the boughs of wych elm so that they formed a tunnel that would in summer be a complete green shade. At regular intervals they spaced out with a measure, they cut holes, twisting the smallest twigs correctly into place. These were to be the vistas through which the enchanted guest would peep, seeing through one a sunken garden where the irises and the water-lilies would rise from a square pond approached by alabaster steps that in their turn would be edged with brilliant flowers, and through the next aperture a long view across the low, rolling English downs that changed so charmingly according as the mist descended or closed in over the landscape, according as the trees wore the pink of spring, the green of summer, or the golden bronze of autumn.

"And in those trivialities they spend their time," thought Nicholas Jerdan with a sneer, and instantly sneered at himself. "If the place was mine, I, too, should be absorbed. It is eating another man's bread that galls . . . a woman's bounty. . . ." He did not spare himself. She had left him money—gold thrust carelessly into his desk. So far he had not touched it, but it might be necessary . . . she must have stolen it from her husband; it was so little.

For ever in his ears was the hammer of the workmen, the sawing of the carpenter, the voices of the architects and the artists as they moved to and fro, debating various points in the decoration of Lyndley Waters—and in his nostrils the smell of turpentine, wet paint and wood newly sawn across.

There was Celia Plaisent, she was still left on the

scene. What was to prevent him, if only as a matter of diversion, finding out what she knew? It was possible that she had heard from London.

He took his way across the gardens that were beginning to assume so ordered an aspect. Plants, still carefully wrapped in straw and tied together with bast, were lying along the edge of the parterres they were to adorn. He thought of the cost, as he bowed to Mr. Swallow standing there as usual with his book and his yard-arm, so self-confident, so pleased.

"Troyes'll be bankrupt . . . after all, Grace's Spanish gold won't last for ever. . . ."

Jerdan came out into the lane and despised the prettiness of honeysuckle, with the coral horns and the honey-coloured trumpets . . . the small leaves of the wild rose . . . the wreathes of clinging creepers whose name was unkown to him, and the tall, flowering grasses that hid the ditch. . . .

He came to Plaisent Manor. This establishment was not important enough to employ a porter, and with no more than some barks from the watch-dog, he reached the front door. There were signs of busy life all about him—a maid fetching water from the spring in the yard, a gardener watching blossoms that were hardening into fruit on the rose-coloured brick of the kitchen-garden wall; no glass-houses here or anything foreign or strange, but all as it had been from one generation to another of English life.

That his presence in his dark clothes, with his brooding face and the book that he delighted to keep always in his hands or under his arms, disturbed these people, he noted with satisfaction. When the woman, who was still tying a white apron over one more suited to work, asked with some tremor his business;

he begged to be allowed a few minutes with Mistress Celia.

There was no difficulty in this.... What was known or not known of him at Plaisent Manor did not interfere with Celia's freedom. How different was this from the way in which Grace had been bred....

The girl was there at once in a little parlour that he supposed she called her own, for it was full of childish curiosities arranged without taste and yet in a charming manner. Everything that she had ever admired, liked or possibly loved was there in the old panelled room that looked on to a garden that was at present full of pinks and wallflowers. There was a magpie in a wicker cage with an open door in the windowplace, and Celia wore a gown of lavender sprigged with a darker shade, and muslin about her neck that she was hastily arranging as she entered.

"Is it bad news?" she asked.

Her native frankness made him smile.

"It's no news at all, Miss Celia. I merely desired to see you. Three people in whom we are all concerned have gone to London, and I for one have heard nothing of them. Have you?"

She was so confounded by this that she forgot for a moment to offer him the courtesy of her home. His methods with her were like Grace's methods with James, so bold as to cause confusion and defeat.

"Yes, I've heard," she stammered, and then, "Pray take a seat, sir. Were you sent—I mean—I cannot quite—"

"Oh, spare me all the conventional excuses," he replied easily, taking the old worn chair beneath the magpie cage and looking up at the brilliant black and white plumage of that cunning bird. "Would not our story come more quickly to its conclusion if we were frank with one another, Miss Celia?"

"But I do not know—why I should be frank—with Sir James's chaplain?" said Celia, calling upon all her sources of strength; guile was required here, she knew, but she had no guile. "Pray spare me, sir, if you have something unhappy or desperate to say. . . ."

"This room," said he, glancing round at the pretty little pictures, the charming little shelves, the screens and stools of needlework, "does not look as if you had ever touched anything desperate or unhappy in all your life."

"I suppose not," she replied. "Why should one? I cannot see that it is so difficult to be happy. . . . I'm sure I've never found it so."

"And yet the only man you cared for first squandered his fortune in building a house that you detest, and then married another woman to have the money to continue his folly."

Celia set her lips and her nostrils flared. She was inclined to rise and in a storm of tears leave the room, but native courage held her in her place; she sat in her old chair by the window, she put her hand into the sunshine that lay on the sill and drew some comfort from the shape and the perfume of the pinks without. Her world was stable about her. . . .

"You're very impertinent," she replied, "at least according to our manners. I do not think I wear my heart on my sleeve for daws to peck at. . . ."

"That is one of your sayings, I suppose?"

He smiled and seemed amused. He still was staring at the magpie as if he had found it more interesting than the girl.

"Well, have you heard from them in London? Nothing even from Mrs. Bateman?"

"Why should Mrs. Bateman write to me? Grace has gone to London to be presented at court. . . ."

"I know why Grace has gone to London," he replied. "What I desire to learn now is whether you have heard from Sir James?"

Celia laughed. This question was such an outrage upon her standard of manners and behaviour as to be amusing.

"James would never write to me."

"I suppose not." He accepted that. "Brian Ormerod might."

"Whatever Brian writes to me I shall not repeat it to you," she replied with much spirit. "Come, sir, what part do you think to play in this comedy?—for I'll never allow it to be a tragedy," she added stoutly. "Why have you come here? You live what seems to me a sad and idle life," and as he did not reply she continued shrewdly, "I suppose you are waiting? I have noticed that, with birds and animals of prey when they mark down their victim they wait, sometimes quite a long time. The fox outside the henroost—why, I've noticed him on a still afternoon when he has thought none about . . . he'll roll over and lick his mask with his tongue and bemuse and fascinate the fowls who sit, poor fools, on the wall—and with every twist of his fine body he will come a little nearer. . . . If I didn't go down to frighten him away he would come near enough to leap on them. The kestrel, too, how long it hovers before it falls upon its prey. . . ."

"I suppose I miscalculated your simplicity," said Mr. Jerdan. "It may be that you are correct."

"Of course I am correct," said Celia. "What should a man of your youth and intelligence and energies do in idleness but plan some future activity?"

"But we get away from why I came to see you," he replied, and having glanced away from the magpie and round the little parlour: "So this is where you have passed your days. . . . I understand you would dislike Lyndley Waters almost as much as poor Grace dislikes it."

"What," asked Celia, "do you intend for her—for yourself?"

She was, underneath her courage and composure, alarmed, saddened, almost in despair. She knew that he would not answer her question frankly, but she might gain some knowledge from the manner of lie he told. She thought that it might help her if she encouraged him, so she added hastily:

"Yes, I have heard from Brian . . . he is in London transacting some business about the selling of his timber and the letting of his farms. He has seen James, who now is living with Grace in their town mansion in Queen's Square. . . ."

"And is there any talk of their return here?" asked Nicholas Jerdan.

"No, Brian does not say that. He sees them often enough."

She spoke as if she derived some comfort from this; as if Brian Ormerod would act as a counsellor, perhaps a guardian, for the unhappily matched couple.

"Two courts have been held—" said Mr. Jerdan.

"Oh, I see you read your gazettes," smiled Celia, interrupting him.

"Two courts have been held," repeated the chaplain, "and Lady Troyes has not been presented at either. Is it not the intention of Sir James that she should lead the life fitted to her station?"

Celia was honestly bewildered.

"I know nothing of all that," she replied. "If you were to read all Brian's letters to me they would tell you nothing of that."

He belived her, and rose with a look of disappointment on his harsh young face. He had hoped that it would be easier than this; but no, it seemed that he would have to work hard for his future.

He rose at once, and she, too, got to her feet.

"Give my compliments to your lady mother and to you father, neither of whom, I suppose, would be pleased to see me here."

"We have no rancour against you, Mr. Jerdan, in this neighbourhood. It is you who have kept yourself close—Even the Rector is willing enough to be friendly. . . . We have nothing against you," she added, trying to reassure herself, "why, nothing at all."

"Of course not," replied Mr. Jerdan. "I should be very careful to see that you had not, shouldn't I?"

She asked him what his intentions were . . . if he were going to remain with no occupation at Lyndley Waters, or if he thought of returning to Scotland.

"Surely that would be the better for you," she urged earnestly. "You would be there among people like yourself who understand you . . . you would, with your gifts and education—for I am sure you have both—be able to make a place for yourself in your own church—by direct means."

He knew well enough that she would have said honest instead of direct had she been completely candid. He knew what lay behind her plea, for plea it was. She wanted him away from the fresh English countryside—she wanted his shadow off Lyndley Waters, because she was afraid for James.

He bowed stiffly, permitting her to see the mockery in his eyes.

"I have no intention of returning to Scotland, Miss Celia," he answered. "All Scots with ambitions and some manner of talent get away from that barren country and seek their fortunes abroad."

She had no more to say, and followed him to the door and stood there watching him as he walked slowly down the modest, neat avenue.

* * * *

That afternoon Mr. Jerdan carefully made his preparations for travelling to London. He selected a good horse. He intended to travel post and to be in the capital as soon as possible. He directed the manservant who was detailed to look after him to pack all his belongings, including a few of the books he had brought with him from Scotland.

"I have received," said he, lying smoothly, "a command from Sir James to join him in London. It appears he will make a long sojourn there and requires his chaplain in attendance."

Nobody believed him. Everyone, from Mr. Swallow to the carpenter's assistant, were glad that he should go, that they would no longer have to see him walking pensively round the bank of Lyndley Waters or, with a chance word or two, inspecting idly their various labours. His figure in the black attire that was neither secular nor clerical, his brooding face on which there seemed to be for ever a quizzical smile, his short sentences with their hint of mockery and their foreign accent, had made him disliked by all. Yet at the same time there was a loyal regret that he should go to London and disturb the problematical yet possible peace of Sir James Troyes and his wife.

* * * *

Mr. Jerdan arrived in London without mishap. He was not an experienced traveller, but he had money and a selfish regard for his own comfort that served as well as knowledge. He went directly to the house in Queen's Square, and before raising the handsome knocker, gave the mansion an appraising look. It resembled those on either side—handsome, stolid, well-kept, betraying nothing of the character or fortunes of the owner.

He knocked and asked if Sir James was within. The servant told him no. He was a man who had been hired in London and who, therefore, did not recognise the Scotch chaplain.

"But I suppose," said Mr. Jerdan at a guess, "Lady Troyes is at home? I am her religious instructor . . . she has sent for me from Lyndley Waters."

The servant at this admitted that the lady was in the upper withdrawing-room, and if Mr. Jerdan would wait in the ante-chamber he would discover if she wished to see him.

Within three minutes Nicholas Jerdan was in the presence of Grace Troyes. He frowned to see the change in her. She was sitting by the hearth; although the weather was warm and moist, a fire was lit and the atmosphere of the room was close. Her skirts and a cloak of thin silk she had dragged about her shoulders were spread over the fender and the carpet and caught small reflections of gold and red. Her hair, after her usual fashion, was undressed and hung in a black fleece to her waist. Her face was pallid and her brows frowning, her eyes had a feverish brightness—she seemed like one in ill health of mind and body.

"Why did you not come before?" she asked sullenly, without moving. "I know all you want to ask me. First, why I did not write to you . . . ? Well, there was nothing to tell you . . . he will not give me a penny piece nor a single ornament . . . save that little I left for you."

Mr. Jerdan did not reply. His dark, cold glance went round the room—there was nothing there that pleased him. Everything was as it should have been—the pictures from Italy, the inlaid furniture—oh yes, a hundred and one nicknacks, but how formal and ordinary. . . . Only Grace, in her untidy, bright clothes, with her haggard face and her glittering eyes, was out of the way.

"Is this the manner in which you pass your time?" he asked.

"More or less. Sometimes his friends come to see me, but they soon go away again. What have I to say to them?"

"And what does he do?"

"I do not know. I think he is trying to induce me to return to Lyndley Waters. He sent a physician once who gave me some medicine that I cast away as soon as I was alone. Mrs. Bateman and the other women spy on me, but not too obviously. . . ." She laughed. "I was expecting you before."

"So you said, Grace. Well—you have failed. I did not think that of you. I thought you had spirit and daring." He drew from his bosom the sapphire she had thrust into the martyr's grave. "Come, where is the art and address with which you secured this?"

"That seemed easy. I don't think you understand how I am hemmed in. . . . I have no ally, none at all. I thought of running away again, of going back to you, of asking your advice, but . . ." She rose with a graceful movement that he unconsciously admired and stood in her glittering silks like a penitent before him. "I could not do it. I could not find anyone to obey me. In short, Nicholas, I cannot get either the money or the jewels."

"Nothing?" he probed. "Nothing whatever?"

He looked at her bare neck, her bare wrists and fingers on which were only the plain marriage ring.

"Nothing!" she replied.

"Then," said he, "we must find means of taking them for ourselves."

"You mean," she asked quickly, and with a flash of hope in her eyes, "the charms. . . . the incantations . . . the mannequin . . . ? All that you taught me in Scotland?"

He looked at her askance and then at the floor. She sensed, remote as she was from his mind, that many crowding considerations were holding him mute. Then, like a cloak quickly thrown about a visage, reticence was between them. He offered her his hand.

"We must be formal," he whispered. "You must remember that I never know who is at the door spying on us."

"The time will come when we are not spied on, will it not?" she asked piteously.

"Oh yes—you must leave that to me."

He gave her the address of his lodging. She protested . . . why could he not stay there, he was her chaplain . . . ? But he replied, with a soothing note such as he might have used to an unreasonable child, that there was no chapel in the London house, and that if he were to reside there, even under the eye of Mrs. Bateman, there would be a great deal said that would not be easy to answer . . . and he was gone, and Grace Troyes was alone.

* * * *

She was not for long held in suspense as to her destiny. For the next few days she watched the quiver of the topmost leaves on the trees in the square waving against the sky, and the cut flowers slowly fading in the crystal bowls. It was a neglected house. She had no spirit, no wish left to make anything about her pleasant or gay, and the servants under Mrs. Bateman's charge below stairs turned the large, stately rooms into a prison for the mistress of the place.

"Mistress of the place . . ." she often repeated the words to herself in mockery. No one could have been more entirely trapped than she was. It was the money . . . it always came back to that . . . the money had been the thorn in the flesh from the first. It had put her in a false position. Had she been but Morrisson of Drumquassel's daughter she would long ago have been wooed and won by some neighbouring laird and lived out her life in such content as she could find in the glens round Moffatt. But it had been the money and her Spanish mother and that strange upbringing —and then the advent into her life of the young pastor who had taught her so much and then left her still in prison.

Sir James rarely came to visit her, and when he did he was deaf to her entreaties, her scoldings as to a change in her position. He urged her to return to Lyndley Waters, and told her that for that journey and none other an equipage would be at her disposal. He gave her a certain amount of credit on the London shops, but this was useless to Grace because it was not sufficient for her to purchase anything on which she could raise money. She had, indeed, written to Nicholas Jerdan telling him of the limit of her resources, and he had not even replied. This showed that he did not think what she had was sufficient means for their adventure.

Of this same adventure she would sometimes dream—the dream that was her sole consolation— sitting in the large room where the shadows fell so early in the spring evenings—for the chamber faced north—with her hands clasped behind her head, staring at the needlework screen that hid the empty grate . . . a dream of freedom, of gaiety, of trellises hung with fine fruits and rich flowers—of an easy, impossible, delightful life with Nicholas Jerdan.

Then this dangerous solitude was broken by the arrival of one of her guardians, Miss Lilias, who had travelled from the north, post-haste, and who appeared without preamble before Grace Troyes. The sight of the old woman, who was in no way altered, save for a heavy travelling cloak over her usual sober attire, alarmed Grace and roused in her that defensive anger that through her childhood and girlhood had been her sole protection.

"You here, Miss Lilias—and what brought you?"

The old lady talked at first of practical details. She summoned Mrs. Bateman, who admitted a match, if not a conqueror—at least temporarily—and addressing the Scotch lady with respect, answered all her shrewd questions as to her chamber and the sleeping closet for the stern-faced serving woman whom she had brought with her on her long journey.

Grace herself, in the middle of her fantastic troubles, was awed by this portentous journey. It must surely have been something of extraordinary importance that had brought Miss Lilias south from the house with the pear orchard.

That lady pulled off her thick leather gauntlets; she had a few curt words to say about the inconveniences and discomforts of London, but she had found where to bait her horses, put up her menservants and house her carriage with as much address as if she had been used to such experiences. Now she came straightly to her point.

"I'm here, Grace, because your husband has sent an investigator to Edinburgh—one Robert Keete is busy in the city, aye, and round Moffatt too, as I fear, trying to learn something of you and Nicholas Jerdan. . . ."

Grace did not speak because she could not readily find words to meet such a startling emergency, and the old woman enlarged with definite phrases on her theme.

"You see what has happened—you've played the fool. I do not know to what extent, but I find you here in his house and he in his lodgings, and the great place that was to have been such a magnificent palace to house both of you, neglected. . . . And you have been indiscreet."

Grace, sullen, muttered, "I do not think so," and plucked at the edge of her shawl. She stared down at the floor as if she saw into an abyss where bright dreams were disappearing like a flight of winging birds, winging their way into an impossible distance.

Miss Lilias continued forcibly, putting aside with the back of her hand the refreshments that Mrs. Bateman with due respect had brought in and placed with ceremony on the burr-walnut table.

"You must go back to Lyndley Waters and take your place as Sir James's wife, whatever you have done. . . ."

"I have done nothing," declared Grace, suddenly glancing up.

"Perhaps that is the mistake," sneered Miss Lilias. "You have been too negative. It was never intended by us that Mr. Jerdan should remain in your service. We decided, the three of us, that he should leave you before now . . . we have written to him to that effect; he took no notice of our letters. We even sent him money—a draft on a London banker—urging him to go abroad."

"Why," asked Grace, "did you ever allow him to come?" She was fumbling into the recesses of the other's mind. "I thought you meant he was to remain with me for ever."

Miss Lilias smiled ironically.

"We allowed him to go with you because to have made any protest would have been to have roused suspicions. Your Englishman was—I will not say a fool, or thick-headed, for I think he is intelligent enough—but absorbed with the building of Lyndley Waters, and so he did not see anything strange in this young man coming to your home. We have not allowed him to travel with you . . . we would not have allowed Sir James to see him before, or soon

279

after the marriage . . . but we thought that he might without harm follow you south. . . ."

"Follow me south. . . ."

The words had a touch of magic for Grace. She remembered the night of the bonfire . . . she remembered their few and furtive interviews, and the occasions when they had rowed upon the lake in the boat where the name had been so newly defaced—the name of Celia Plaisent. . . .

"He ought never to have married me," she said negligently; "there is another—Celia, her name is—she would have been the wife for him."

"I daresay," nodded Miss Lilias brusquely, "but she possibly has not got a penny to her dower and you *have* got the money. But you must return—don't you see that?" And then she began to probe the young woman as to where the pastor was. Grace would not answer. The older woman then became in a controlled way indignant and contemptuous.

"I was always the one who considered you half-witted, Grace," she remarked coldly. "You ruined all chances of a really splendid match by behaving—I won't say like a wanton—no, it was like a child, for what was there in any of it but a secret kiss or two beneath a pear tree. . . ."

"Indeed, there was no more than that," sighed Grace seriously, with regret. "You should have let me marry him."

"It was not in my power to decide about your marriage." replied the other impatiently, "and who could have permitted you to have married a rascal like that?"

"I thought that you considered him a very saintly man."

Miss Lilias struck lightly on the table with her gloves.

"I've not come here to argue. You know, that by your—what shall I call it—?" She spoke not without sympathy and seemed desirous to discover words that would not hurt, "—your indiscretion with this young man, this penniless student, you raised a scandal and got yourself a name that cut you off from a fine match, and therefore we were all of us glad to marry you off to a foreigner who knew nothing about the matter."

"I was glad also," agreed Grace quickly. "I decided that I would take the first suitor that came who allowed me to keep Nicholas as a chaplain."

"Yes, I supposed that was your intention," said Miss Lilias. She looked round. "This room is very ill-kept . . . I infer this is English splendour . . . ? For myself I would rather have less ostentation and more cleanliness."

But Grace gave no attention to these harsh complaints. She was pursuing her own vanishing dream.

"I thought that we would go away together after a while—besides, he had taught me something that would have taken us far away. . . ."

She said no more than that, but Miss Lilias pursed up her lips as if she understood.

"I suspected something of the kind . . . cantrips and incantations. . . . He was amusing you, child—there's no such thing as magic, there's no such thing as winning love, or satisfying hate by a few herbs thrown into a fire, or a few sticks cast criss-cross on the ground. . . . It's only the peasants who think so."

"There's no such thing?" said Grace, frowning.

"My father told me many stories of glammer, and Nicholas was what they call a grammarian or magician."

"All that is but moonshine," insisted Miss Lilias. "Who would have supposed that you would have believed it, even though you always were on the sly reading chap-books and ballads and listening to old Elspeth's tales. . . . What did she do in the end when she thought you were lost in this world and damned in the next? She left us and did her best to warn the man who is now your husband against marrying you."

But Grace was too set on the one matter to take any notice of this. What did it matter to her that Elspeth, who had at one time encouraged her, had, in turn, betrayed her?

"My father," she repeated. "What reason had he for deceiving me?"

"I suppose," replied Miss Lilias, "he disliked you in a way because yours was the money. The love he had for your mother must have come to an end very long ago, and he's a poor man and one who lacks wealth. What do you suppose it was to him, in his rude, isolated home, thinking of all that money tied up with foreigners, waiting, increasing every year—to be handed over to some stranger—your future husband . . . ? I daresay your father, my dear child, enjoyed the scandal that prevented this happy conclusion to your fortunes. And, of course, he must have hated Sir James from the first."

Grace rose and went to the hearth. Never had the room seemed to her more foreign, more dismal; but she controlled herself, feeling that there would be but little sympathy for her from the stern-faced, capable woman who sat by the long table.

"You will go back to Lyndley Waters," commanded Miss Lilias, "and I shall go with you. . . . And Nicholas Jerdan will not dare to show his face there again. If I can find him I shall be able to get rid of him and for ever. . . ." And then, with feminine impatience at an elaborate intrigue that had gone wrong, she exclaimed, "How is it that you were so foolish as to be discovered? I thought that when you came to England all this infatuation would cease."

"It was not an infatuation, it was true love."

Miss Lilias made an impatient motion of her head.

"I'll stay here until you are re-established at Lyndley Waters . . . until I have seen your husband and this wretched student," she remarked with the air of one who pronounces an ultimatum.

* * * *

Grace could only think of one action to take—to see Nicholas and to see him quickly. She put on her quietest garments and did contrive, after many hours of painful watching, in the dusk, to slip noiselessly out of the house, escaping the scrutiny both of Mrs. Bateman and Miss Lilias. . . .After all, it was not so difficult. She had but to pretend to be in her room, close the door noisily, and then, without sound, creep down the stairs, and without sound open the great door—and down the steps and so away.

But it was not easy to find his lodgings, for she knew London hardly at all, only by glimpses she had had from her carriage when abroad on her futile journeyings to the shops. But by asking this person and that, she did find the alley (that was not far away) where he lodged, and she did find him in his room. Indeed, he usually spent his time there, having no incentive to go abroad, having much leisure on his hands and believing that it was safer to remain hidden—for he was not as unsuspecting as Grace had been; he supposed that those three women who lived in the Edinburgh house would sooner or later make a move.

"You've done the maddest folly!" he exclaimed as Grace opened his door, having been told by the cobbler who kept the house that the lodger was upstairs and she might, if she pleased, visit him.

"But everything is mad," smiled Grace. "Miss Lilias has come to London—she says my husband has sent a spy to Edinburgh to find out all there is to find about you and me."

"And that will be remarkably little," replied the young man sullenly. "I suspected no less. This has gone too slowly, you have been so stupid, as if you were drowsy from a drug."

"I did what I could. I can get nothing—nothing at all. Why, to-night I would have brought something with me—they do allow me a brooch or so—but when I went to my jewel casket I found all had gone."

"Miss Lilias has taken everything," said Nicholas Jerdan. "They will see that you have no means to escape. Well," he rose and pulled his hat from the peg where it hung inside the door, "the last service I can do you is to take you back to your house. I hope none will have noticed this escapade."

Grace could not understand, much less believe his words. They might have been the water flowing over the ears of a drowned person for all they meant to her.

"We must get away," she whispered. "We can get

the money somehow ... we can work out the ways. ... Could you not obtain some employment on a ship at the docks ... ?"

He looked at her with a little amusement. He had been prepared for much childishness, but not quite such foolishness as this prattling.

"Without money," he replied, "we can do nothing."

She stared at him very intently, approached him and asked, "Was it because of the money you wanted me?"

"Of course," he replied harshly. "What do you suppose?"

She checked the words "I thought you loved me," and sighed, and he was relieved that she made so little ado.

"And the incantations ... and the manne-quin ... and the books of magic ... ?" she asked.

"They were so much nonsense to keep you, who are little more than a child, amused."

"That is true?"

She peered at him quickly, coming nearer, and he did turn aside before the stare in her dark eyes.

"That is all true?" she repeated.

"Of course it is true," he answered. "I've tossed a hazard and lost. With another sort of woman," he added regretfully, "it would have been a success—but you were always in the clouds. I was glad to have you bemused with the ballads and the silly plays we made with sticks and dolls ... but not ...." He shrugged at this point.

"Then you don't want me, and all those dreams and all we might have done with the money and the magic were so many lies?" asked Grace steadily.

"So many lies," he said bluntly, willing to put the scene, which, after all, was so much quieter than he might have feared, to an end.

He had himself to think of . . . there were powerful people trying to nose him out. Keete would, of course, in no time discover the whole story; he, Jerdan, was in every way ruined. All there remained for him to do was to escape—to leave the country. He had a little hoard against such an emergency.

"I will take you back to your house," he repeated.

She made no demur but, walking stiffly, silent as a puppet, went behind him through the ways he knew so much quicker than those she had taken to the house in Queen's Square. She found the door still open, for there had been a good deal of coming and going that evening, and she passed in, not looking back at him, and went upstairs to her room.

As he had seen but one action to take, so Grace Troyes saw but one action to take; that was, to return to the north, the wild, haunted, enchanted north. There, perhaps, some of the old magic might return. She had dreams of trying her incantations there . . . and yet he had said they were no use. . . . But in those early mists, close to the grave of the martyrs, might not someone, god or devil, come to her assistance and take her away to all that beauty and softness and love and kindness of which she had dreamed?

She would be able to reach Lyndley Waters without any trouble, and when she was at her husband's home she would be able to get a horse also without any question, and she would ride straight to her father's native mountains.

This resolution, in the midst of her unspeakable pain, gave her the consolation of a settled project. She need not even listen to any more reproaches or sermonising from Miss Lilias; she need not have any more debates with her distracted and sullen husband. Everything would be perfectly easy.

* * * *

When Sir James next visited his town house he was immensely relieved to find that Miss Lilias, with all the adroit arts of which a gentlewoman of her age might be supposed capable, had brought his rebellious wife to reason. Grace was willing to return to Lyndley Waters and to take up her position as mistress of that magnificent but yet unfinished mansion.

Here, then, were all the problems solved. Sir James felt as if the world was once more rolling in its proper orbit. The house . . . after all, it was only the house that mattered, even Celia was of no importance compared to that. . . .

"I wonder," said Miss Lilias in grim rebuke, "Sir James, that you allowed your affairs to get into this clutter," and he was willing to grant the old gentlewoman her triumph. Yes, everything was settled without trouble. They would return to Lyndley Waters; Miss Lilias consented to make a brief stay in her ward's mansion.

"I might be able," she remarked slyly, "to assist Grace," and she looked at Mrs. Bateman as if her main intention was to put the housekeeper in what Miss Lilias would have termed "her place," which was as head of the servants' hall, not as chief spy on her mistress; though Lady Ladelle was willing to admit that a spy had been very necessary.

All that the old Scotch woman regretted in leaving London was that she had not been able to come to an issue with Nicholas Jerdan, but she believed that he would not, as she termed it, "show his face again." She rightly divined that he now, in every way discredited, would have no thought save that of making an escape—"probably to those foreign parts he's always longed for," thought the old woman sourly, "but not as the great prince he fancied he might be, flourishing on stolen money, but in some mean position—a footboy or a lackey. . . ."

Brian Ormerod, who still remained in London and made discreet visits to the Queen's Square house, shared Sir James's pleasure in "the reformation," as Miss Lilias termed it, of Grace Troyes; and with a discretion that is usual in his type, withdrew altogether from the affairs of his neighbour and returned to Lyndley Waters.

"Do you think, James," asked Grace, the day that they were to return, "that I am really going in future to—as you say—as Miss Lilias would say—as Mrs. Bateman would say—indeed, as I suppose, Celia Plaisent and Brian Ormerod would say—behave myself? That I shall learn all I ought to learn as mistress of your great house, and be diligent and careful with keys on my waist, and my books—account books—locked in my desk?"

"I suppose," he replied uneasily, "you will in time learn all this. Those of whom you speak will help to teach you, and so shall I. . . . Indeed, Grace, I mean—and I speak honestly—to do my utmost to help you."

"And I shall not have a chaplain any more?"

"No," he replied, with a deepening of his anxiety.

He disliked having to talk of intangible matters, half understood, that troubled the even surface of life.

"The Rector can come over when we desire a service in the chapel—Miss Lilias says that you are prepared to leave your Calvinist faith—or is it the Church of Scotland?—and to join the Church of England."

Grace had never said this, but she did not trouble to deny it.

"I thought Miss Lilias was a fanatic," was all she remarked, "and more inclined to the Covenant than the Church."

But she gave only a passing reflection to the curious attitude of Miss Lilias, who was certainly bigoted but who, it seemed, was very worldy-wise as well, and who, ever since she had discovered the truth about Nicholas Jerdan, had vowed to bring him down.

And so Sir James and Lady Troyes left London and the house in Queen's Square was closed up again, the holland covers put over the chairs, and the muslin bags over the chandeliers, and the tapestries unhooked and laid away in the tapestry room, and the glass and silver that had been set out in honour of the young mistress, who had never glanced at them, packed carefully and the shutters closed in all but the basement rooms; while on the high road rolled the Mulberry carriage with the baggage waggons behind and the escort, the footmen and the armed servants who were to look out for robbers . . . and Grace Troyes in a cloak of vivid green silk and a hat with a purple feather, looking like a doll that has been carelessly dressed by one with extravagant taste, sat in her corner, with Miss Lilias, grey and correct, opposite her, and Mrs. Bateman, neat, pale and decorous, beside her on the grey-padded seat.

Grace was silent, taking no part in such conversation as Miss Lilias permitted. The leathers were up for most of the journey, and what light the women had came from an inch or so of lowered window, and was pale and misty. But Grace was in another world. When she closed her eyes she was able to gather round her, even though in false and fleeting shapes, something of her old dreams . . . her old delusions. Her last speech with Nicholas Jerdan in the neat room above the cobbler's shop was not impressed on her mind with anything like reality . . . the ordinary routine of the London house had already gone into the background of her thoughts; these ranged wild and free over an uncertain, an unglimpsed region where alone she was at ease, where alone she could be happy.

* * * *

Lyndley Waters was to Grace Troyes in one sense a prison, in another sense like an inn that was the first stage on the road to freedom. She noted that her husband was endeavouring to be civil, if not kind; that everyone treated her with respect; that nothing was done that was likely to make her feel the loss of Nicholas Jerdan or her own escapade, as no doubt they thought of it, in London.

Mrs. Bateman, completely subdued by the presence of Miss Lilias, again presented her mistress with the keys, and this time she accepted them, though it was only to throw them carelessly on her toilet-table. What did anything like that—keys or respect or civility—matter now? She had learned, both from Miss Lilias and from Nicholas Jerdan, the truth—or at

290

least that facet of the truth that most concerned herself. . . . She waited her chance.

Celia, making an effort over many complex emotions, came to see her and endeavoured, even, to get into her confidence; but Grace smiled at her and said as little as possible and allowed her to go as soon as she would.

The only person with whom she felt even a glimpse of sympathy was a man to whom she had paid little attention hitherto—Brian Ormerod. Coming one day on to the terrace where the workmen were still employed in setting in place the great vases to hold the arbutus and brilliant dahlia flowers of a later season, she found him there as if waiting for someone. Her tone, her manner, were at once conventional. She had great skill in keeping the mask in its place.

"I suppose you desire to see Sir James?" she asked.

The young man replied, "No, yourself."

She was surprised at this, and in a way pleased.

"How could anyone have an interest in me?" she demanded.

"I thought you might be lonely and unhappy," he replied. "James has got his house—Lyndley Waters. You, since your chaplain went overseas, have nothing but trifles—and I never thought you were a woman to be satisfed with trifles. . . ."

"*Did* Nicholas Jerdan go overseas?" she asked.

Brian Ormerod could not answer that question, but he told her with tact that he believed the chaplain was a wild, adventurous spirit who had now slipped the country and disappeared, either to Ireland, or, what was more likely, to the Indies or Jamaica. . . .

"No one would concern themselves about him, you know, Lady Troyes, once he has left your establishment. You, too, must put him beyond your consideration. I know nothing of your Scotch life, and perhaps you will consider it an impertinence . . ."

She interrupted the kind, conventional words. "Not an impertinence," she said earnestly. "I like to talk to somebody who seems to understand."

"I do not understand," said Brian frankly. "I only see that you are lonely and this fellow was some company to you."

"What is it thought? What is it believed about him?" she asked.

Brian made an effort over his own good nature. He had been asked by Sir James to undertake this business of finally enlightening his lady as to Nicholas Jerdan, and had at first refused. . . .

"One supposes that he came south because he was weary of the north . . . that he, in a fashion, deceived the three old ladies who were your guardians. . . ."

"But you know better than that?" interrupted Grace. "You know that I—well, I would have married him if he had been anything but a poor pastor . . . we were discovered kissing under a pear tree, and then it was supposed that I was ruined, and he was cast out of the church . . . and had no money, nor chances at all . . . and I had nothing to give him because, although I was an heiress to so much, I had not a mere penny piece in my pocket. . . . I don't know what he did, but sometimes he contrived to send me a letter, and sometimes I, on my rides in the Highlands, contrived to see him. My father favoured him, you see. I don't know what that was . . ."

"I can tell you," said Ormerod, "and it may help

to put it out of your mind. Mr. Morrisson helped Mr. Jerdan because of the great spite he had against you, as your mother's daughter. You see, all the while he appeared to live in content in Drumquassel, he was thinking of the mighty fortune that had escaped his hands. He married your mother no doubt in a passion of love and agreed easily enough to the contract that set all her money aside for her children—and when she died leaving but a girl . . . Well, perhaps you can guess—at least another man could guess—what he felt."

"And so he helped Nicholas Jerdan to make a mock of me?"

"To make a mock of Sir James Troyes, shall we say?" replied Brian Ormerod, trying to put the matter in a light that would be less hurtful to the lady, but she seemed indifferent.

"I resolved to marry the first man who would have me after I was twenty-one—I had a free choice then, you know—and I thought Nicholas would come to me as my chaplain, and then that we would . . ." She paused, and with a return of her own silence, looked at her companion. "Never mind, we had our plans—and now I see that they were but follies."

"Follies indeed, and you have your own life before you—and Sir James is a good fellow at heart and well inclined to be your devoted servant."

"All his goodness and all his devotion is for Celia Plaisent," said Grace. "But I am glad to have spoken to you." She gave him her hand. "You have helped me in many ways. . . ."

Her gesture seemd to indicate that she wished to be rid of him. He believed that his prosaic words had had a certain response and that the poor lady had been roused from her moodiness and brooding by his cheerful indications of what life, that was so broad and so pleasant, might have for the mistress of Lyndley Waters.

But the truth was that Grace had given no heed at all to this part of the conversation. What she was concerned with was the certain knowledge that she had now gained—that Nicholas Jerdan had gone abroad, and that they all knew, even though it was in a pitying way, of her wild and, as she now felt, foolish affection . . . passion . . . for him. Even her father had been in the plot to confound her, to make a fool of her . . . because of spite about the money.

She had not been in the least affected when she had first realised, through the horrified and harsh discourses of Miss Lilias and her sisters, that her behaviour with the young chaplain had ruined all her chances of a fine match in Scotland, and that she must marry the first stranger who came asking for her; but now horror, and worse than horror, seized her lonely spirit.

Yet it was, after all, she reminded herself, only the culmination of everything she had felt since Nicholas himself and Miss Lilias had spoken to her in London. All had been what they would call in the Highlands, a glammer—that mist or coloured light that is seen over the bare thorn bushes after rain . . . that impalpable spectre that haunts the lonely lakes and valleys where the martyrs lie buried. Her feeling for Nicholas Jerdan had been compounded of a wild, earthly passion and an unearthly devotion. She had seen him as the descendant of men who had died for their faith, or rather, as she put it in her mind, would die rather than give in to a superior force. She had seen him also as a man who was, like herself, starved of all that was splendid and beautiful; and she had looked upon her fortune, that had been locked away from her so long, that would be hers, she had supposed, when she was twenty-one years of age, as that which might have given them both these treasures.

He had talked of such prospects, and so had she, when the pear trees were bare, covered with frosted-looking blossoms, or with brownish leaves, or with long, unripe fruit; to her they had always appeared to be burdended with the most delicious blooms that were outlined against the most radiant of skies.

While she was thinking thus, walking up and down the terrace at Lyndley Waters, where the workmen, with an uneasy glance now and then at her unwelcome presence, were setting into the sockets the handsomely carved vases, Nicholas Jerdan was not yet on any such romantic voyage as she or Brian Ormerod supposed; he was, in fact, going from one dubious resort to another in Whitefriars; it had not taken him long to discover the underworld of London, and his object was to see how large a sum he could raise on the Kashmir sapphire.

* * * *

Grace Troyes did not find it difficult, with due exercise of discretion and skill, to run over one afternoon to the stables, to take out from his stall a fine bay that she had often ridden before; to harness him (for she was used in the Highlands to harnessing her own mount), and to ride out of her husband's lands on to the high road. She had never left his domain before without someone, if it were only a groom, in attendance; but this time she had escaped the vigilance even of Thomas Pratt.

They had begun, indeed, to look upon her as no longer dangerous, a person whom it was not necessary any more to watch. Miss Lilias was soon returning to Edinburgh. Mrs. Bateman had taken up again her usual place as housekeeper, taking, when she wished, the keys from her mistress's toilet-table, but always replacing them.

Sir James, who, in the common sense of the word neglected his wife, yet had a certain trust in her and vaguely thought of the future as bringing about . . . well, at least sufficient reconciliation to provide an heir for Lyndley Waters. For the rest, he had allowed his obsession to take hold of him again, and he was soon so occupied in watching the architects, the carpenters, the painters at their various occupations, that he had very little time to think of his wife.

So Grace Troyes found herself on the road and Lyndley Waters was out of sight and she was not followed.

Of the practical side of her enterprise she had not thought. She had, as usual, very little money; only the few coins that were given her under some excuse or other by her husband. What had these been given to her for? she wondered idly. Some charity, she supposed. Well, for a charity they should be spent. The horse was in fine fettle and she rode well. She had put on an inconspicuous riding-gown of russet brown and a hat with a plume. When she came to the two crossroads that she had not seen before, but that were not far from Lyndley Waters, she stopped a rustic in a smock and asked him which way lay north.

He looked at her with slow consideration; he was

not himself clear as to the answer.

"North?" He ran over the towns that were in the immediate neighbourhood. She shook her head, not even knowing the names—she wanted to know which road lay northward.

At last he indicated one that he believed might lie in that direction, but she was to ask again, and as soon as she could. She thanked him and proceeded slowly on her way.

She had no money for posting, even for baiting her horse; but she believed that he might crop on the roadside and she could drink at the springing rills that she had seen on every hillside she had ever known since she was a child; and as for food—well, she could live without food until she reached the north, until those hills again encompassed her and she could, through the mists and the rainbow and the uncertain lights and shades, glimpse the world with which she was familiar, where once more she and Nicholas Jerdan, or the fiend who had inhabited his shape, would be able to cast themselves free of this earth into that other existence where they might be, if not happy, at home.

* * *

It was at the evening meal that Sir James noted the absence of his wife. He made no comment on it because she was apt to spend many hours in her chamber, and he was weary of hearing the excuses given by Mrs. Bateman and the maid for her absence. Neither did those who were his guests—the architect and the painter and, as it chanced that evening, Brian Ormerod—say anything either. It was not their part to interfere in the domestic felicities of Lyndley Waters.

But the next morning, when Mrs. Bateman asked

Sir James if he had seen his lady, if she had changed her apartment, or was sick and had been attended by the apothecary, the young man was startled.

"Why, I thought she was in your charge?" he said brusquely, but the housekeeper reminded him primly that Grace Troyes had never been put in her charge.

There was then a summoning of Miss Lilias, and she, too, knew nothing. A few enquiries made discreetly by Thomas Pratt showed that the lady was not, to all appearances, in the house. Large as it was, she could scarcely have kept herself concealed for so many hours unless she was in some closet or secret apartment; such as there were of these in Lyndley Waters the architect knew of perfectly well, and they did not take long to ascertain that they were all empty.

Sir James himself, with a sullen look and a remorseful air, went to the chapel. How cold and gaudy it looked—neither like a place to pray in nor a place in which one might have normal human thoughts. He had glanced at the niche where she had hung the mannequin. She must be abroad and alone.

He blamed, and severely, Thomas Pratt, and the faithful servant had no defence to make, though he had not actually been put in charge of the lady, and there had been no indication that she intended to leave the house.

"Perhaps she has gone to stay with Mistress Celia Plaisent?" he suggested, and Sir James snatched at this, and he and Brian Ormerod, leaving Miss Lilias in charge of Lyndley Waters, and refusing the company of the architect and the painter, rode over to Plaisent Manor.

Celia was there in her pleasant little room with

the spinet, the water-colours and the gay little bird in his cage, and her own charming little occupations; she had not seen Grace Troyes.

"Perhaps she has gone back to London?" suggested Sir James, standing haggard in the doorway.

But Brian Ormerod, who knew her better, said, "No, she'll have returned north—of that you may be assured."

He spoke with a conviction that impressed the other man. ... To him the word " *north* " brought up a picture impressive, sombre and in a way horrible; the house in Edinburgh, the orchard with the pear trees ... Grace in her incongruous splendour ... the young man riding across the River Almond over Cramond Brig. ... Sir James did not wish to return north—nay, he did not intend to do so. How far could his wife have got? A very little way. She had no money, no equipment, and the horse—she would not be able to do more than exchange him once for a nag at some posting station. ...

These practical considerations flashed through his mind while Brian Ormerod was urging him to action.

"I will come with you," said Celia.

Sir James was startled at these words.

"When we find her it may be that she'll like to see a woman—even though she does not like me, she may like to see a woman," insisted Celia, tacking up her skirt.

She had come out with the men into her privy garden where the spring flowers were blowing before that wind that is the harbinger of a storm. The sky, even since the two men had left Lyndley Waters, had become overcast and purple clouds were obscuring the blue. ...

"There is a tempest coming up," said Brian, and he pointed to where the lightning was darting on the horizon.

"Then she could not have been so foolish as to go riding away alone . . . she is somewhere in Lyndley Waters. . . ."

"You do not understand her like I do, James," said Celia. "Wait but five minutes while I change my gown and get my mount and I'll go with you. . . ."

"Why should we be hampered with you?" said James unkindly, but Brian Ormerod told him to be silent—the girl was as good a horsewoman as they were horsemen . . . she would be no drag upon their action, and far from hampering their errand would help it. . . . Grace Troyes had been many hours—nearly twenty-four hours—absent.

James was silent . . . frowning, not quite understanding. Was he then so stupid that he could not grasp what these two people seemed to see so easily? Brian noticed his bewilderment and remarked:

"You may trust us, James. Remember that your obsession is Lyndley Waters and that we, as outsiders, perhaps see or understand more of this poor lady than you do."

So the three of them without more ado and with no more words were on the high road. They knew not which direction to take, but both Ormerod and Celia declared it should be northward. They had not the trouble that Grace had had in finding the north road, and the three of them, well mounted and earnest in their intention, proceeded at a brisk canter, passing familiar cottages, homesteads and scenery.

James said now and then, "Why should she have left me? Why should she have gone north?" and the

300

other two did not answer.

The storm increased; it seemed to follow them. It came up from behind them in clouds of purple and violet that overspread one another and blotted out the sky. There were loud cracks of thunder and livid darts of lightning. James once turned in his saddle and harshly suggested that Celia should return, but the girl, with her hood buckled firmly under her chin, shook her head without replying, and it was Brian Ormerod who muttered, bending his head before the sudden spurts of rain, "Of course Celia will not return."

At one moment the wind and rain were so severe that they could not proceed; the horses could not obtain a foothold in the soggy road, and the rain, having veered, was full in their faces for a few moments and caused them to bend low on their saddles and so blinded them they could not see the way before them. Then, with the shifting of the wind, it changed again, and once more was behind them . . . and then, for all the soaking of their heavy cloaks and the impediment that the rain caused them and their beasts, they went forward, the animals starting now and then when the thunder crashed or the lightning rolled, but firmly held on their way by their expert riders.

They none of them knew what they expected to find, though in Celia's mind was a sorrow that did not amount to a dread, for she felt that this was the only possible end to the story . . . a prophetic sorrow of what would be the end of all that was human in Grace Troyes.

Through the grey mist they saw the horse, wandering wet and frightened, now cantering, now at a trot down the road, returning home. Sir James knew the bay at once. She was not in the saddle. None of them remarked on that; allowing the horse to pass them they rode the faster, and when nearly spent found what they had come to seek.

She was visible from some yards off, cast into a ditch, her head struck on to the trunk of a tree that had been uprooted in some other storm and rolled away so that it should not obstruct the highroad, but left to lie across the tangle of elder blossom and parsley flowers. Her garments—and she had taken no particular care to choose these thick or weather-proof—were wound about her and so wet that all her limbs were shown clearly moulded.

Celia was the first out of the saddle, throwing the reins to Brian, and quickly on her knees beside the other woman.

"Grace is dead," she cried, speaking truth in her ignorance, and then James was down, giving his horse's reins to the other man, who sat there with an ironical smile on his face; he had done what he could and had done it to no purpose.

James Troyes had lost his hat in the storm some miles back, so there was no chance for him to uncover his head; he tried to lift his wife's body, but Celia cried, "Don't touch her—you take the horses and bid Brian come."

And this the man did heavily, but without objection.

When she had Brian to do her bidding, Celia asked him to raise Grace so that she lay in a less huddled position, and to arrange her cloak under her head so that it had the semblance of a pillow. The blood that had stained her temple had clotted; she had been dead for some time. Good horsewoman as she was, she had become fatigued, something had caused the animal to bolt and throw her from the side-saddle, so heavy and dangerous.

"See what she has scattered about her," whispered Brian. "She must have been carrying them with her, as if they were something precious."

Celia stared—there was the wooden mannequin, a few sticks, a few soaked packets of what had been powders, a few lengths of chalk . . . nonsense . . . rubbish . . . Grace Troyes' paraphernalia for obtaining an entry into paradise.

Celia gathered them all up, broke them as well as she could and threw them into the ditch underneath the tall, strong flowering weeds that seemed to thrive in the storm and to receive on their glossy leaves, without shrinking, the large drops of rain.

James had come nearer, bringing the horses with him.

"She is dead," he muttered, and repeated it several times.

Then he stooped and, lengthening the reins, helped Celia to her feet.

"Yes." The girl had no more to say than that. She stared up at him and put back with her cold hand the wet hair from her cold face.

"Then you belong to me," said James Troyes, all decorum and even sense being driven out of him by the terror and splendour of the moment.

But Celia took her hand, that he had snatched, away from him and returned to Brian Ormerod, who had drawn from his pocket his large silk kerchief, and knotting it, had placed it over the face of the dead woman.

"No, I belong to Brian if he will have me. Do you

take the horses home, sir, and send your people with what is necessary here. You have Lyndley Waters . . . concern yourself with that. . . . "

James Troyes turned aside, mounted his own beast and led the others away on the road to Lyndley Waters.

"You and I will have to sit by her till they come," whispered Celia to Brian. "I will stay with her alone a little, if you would rather walk aside. And what I said let us now forget. She must have lost her way and perhaps crouched in the woods all night—then was up—trying again to escape."

"She must have been dreaming of something. . . ."

"Never mind of what she was dreaming. She was distracted or she would not have been thrown. She was freed in the way she would wish to be freed . . . she will not now have to give any explanations to James, to Mr. Morrisson, to Miss Lilias—or even to you and me, Brian."

The rain had slowly ceased. The thunder was rumbling away across the forest that bordered the wood to the left. Brian Ormerod drew Celia to her feet; she shivered against his heart.

"What did I hear you say, Celia? That I must forget?"

"You know I am yours, Brian—if you want me. . . . I believed at one time that no man existed for me but James Troyes."

"I knew we should be happy one day."

"But you are not to talk of that," she whispered. "We're fatigued and in a strange situation—there is a dead woman between us. Let us think of her. . . . If you know any prayers for such as she was, offer them, Brian. It does not matter to what god—"